INDULGENT

THE CULT OF SERENDEE

ANGEL LAWSON

FOREWORD

Readers,

This is your friendly little author note reminding you that is part three of the Cult of Serendee Series (and yes, it's a series so go back and read the first two if you haven't. This will make no sense otherwise.)

The Cult of Serendee is a reverse harem, dark romance. A cult romance, which I am not exactly sure is a thing, but when has that ever stopped me before?

So onto trigger warnings: This series deals members of a high control cult who are deeply immersed in their community. I've taken elements from a variety of documented cults that inevitably all use the same methods to control their victims. This includes controlling food, sleep, clothing, sex, money, isolation, relationships and demolishing personal boundaries to make victims more malleable for abuse.

Specific TW include: dub/non-con, medical abuse, manipulative sex, blood play, arranged marriage, self-harm, occult activities, sex trafficking and captivity.

UNTITLED

Indulgent

1

Imogene

"Twelve pounds."

As I stare at the number on the scale, Healer Bloom's disappointment is obvious. The weight that Rex wanted me to gain, to become more like the women he found appealing, is no longer acceptable.

She sighs and jots the number down on my chart. "At least you lost three."

We're in the exam room at the new childcare center. The center is also my new home. I eat, sleep, work, and attend these appointments, ordered by Anex, weekly. I come in, strip, get weighed and checked for any changes in my body. Healer Bloom's eyes always linger on the pale white scars crisscrossing my wrists, or the newer pink ones on my inner thigh. I lied when she asked how I got it—saying it was an accident. I know better than to tell her Levi gave them to me—that I asked him to. That memory is mine, and I refuse to give it up. Especially now that he's gone.

"I've cut back on my portions and have maintained my caloric logs." I swallow. "The rest of the weight should come off."

She grunts, clearly not impressed with my results. "Menstruation?"

"No, not yet." Anex discontinued my birth control the day I moved into the facility, but my period hasn't returned, despite the fact it's been a full month.

"No spotting?"

"No." I shake my head and fight the chill that ripples across my bare skin. I've learned not to complain, or she'll drag the process out longer.

She sets the clipboard on the counter and approaches. Her eyes are focused on my hip—or rather the spot just below. The brand is healing—still red, but the scab is almost gone. "Are you picking at it?"

"No." I pretend it isn't there. That I haven't been marked with Anex's initials. That things are like they used to be when we were all together, before he exiled my lovers, and forced my mate into submission.

I didn't realize how good we had it—even if it was just for a short time. It all feels like a trick now. Anex's way of fucking with our minds, our bodies, our souls. He dangled something in front of us—hope, love, companionship—and snatched it away. The way the pieces fell into place, I have to think he planned it all from the start.

He wanted me like this from the beginning: marked, isolated, controlled.

Broken.

"You need to lose the remaining twelve pounds," Healer Bloom says. She reaches into a cabinet and pulls out a bottle. I recognize the sticker on the side. It was made at the Serendee Apothecary. "Mix this into your tea. It should stimulate your hormones."

"My hormones?" I ask.

She nods at my clothing—permission to dress. I don't hesitate, pulling on the approved undergarments and dress quickly. I have no idea where the clothes Elon bought for me are. Burned probably. Maybe in effigy in front of the whole town as an example.

I'm the example of who you don't want to become.

"I'll be honest with you, Imogene," she says. "You need to become fertile. Preferably before the winter equinox."

My heart lunges at her reference to the winter equinox. That's the date when Rex and I were to be truly mated. Where we'd be "married" in the eyes of Serendee.

Or it was until I was sent here, while Rex was sent to Re-education. It's foolish, but hope swells in my chest. Maybe all of this was a different kind of test. I've done everything Anex has asked. Maybe Rex is doing that as well. Maybe our leader understands we are fated to be together—and he wants me fertile so that I can give him a grandchild.

"Has Anex changed his mind? Is he going to let Rex and I have our Mating Ceremony?" I'm already planning what I can do to earn his favor. Eat less. Work harder. Study more. Submit to Corrections...

"Our leader needs you strong and fertile for the Mating Ceremony, but not for his blasphemous son." When she looks at me, I spot the small smirk on her mouth—the dark glint in her eye. "He has plans for you, Imogene, and they don't involve any of the men you've been fornicating with for the last six months."

My jaw drops, shocked at her tone—at her condemnation. She hands me the bottle.

"Take your medicine," she says, gathering her clipboard and walking to the door. "And don't forget, we're watching."

As much as they're watching me, I'm watching back.

I keep an eye on Margaret as her stomach swells, growing bigger every day with Anex's child. I assess the other pregnant women that come in the center with their luggage, kissing their spouse's goodbyes, so that they can immerse themselves and the fetuses they carry with the purest form of The Way.

I watch the big window that looks out over the fields, gaze trained for broad shoulders and a halo of hair. Sometimes I see him, dirty after a hard day's work. His hair darkened, damp with sweat. The hands that were so harsh on my body, so deliberate, are now coated in grime. He's almost unrecognizable, except for the fact that I'd know him anywhere. My Ordered. My Bonded. My first, callous and violent. Shining and bright.

Rex.

Now he's a shell, broken down by his father for Regressive intent, for daring to choose me.

I watch the door, praying that Elon will kick it down, the hinges cracking under the force. Levi will follow him through it, all traces of pain and betrayal clear from his face. Silas will be there too, scooping me into his arms, tell me everything is okay, kiss me—

"Imogene."

I blink, looking up from the cutting board and the sweet potato diced in a pile. I'm chopping air. Margaret stands in the doorway, hand on her belly. "Sorry." I brush my hands together and hope she doesn't see the flush on my cheeks. "Did you say something?"

"There's a new addition in the waiting room."

"Oh," I say, coming back to myself. "Yes, of course."

She smiles gently. Despite everything that happened with Anex the night he banished Elon and Levi from the community and punished the rest of us, she's remained true to our bond. "Sisters" is what she calls us. But like everything, there's a power imbalance, and like always, I seem to be at the bottom.

"I think you'll be excited to greet our new housemate," she says, walking down the hallway.

I'm not sure why she says that, not until I walk into the registration office and see her. Maria, my best friend from the Domum. My eyes drop to her stomach and under her cotton dress is the smallest swell. Pregnant women are required to report to the child center once they reach the second trimester.

"You're pregnant," I blurt, unable to present the happy façade I give to every expectant mother that walks in the door.

"Three months," she says, not quite making eye contact. No one does. The whole community is aware that I'm being punished for sleeping with men other than my mate. What they don't know, or believe, is that Anex commanded them to train me. He set me up.

"Welcome." I force a grin. "We're here to celebrate the growth of our community and ensure the future by nourishing the body, mind, and soul of the mothers and children born here."

The words come on command, memorized from my training with Healer Bloom. Margaret watches me carefully, probably aware of my history with Maria. How we'd been so close when we were teenagers —before we were Ordered. I don't reveal my true feelings, how I mourn for who Maria was before she walked into this facility.

It's not a place of care and support.

It's a noose tightening around our necks, and like everything else in Serendee, Anex is holding the rope.

2

Rex

Every part of my body aches.

My back, my legs, my cracked and bleeding knuckles. Manual labor sucks, and I'll be the first to admit it, I had no fucking clue how shitty most of the jobs in Serendee were before I was forced to do them myself. The farm work I've been assigned to isn't just back breaking. It's soul crushing.

Never think my father doesn't know exactly what he's doing.

At the end of the day, I'm too exhausted to think about running. I'm too hungry to worry about anything but my next meal. My brain feels fuzzy. My reaction time is slow. Every symptom is intentional—a way to make me complacent.

"Pick up the pace, Rex."

I don't look back to see who's speaking to me. It's a guard, assigned specifically to follow me around all day. They rotate, and I know them. Grew up with them. The one following five steps behind me right now, Erik, lived in my Donum. Another one of my father's games.

God, I want to kill him.

Hence the guard.

I take a small amount of pride in knowing that despite how run down I've become in the last month, Anex still views me as a threat. More than the others. I know Elon and Levi, wherever they are, won't be able to see it, but my father gave them a gift. Freedom. He's kept me a prisoner because he knows this is the worst punishment he can give.

He took my money, my cars, my ability to move in and out of Serendee. He took away my job of recruiting rich, attractive women into the community. All those privileges I didn't fully understand until they were gone.

And none of them are even the most important.

"Seriously, man," Erik says, nudging me along with a hard shove. "You do this every day."

He's right, I think, glancing over at the building as we pass. Wide glass windows make up the walls of the Child Care facility. I drag my feet when I'm passing the building—a route my father surely chose with intention. I don't care about his conniving, or how I'm sure he thinks parading me in front of her facility every day is a punishment. I've caught a glimpse of her once or twice. Her blonde hair is hard to miss—her gorgeous face.

That's all I need. A glimpse. Something to tell me she's okay.

"Why are you doing this to yourself?" he asks, voice low and close. It comes with the sensation of hard metal pressed into my back. "She's not yours, and the longer it takes for you to understand that, the longer he'll keep you here."

Erik probably believes there is a way out of Reeducation. That Anex's pathway from the Fallen back to the fold is possible. It's not. There are no second chances. No test we can pass, and I'm paraded through the community like this, every day, as a reminder to everyone of what happens when you cross our great and infallible leader.

My eyes linger on the building, but the windows are clear. I push aside the nagging worry of what could happen to her without my protection—without the others.

Even if I couldn't have her, I'd be okay if he left her with one of my friends. But no, that wouldn't have been painful enough. It's also not what he wants. I see it now. My father has wanted Imogene from the start. Probably as revenge against her mother for leaving, but I know it's more than that. Imogene is special. Beautiful. So fucking strong.

The men in our family clearly have a type.

The walkie-talkie on Erik's belt crackles as we continue down the path. There's no speed in my step. Once work is complete, I'm forced to stay in my room until the next morning. Room is an exaggeration. Closet? Cell? My food is delivered to me. My toilet is two feet from my bed. There's no window. But I do hear the cries at night. The Fallen as they go through Corrections. As they're tested and fail.

Some nights I even hear his voice and I know he's down there, looking to see who he can break next. Who he can use, abuse, and worst of all, sell.

Erik pauses, turning his head to speak into the device. His eyes flick to mine, then away, but not before I see a shift in them.

"Understood. We're on the way." He clips the walkie-talkie back to his belt, his movements hurried.

"Everything okay?" I ask, the smallest hope that the day I've been waiting for has come. This underlying hope that my brothers will return for us. Elon and Levi are out there, and I know they'll fight for us. It's just taking longer than I'd hoped.

"Everything's fine," he says, lifting his chin to the east. Toward the Main House. "You're not going to your room... not yet."

My hope sinks, but I'm curious. My days have been a strict routine since my father put me to work. Rise at dawn. Work 'til dusk. Locked up overnight.

"Where are we going?"

His jaw tightens and his hand rests on the weapon attached to his side. Like he's afraid he'll have to use it. "To see your father."

Anex sits in his chair—what the hell, let's call it what it really is—his *throne*, as if we've seen one another since he took my mate from me and banished my friends from Serendee.

He's got that same smug expression on his face, his hair slightly disheveled, and a knowing glint in his eye. It's all a con. I know it well. He's the one that taught me the methods of persuasion. While other dads were teaching their kids how to play ball, he was refining my skills in manipulation. In seduction.

I can get just about anyone to hand over their money, their clothes, their *pussy*, but most of all, their integrity. Just like my father.

He waits patiently, Erik bowing before him and touching his forehead in reverence. Anex's crystal blue eyes, another matching trait passed down, dart from the guard to me. He wants me to honor and respect him? Fuck no.

Finally, he says, "I see your attitude hasn't adjusted."

"By plowing fields? Is that the outcome you expected?"

"I thought maybe some manual labor would set you straight. Show you how entitled I've let you become."

I sigh. Every muscle in my body screams with exhaustion. I just want to go to my room, eat dinner, and sleep until the day repeats itself. I'm too tired to even jerk off. "What do you want?"

"A father can't check up on his son?" he asks, waving over one of the girls standing by the wall. I scanned their faces the instant we walked in, both hopeful and horrified that Imogene may be one of them. She's not. These girls are young. Probably underage. Children, I assume, of members of our community, unless he's started recruiting at the local high school.

The girl that steps forward is waif thin, dark circles under her eyes. She carries over a tray of fresh fruit, her arms shaking from lack of strength. Disgust builds in the back of my throat. No, this one has been here for a while, probably grew up in Serendee, but somehow managed to offend my father.

How did this happen to my community? When?

Serendee—my father—he wasn't always like this.

Or has it? Has *he*?

"I'm sure you have your methods of keeping track of me." I tilt my head toward Erik, who shadows me most of the day. "It's not like you trust me."

"You're right about that." He grabs a handful of grapes and pops one in his mouth. "You haven't earned back my trust." He reaches out, tucking a strand of hair behind the girl's ear. "At least not yet."

Ah, here it is. The big play. Dangle hope in front of me—an opportunity—see if I take the bait.

"I'm not interested in regaining your trust or anything else." I take a step back, as if to leave, but Erik's hand comes down on my shoulder. Hard. "I'm done with you."

Anex waves the girl off and leans forward. "I'm trying to be patient here, Rex. Rebellion is normal in a man your age. You want to spread your wings—your seed." He grins knowingly. "And I gave you a lot of leeway. Much more than anyone else in Serendee, because I knew for you to step into your rightful role, you had to experience what we are keeping the community safe from." He adjusts the gold watch on his wrist. "But things changed when you infected our circle with Secularism. When you pushed your Regressive, blasphemous views on the weak minded. I had no choice but to step in."

For the last month, hell, the last few years, there's been this dark ball in the center of my chest. Most of the time, I keep it still, smothering it down, but at night, alone in my room, I see it for what it is: a ticking bomb. *Tick, tick, tick.*

"By stepping in, do you mean branding my mate?" I ask, fingers twitching.

A beat of silence runs between us, dark and feral, the bomb in me ready to explode, but Anex is more calculating than that. He ignores me and gets to the point of this sham of a meeting.

"As much as I'd like to keep you toiling in the fields, your skill set is better used elsewhere." My skill set. Conning women into taking classes at the Center, handing over their personal details, bank accounts, bodies... "One of your recruits, Jasmine, is insisting on working with you." He snorts. "Apparently, her pussy and Daddy's pocketbook only open for you."

Tick, tick, tick.

"So, you're willing to pull me off grunt work, so I can seduce a heiress."

He shrugs. "Under supervision."

"You can force me to work in the fields, but what? You are going to make Erik stand over me with a gun while I fuck this girl?" I shake my head. "I don't think she'll be into it."

A line creases between his eyes. It's his tell. He's pissed. The first time I noticed it was when me and the guys came home late one night, rolling on molly and rummaging through the kitchen in the Main House. We'd trashed one of the cars, wrapping it around the mailbox of a professor's house just off Wittmore's campus. He didn't lose control then, and I don't expect him to now.

But that doesn't mean I won't pay.

"I think you've forgotten your roots. The Why of this community. How we are One and work together for The Way. How your petty, rebellious actions affect everyone."

His tone drops at the word everyone. Even if I'm isolated here, I know I'm not alone. Imogene and Silas are both bound to me. From the quirk on Anex's lips, I know where this is leading.

"You're upset about Imogene," he suggests.

"*Don't* say her name."

He stands, slowly walking toward me. When he speaks his voice is low. "You seem to be confused about how Serendee operates. This is my community, and these are my people. I *gave* you Imogene, which means I can, and have taken her away. The fact she kept the women's group and their actions a secret from you, fucked your friends on *my* command, and subjects herself to intense sessions of Corrections, means she never belonged to you. That's why I branded her. She's *mine*." His voice shakes, anger pushing through. "By the equinox she will be claimed," he smirks, "intimately."

My hand shoots out, clamping around his throat. His eyes bulge, jaw parts, fingers grabbing for release. "Not if I kill you first."

My fingers squeeze, tightening, but around me the guards, Erik, in particular, have sprung into action.

"Get off! Get him off!" a voice shouts. Hands grab at me, weapons are drawn. I have Anex too close for them to shoot me and I take advantage of the chaos swirling around us.

Another trick he taught me.

I don't stop, gritting my teeth as I try to snuff the life out of my father. "You will die for this. I will wring the life from you before I allow you to defile Imogene."

I grin down at him, he's losing strength—air—just a few more seconds and—

Slam!

A hard weight crashes down on the back of my head, I stumble back, dragging Anex with me, but my brain is fuzzy, consumed by distant echoing clicks. I blink, looking up at the barrel of Erik's gun, wishing for him to end it. To take me out.

Finish this for good, because the pain in my head, in my limbs, in my fucking gut is too damn much.

Our eyes meet, and he rears back, dropping the gun and the last thing I see is his fist slamming into my face.

Then I black out.

3

Silas

I've got one last person to visit when I see the burly guards drag Rex into his room. He's unconscious—he has to be. Otherwise, I can't envision any scenario where he's manhandled like this without a fight.

"Jesus, he's heavy," one of the guards says. I duck around the corner, hoping they didn't notice me. I may not be on lockdown, or outright banished like Levi and Elon, but I'm being closely monitored.

"Get him in there before he wakes up," the other replies. "I saw what he did to his father. I'm sure he'd have no problem taking us out too."

Rex did something to Anex?

"Do you blame him?" I hear one say. "Look at him, his father is the leader and he's locked in here like the rest of the Fallen."

"What did you say?" The voice is curt, tone hard. "You're questioning Anex's decisions?"

"N-no." He clears his voice. "No. That's not what I said. I just—

nothing." I hear them back in the hall, door closing behind them. "Let's get out of here. It creeps me out."

They move quickly, exiting the locked door down on the end of the corridor. I understand their haste. There's an underlying fear in Serendee that Regressive thoughts are contagious.

I wonder where they got that idea?

As the days pass, I'm learning more and more that the people down here have done little to deserve their fate. I sensed it before, the punishments seemed too swift, too severe, the conditions the Fallen are held in, demoralizing and dangerous. The younger women are used as a receptacle for Anex's hypersexual needs. The young men? An example to the rest of us about what can happen if you disobey.

Which is why, even though I'm worried, I don't go straight to check on Rex. It's too risky. Instead, I punch in the code to the room next door, pausing for a moment after the lock disengages. I've been avoiding this visit all day.

Charlotte is curled up on her bed, eyes darting to mine when I walk in.

"Silas," she says, rising. Her eyes brighten a little and it just makes me feel worse. "I hoped you were coming today."

I shut the door behind me. Charlotte is one of the Fallen I supervise now—a role given to me by Anex the night all hell broke loose. Charlotte, and the others down in this ward think they are being Reeducated to reenter Serendee. The truth is that Anex has bigger plans for them. They're being groomed for sale, and I've been assigned to prepare them.

"How are you?" I ask, noticing her dinner plate is empty. Stacks of Anex's books are on the small desk, pages dog eared and well-read. A food log is open. I stop by it and run my finger down. She's counted every calorie and every bodily function. "You ate all your dinner."

"I did," she says beaming. When I came down here before, with Elon and Imogene, Charlotte was in bad shape. Her weight was tragically low and she had an infection. She was bruised, her hair a stringy nest. She was desperate for Anex's approval, which was deranged. He was the one hurting her.

But as it became clear he wants to put her up for trade, he's allowed me to increase her caloric intake, provide her extra grooming time, and a few additional rewards. She looks better, eyes brighter, hair cleaner, although there's no mistaking her exhaustion. Anex is all about product, be it his classes or produce from the farm, or weed grown under the barn. He wants a superior product and Charlotte is nothing more than that.

An object to sell.

The craziest thing is that he managed to break her down to the point that she was afraid to eat the extra food at first. Terrified of accepting new things. Her brain was so twisted up, so wired to meeting Anex's insane demands, that she felt better starving herself than being healthy.

"Good," I say, and her smile widens, encouraged by my praise. I walk over and sit on the edge of the bed, taking her arm to assess her skin. The rash on her wrist from the shackles is finally healing. "I'm glad to see that it's better." It took a while, but I finally convinced Anex that the chains were unnecessary. Unfortunately, Charlotte is as passive as they come. "How are you sleeping?"

"Better. The meditation techniques you showed me help." She grins but ducks her head. "Do you think he'll come tonight?"

She asks me that every time I come—sometimes they are the first words out of her mouth. He's fully convinced her that the only way to reach Enlightenment is through his approval. She'll do anything to attain his favor. Even with extra calories and hygiene, her devotion to Anex is no less intense. Again, our leader knows how to manufacture the perfect product. Docile. Submissive.

"I'm not sure." I think about what the guards said, how they said Rex injured his father. "I think he may have other obligations."

"Oh." Her expression falls. "It's been a few days."

According to her journals, Anex used to visit her regularly—enacting Corrections personally as part of her Reeducation. Being in his presence is considered a gift, and for the Fallen, it was like being visited by God himself. What Charlotte doesn't understand is that she is no longer of interest to him outside the amount of money she can add to his coffers. He's done his work, broken her down, stoked her insecurities and lack of self-esteem. She's putty, primed and ready for trade.

"You seem tense," she says. "Everything okay?"

No, I want to say. Nothing is okay. My best friend was just dragged, unconscious, into the room down the hall. My other friends have been banished from the only home they've ever known, and the woman I love is being locked up in a fortress created to house and control the women of Serendee even more than before.

And the woman in front of me—girl really—is being expertly groomed for trade.

Nothing is fucking okay.

"I'm fine," I say, instead. "Just a long day."

"Maybe you want to hang around for a while?" Her hand rests on my thigh, falling into the role she's been taught so well. "I can help you out for once."

Bile rolls in my stomach, squelching any possible desire. Even though she's completely out of reach, the only woman I think about like that is Imogene.

I miss her so much. Her innocent smile, her kindness and compassion, the way she instinctively knows how to take care of those around her. It's what I thought I was doing all those years, but I was really just another layer in the system of abuse.

Still am.

Despite Imogene, the idea of having sex with Charlotte makes me physically ill. In a few days she'll be sent off to her new owner.

And I'll be the one making the trade.

Her hand drags upward, toward my crotch, while she leans forward, pressing a soft kiss against my neck. I swallow, trying to still my stomach, and ease Charlotte's hand off my leg. "I don't think so, sweetheart. I have a few other people to check up on tonight."

"Oh," she pulls back, but takes my rejection in stride. I don't sleep with the Fallen, even though Anex would approve. Someone needs to be there for them, look out for their health and needs. I know it's not much, but it's all I can do, at least while they're still here.

"Any update on my Rising?"

"Soon," I tell her, standing to create some distance.

Rising. That's what he—we—are calling it. Rising back into society. The first step out of the status of Fallen. From the ashes, blah blah blah. Anex has waxed poetically about it to me for the last month. It's just a shiny word for an ugly, terrifying thing. Sex-trafficking.

"I hope I've passed all my tests."

She has. Medically, psychologically, physically. Charlotte is the perfect fit for our first trade. She's pretty, docile, compliant, and willing to do anything Anex asks of her.

"You're going to do great," I tell her, hating myself for every word. Hating myself more for what I do next. My hand dips into my pocket and I pull out the green pill. "Here you go."

Her eyes light up. She gets one every morning and every night. A special blend of narcotics created here in Serendee. It's to keep the Fallen complacent, enough not to fight back while regaining enough strength not to look like shit for the buyers.

She happily takes it, swallowing it as fast as she can, then curls back on the bed, like she was when I came in. "Thanks, Silas."

I don't respond, I don't even breathe again until I'm out of the room, door locked tight. What I'm doing is so fucking wrong, but what other choice do I have?

I hear footsteps coming down the hallway and tense, but it's just the food delivery person. I watch as he stops at each door. I don't miss the taser on his hip, and he does his job expertly, no engagement, no conversation, just dropping off one plate and retrieving the one from the prior meal. The heavy doors click into place as he walks to the next room.

He nods as he passes, popping into Charlotte's room. I start to make my way down the hall, but then he pauses in front of Rex's room, and I stop.

I don't have access to his room. Anex didn't give me the passcode, which is understandable. Keeping us apart is just another nail in our punishment. I watch as he hesitantly approaches Rex's room, free hand shifting to the taser. This is also understandable. There's no fucking way Rex makes anything easy on anyone in here. He visibly braces himself and punches in the code. This time he doesn't go in, just slides the food across the floor and jumps back out.

Like Rex is a wild animal or something.

He scurries off, and on instinct I dart forward, shoving my foot in the empty space before the door catches. I know it's possible I'm being watched, but fuck it. My friend is hurt and I'm going to check on him.

I duck inside, wedging a handkerchief between the jamb and the door to keep it from locking.

Rex is flat on his back, the skin under his eye swelling and discolored. Blood oozes from a split lip. From my vantage, I see his chest rise and fall, confirming he's at least breathing.

"Hey," I say, nudging his shoulder. "Rex."

He shifts, a groan caught in his throat, and relief washes over me. It's been weeks since I've seen him and it's clear the time has been hard on him, at least physically. Although he's still big—tall and broad shouldered—his muscle mass is waning, his cheeks gaunt and under the forming bruises I see dark shadows under his eyes.

"Brother, wake up," I say, trying to push his frame closer to the wall. It takes both hands to move him over enough for me to sit next to him.

He blinks and our eyes meet. "Silas?"

"Yeah, it's me. You look like shit." He grunts, eyes fluttering shut. "Stay with me, okay? You definitely have a head injury, and you need to stay awake. Tell me what happened."

"Anex happened," he says as I unzip my bag, rummaging through for the scissors I carry with me. The blades are short, surgical, and I use them to cut the front of his shirt, ripping off a strip of fabric. I reach for the cup on his tray of food and dunk the fabric in the water. Balling it, I shove it in his hand and lift it to his mouth. "Apply pressure if you can."

I fall into routine, finding the package of bandages, rubbing alcohol, and salve I carry with me. Pretending the ache in my chest isn't one of revenge and anger. This is my friend, my best friend, and his father is the one that hurt him like this. It's wrong. Everything about this hell of the Fallen is wrong, but there's nothing I can do about it but tend to his wounds.

"Do you want to tell me what happened?" I ask, cleaning his knuckles with the alcohol.

He winces at the sting. "You know what happened."

Imogene.

My heart leaps in my throat. "Did he do or say something specific?"

His eyes open and his crystal blue gaze holds mine. "He wants her."

There's no mistaking what he means. I see it every day down here, the girls Anex keeps for his own services. "I think he made that clear when he branded her with his initials."

"No, Silas," he pushes up on his elbows, a struggled huff of air escaping his lungs. "He *wants* her, for his own. For his pleasure and under his control." He hisses when I swipe the ointment over the scraps on his hand. "He's going to claim her on the equinox."

"What?" I ask, a tremor rolling up my spine. "The equinox?" There's no mistaking what that means. It's a ceremony. It was to be Rex and Imogene's ceremony before everything fell apart. "He wants to mate with her."

"He's going to, Silas." There's an undeniable pain in his voice. "He will unless…"

"Unless we save her."

We fall into silence, both of us well aware that the other would have done something if we could. We have no freedom. No money. No confidence we can get her to safety.

Rex sighs. "Any word from the guys?"

"Nothing." I gesture for him to turn. "Let me check your head."

The contusion is about the size of my fist—but there's a clear outline—the butt of a gun. I gingerly press my thumb against the spot, and he shouts, "Son of a bitch, Silas!"

"Sorry, I was just testing it."

"Well, it hurts like a motherfucker."

I stand, walking across the room to lean against the small metal desk. "It's a bad injury. Like I said, you probably have a concussion, but this isn't my area of expertise."

"Yeah, you're better at massaging vaginas and soothing psychic trauma."

His tone is snide—dismissive, but I know he's just upset. I'm upset. "You're right. The damage your father does to the Fallen down here—it's not as violent, but it's also no less brutal."

"So, he still plans on selling them?"

"Any day now, I suspect."

"And you?" There's no mistaking his concern. "What's he going to do with you?"

"I don't know." I push off the table and start to collect my supplies. "But I'm pretty sure if he found out I'm in here helping you, he'd put me out there with them."

"You're right." Something in his eyes is clear, like he's struggling through the fog. "You being here is dangerous. Not just for me and you but—"

"For Imogene." I straighten and grab my bag. Not wanting to leave my friend, not hurt, not ever. I start for the door, pausing with my hand on the knob. "I'll get to her," I tell him. "I'll make sure she's okay."

"No," Rex snaps.

"You don't want me to check on her?"

"I want you to make sure she's safe," he says, expression turning hard—looking more like his father than I've ever seen him. "But what I need you to do is make sure she gets away from here—from him." He holds my eye, understanding passing between us. Still, he asks unnecessarily, "Got it?"

"Rex," I say, shaking my head.

"Silas, I'm serious. Promise me."

I swallow past the knot in my throat, a wave of nausea not far behind. Rex isn't just my best friend, he's also the leader's son. The heir. My loyalty to him is greater than it is to anyone else, including Anex. That's the reason I nod and accept his directive, even though it goes against every instinct I have.

Rex wants me to do whatever it takes to get Imogene out of here.

Even if that means leaving him behind.

4

Elon

"Make it a double this time," I say, gesturing to my empty glass. The bartender, a woman named Shelly, eyes both me and the glass before grabbing the bottle from the shelf and pouring the amber liquid to the rim.

"You're a big guy," she says, gently pushing it my way, "but even big guys have limits. I think you've about reached yours."

"Sweetheart," I say, pulling the glass close, "you have no fucking idea about my limits."

Trust me, I've been testing them. Day after day. Night after night. Just trying to see if I can reach them—reach the point where I can feel something other than the all-consuming rage that festers in my chest. The alcohol, well, it's an attempt to numb it a little bit.

There's only one thing—one person—that can quell the dark anger coursing through me, and she's locked away, out of reach. She's lost to me.

Who am I kidding? She was never mine to begin with.

I swallow the liquid in one gulp, letting the burn take over for a brief moment.

"You come in here, night after night, looking like hell and then head down to the ring," the bartender says, dark ponytail swinging against the column of her neck. She takes my empty glass and drops it into the sink. The message is clear. She's done serving me. "What's your deal?"

I catch my reflection in the mirror behind the bar—my dark hair messy, a thick beard covers my cheeks and chin—as well as the gauntness of my cheekbones. It does nothing to hide the dark circles visible under my eyes that give me a look of worn-out desperation. The dried blood on my split lip I received during last night's fight only accentuates it. I look homeless, which is apt.

I'm without a home.

Without my community.

Without my leader.

Banished.

"Don't people come to these places to get lost?" I ask, reaching for the cash in my pocket—cash I earned downstairs—and peel off a few bills. "Isn't it your job to make your patrons feel at home? Or at the very least, not ask a lot of intrusive questions?"

She leans over the bar, tits pressed against the thin fabric of her tank. She's not wearing a bra, she never does, and her nipples seem perpetually hard. She's the kind of girl Anex warned us about, tempting like a sweet, delicious, fruit, but she's not the kind of secular girl we pursue. Too independent. Too confident. Trouble.

"You're right. That was rude of me, but let me make it up to you." She looks at the clock over the bar. "How about you come find me after your match."

The bar is on the other side of the Whittmore campus, a shithole frequented by students trying to pretend they're something more than entitled frat boys. It's not the usual haunt Rex and I would frequent while working the University. This place doesn't have the right clientele for Anex's recruitment. That's why I'm here. Well, that and the fact that downstairs is a fighting ring, a place for petty grudge matches and high stakes bets. I've spent most of my nights drinking and then going down to blow off some steam and earn a little cash. It's not like Anex is funding my life outside Serendee.

"You in?" Shelly asks.

Fighting makes sense. Fucking, not so much, but I hold her eye, wondering how it would feel to lose myself in her—in someone. To find a reprieve from the anger and ache.

"Don't embarrass yourself, doll," a voice says from next seat over. "You're not his type."

Shelly's gaze flicks to him. "Mind your own business, Royer."

"He likes his women a little more subservient," he grins over at me with a crooked and clearly drunk smile. "Isn't that, right?"

My eyes shift to study the asshole's face in the mirror reflection and realize I've seen him before. He's one of the frat presidents over at Whittmore. We've done business—which means he may know more about me than I realize.

Shelly's eyebrow rises. "What's he's going on about?"

"Nothing." I stand. My history isn't anyone's business, especially these two. "Night."

"He's one of those wackos," Royer says, apparently not ready to give this up. His voice lifts over the music and crowd. "From that cult."

My spine tenses at the word, my heart racing. Instinct is hard to alter, and a lifetime of defending Serendee is second nature. My fingers curl into a fist.

"You know, where the girls wear those creepy dresses and act all pure and innocent." He snorts. "I heard a rumor that they can't actually leave —the girls in particular. That the freak leader has more than one wife."

I turn on him. "You're really going to talk to me about subjecting women? I know what your parties are like, how you treat the women let in the door. They're nothing but glorified whores."

Behind the bar Shelly's eyes are wide. "You're in a sex cult?"

The weird thing is that she doesn't seem entirely disinterested. Maybe she's a better target than I realized. The kind of girl I can introduce to Rex, and he can—

Fuck. I rub my hand over my face.

I keep doing it. I fall back into the routine over and over. That life is over. Rex and Silas are trapped behind the walls, suffering God knows what kind of punishment. Imogene is—I can't even think of what could be happening to her.

And Levi.

Shit.

There's no doubt he's taking the banishment harder than I am. His entire life was wrapped up in Anex and The Way. His entire identity. Where Rex, Silas, and I succumbed to the temptations of the secular world, Levi... he held firm to his faith.

And now he truly has nothing but me, a Regressive, with no path to Enlightenment.

"Is that true?" Shelly asks again. "Is the leader a polygamist?"

The argument that Serendee isn't a cult—isn't a sex cult—is on the tip of my tongue, but for the first time in my life I'm too tired to say it. Or maybe, for the first time I don't believe it, which is why the following falls from my lips.

"Why?" I ask. "Do you want an introduction? Do you want to go in and see if he'll take you?" I look her up and down, at the outline of her nipples, at all the flesh and exposed skin. "You can try, but before you even get in the door he'll break you down, bleed your bank account, isolate you from your family, and force you to submit to his whims." She swallows, my bluntness shaking her confidence. "Is that what you want? Someone to demean you? Control you?" I snap my arm out and grab her wrist, leaning over the bar until we're inches apart. "If that's what you want, you and I can go to the back, and I can give you a taste of what it's like personally."

A tremor runs down her spine, spreading goosebumps across her skin, tightening those nipples into hard peaks.

"Don't hurt me," she says in a quiet voice. "Please."

Royer's hand comes down on my shoulder. "Let her go, asshole, or lose the hand."

I release her, dropping her wrist like her skin is made of fire. I need to get out of the bar. Get away from these people. Fuck the money from the fight. We'll make due or maybe we can try to—

No. I shake the thought from my head for the millionth time since we were tossed outside the gates. We can't go back. Not just because Anex is a fraud, but because he won't let us. I'm certain of that.

And that, I think, exiting the bar and heading into the night, is the worst part of it all.

If he let me come back, I'd probably go.

Because without Serendee, without Anex, I not only don't know who I am, but I'm not sure I'm anything at all.

"Hey," Royer calls, grabbing me by the shoulder and spinning me around. "Don't think you can manhandle her and walk out of here."

I snort, head swimming from the night of drinking. "And you're going to stop me?"

"Someone needs to."

Gazing down at the guy, it's easy to see that I'm not just taller than him, but I probably have him by thirty pounds. It's when I meet his eyes that I see there's something wicked lurking in there—a wildness I've seen before. Rex gets that look when he wants to cause trouble and that's what this guy wants—trouble.

Maybe I'm the one that should give it to him.

I look over at Shelly, her hand rubbing the spot on her wrist where I had hold of her and the reality hits me harder—I'm not any better than Anex. I hurt. I take. I abuse.

"You want to fight me?" I ask.

"More than anything," he says, pushing up his sleeves.

I jerk my chin toward the stairs. Someone should have stopped Anex a long time ago. And even though I doubt this kid can take me, I should at least give him a shot.

Someone needs to stop me, too.

"You've got to stop doing this." The bag of frozen corn lands on my stomach. I jump, as much from the cold as the aching pain in my side.

"I was made for this," is my short reply. Born for it. Cultivated like the weed growing under Anex's barn. Wincing, I lean over and shove my hand in my pocket, pulling out the wad of cash and tossing it at Levi. He lets it fall to the floor, like it's too dirty for him to touch.

"You're welcome." I lift the bag and press it against my temple. That Royer prick may be a dumbass, but he's got a solid right hook. Too bad for him, all those years of corrections make taking a few hits seem like a cake walk. More than that, I enjoy it—*deserve* it.

"There are other ways to make money," Levi says, sitting on the chair across from mine. With his red hair in disarray, and slumped in his seat, he looks as beat up as I feel.

"Name one that I'm qualified for other than drug dealer or fighter."

After Anex banished us, we were forcibly removed from the property. Tossed in the back of a van and driven miles from town. Dumped by Anex's guards in a park with nothing but a bag of generic clothing and supplies. He'd given us both a hundred dollars in cash, along with our ID's, but we had no idea what to do with it. Sure, I'd spent time outside the walls of Serendee, but due to my position as one of the Chosen, I had stacks of cash, nice cars, clothes, and access to clubs and restaurants. Living a life of secular poverty was an unknown.

We didn't go quietly. At least I didn't. I had one goal, get back to Serendee, breach the walls and find Imogene, Silas, and Rex. But as the hours passed, and Levi managed to get us a ride back to town, my plot altered. I knew getting inside the walls would be impossible, especially unarmed. We'd need supplies. Weapons. A plan. Intelligence.

I wanted my woman back in one piece and I wanted Anex dead.

To his credit, while I wallowed, Levi stepped up and found this crappy little apartment two miles from campus. It's an efficiency. With a double bed, a scratchy couch, and an ancient, avocado green refrigerator that rattles all day and night. We at least had shelter. But we needed money. I'd heard rumors about the bar that held nightly fights and decided to check it out.

"There are legitimate jobs," Levi continues.

I switch the bag to my swollen knuckles. "Have you had any success finding one of these magical jobs?"

He shoots me a resigned look. We both know he hasn't. Why? Because we were raised with no real skills. Anex hamstrung us for living a life outside of Serendee. For living a life *inside* Serendee.

"So, you're struggling to find a job where you can lecture people in the glory of basking in the glow of Anex's genius? Or no one will allow you to dole out Corrections for personal failures?"

"Elon…"

"Fuck, Levi, at least he taught Silas how to be a whore! He could survive out here! We're just…."

"Fucked. We're fucked, I know!" He shouts, the last thread of his patience snapping. "You don't have to keep reminding me!"

If I thought rattling Levi would make me feel better, I was wrong.

Now I just feel like shit. Faith is all he has. It's all he's ever had and watching those beliefs slip away is like watching a man drown.

I sigh. "You know what I think about when I'm in the ring, letting those assholes get in a few punches?"

"What?"

"How much of our world was orchestrated by Anex. Did he sense who we are, who we could be, from childhood? I don't misunderstand that he used us to build Serendee. At what point did he realize my body, my strength and power, could be honed to pressure and compel? To enforce? That Silas's was nothing more than a vessel to be exploited, his body used to manipulate and convert?" Levi's face pales, his hands gripping the arms of the chair, knuckles white. I continue, "Or when did he recognize that your mind, your faith and loyalty, would keep the rest of us on the path to Enlightenment even when we knew better."

"Don't—"

I'm not finished. I lean forward, feeling the burn against my rib—

relishing the pain. "And what about Rex? The heir. Gifted and powerful. He always had the ability, and freedom, to become the greatest of us all. But was there ever any real freedom? Were we really friends? Were any of us more than pawns?"

"I don't know the answer to any of those things." His eyes are cast down and my heart sinks, because Levi always knows the answer to these questions. He's always a rock, reliant on faith even when the rest of us aren't. And if he can no longer draw on that, then what are we supposed to do? "I don't know who I am outside those walls, outside the classroom and literature and books." His gaze meets mine. "Outside of Anex's approval."

I haven't told Levi about my plan. About the lists I keep in my head. The number of guns. The knives and explosives. How I will get Imogene first. Then Rex and Silas. And after they are safe, I will find Timothy Wray, the man that started all of this, the man that destroyed our lives, and I will end him.

5

Imogene

"I understand it's hard for you to be away from your mates and your homes right now, but starting your child's life in our new Childcare Center will allow them to be one step closer to Enlightenment and The Way. Their entire foundation will come from a place of hope and love—from a compounded energy passed from each of you, from me, and my wives. We're no longer just members of a community, we're a family. I will be the father to all of your children, just as you will mother each other's children."

Anex's words create a cold ball in my belly, a reaction to the lies and manipulation. Even though I can see it so clearly now, how he uses his gifted tongue to draw people to his will, there's part of me that is surprised I'm no longer influenced by his lectures. I know better now. He isn't a good man.

I stand just outside the room, uninvited to the meeting as I am both Fallen and not pregnant, waiting to clean up when he dismisses them. I can see the women, including my former friend, Maria, whose face is bright with Anex's declaration of a shared family unit.

"Before I go," he uses his hands to gesture to the women, "come forward, and I will bless each of you and your unborn child."

Bile rises to the back of my throat, nausea from watching these women so easily manipulated. Margaret goes first, her belly exposed, in one of her unconventional outfits. Clothing forbidden by other women in Serendee. Her skirt is long, but her top cinches under her swollen breasts, revealing the exposed skin of her protruding belly. The top is cut low, and it's the kind of clothing we'd always been warned against, but rules don't seem to apply to Anex's favored wife. Still, she goes through the motions, touching her forehead and bowing before our leader. When she stands, Anex rests his hands on her stomach and he bends, kissing the stretched skin softly. It's an intimate act between a man and his mate—she's carrying his child, after all. Margaret smiles and steps to the side, and the next woman is waved forward. She goes through the same motions of honoring Anex.

"Sweet Doris," he says to the woman. She was Ordered and Mated a few years ago. "It's no secret you've struggled with conception. And you went through the process to discern what you were doing to block this gift from your life. You spent your time in Reflection and Correction. You've studied and meditated over The Way. You've searched for Enlightenment and ultimately, you allowed your body to accept the seed of life. A seed we shall cultivate and foster in our family garden."

His words are a twist of confusion—a blessing and a condemnation at the same time.

"Lift your skirts," he commands. Without hesitation, Doris does as she's asked, lifting the fabric and revealing herself to the room—to him. Anex's hands splay across her stomach, a gentle caress, similar to the one he gave his wife. "This baby shall be a gift to Serendee— the future of our community. The hope for alignment and peace." He bends, kissing the pale skin. A sick feeling heats my throat as I watch the scene unfold. The way Doris smiles down at him. The way Margaret looks at them with such loving confidence.

Everything in this room is wrong—so wrong. I look up to my

friend Maria, waiting for her blessing, aware of the shiny glaze in her eye. It's awe and respect. Devotion.

I stumble back, away from the intensity of the room, struck with my own emotion. Grief. Jealousy. Abandonment. It's too much to comprehend and I turn away, escaping down the hall. I enter the first door I come to. Inside, the room is dark other than a small lamp over the exam table. Pressing my back to the door I shudder out an exhale.

"Imogene?"

My heart lurches and I turn to the dark corner I heard the voice.

The *familiar* voice.

"Silas?"

The instant his name is out of my mouth, I wish it back. It's foolish. Ridiculous. I'm losing my mind. This place, the isolation, is making me crazy. Silas isn't welcome here.

"Imogene, it's me." I don't believe it until I feel his hands on me, one on my hip, the other sliding behind my neck. His eyes dart from my face across my body, assessing. "God, tell me you're okay."

I nod, unable to speak past the lump in my throat. Fear that this isn't real. A tear slides down my cheek, and he catches it with the warm pad of his thumb. "Baby, it's okay. Take a deep breath."

I inhale, allowing the air into my lungs and when I exhale, I ask, "What are you doing here? How did you get in?"

"The apothecary." He nods over to the corner he'd come from. A box sits on the counter, stamped with Serendee Apothecary on the side. "The Center requested a delivery and I volunteered to bring it."

"Anex is here," I warn him, pressing my body to his. "Talking to the mothers. If he finds you—"

"I don't care." His hands roam my face, like he's searching for something. "I needed to see you—make sure you were okay." He swallows, Adam's apple bobbing in his throat. "Has he hurt you?"

I shake my head. "No."

His hand runs along my side. "You've lost weight."

"He... he prefers me this way."

Silas swears, a secular, forbidden word. "You don't belong to him."

"Do I not? Do I not wear his brand? Live with his wife? Do his bidding?" I whisper, looking into his darkening eyes. "Are you not under his thumb, too?"

"Let me see it."

My head tilts. "What?"

"The brand."

Heat prickles my skin. "No."

He grabs my wrist, but it's not harsh. It's warm. Strong. Touch I've craved for weeks now. "*Yes*. Let me make sure it's healing correctly."

"It's humiliating," I confess. "It's embarrassing to wear his mark like this."

Silas' sharp, angular, jaw clenches tight. "You think it's not degrading to do the work he forces on me? Preparing the Fallen to be whored out to the depraved and perverted?"

"Silas—"

"We were raised to protect one another, Imogene. Community at all costs, but I spend my days and nights doing the opposite. I am a traitor to my brothers and sisters, and that has left me as marked as you are, mine is just under the flesh, burned into my soul." His skin pales. "What he's asked me to do to the Fallen—"

"And Banished," I interject. He stops, worry drawing his eyebrows together. I see he's afraid to say their names too. Elon. Levi. Rex.

"So," he says, licking his lips, hand firm on my hip, just above the branding, "let me see it."

I don't fight as Silas reaches for the hem, lifting the gray jumper to my waist. He hooks a finger at the waist of my underclothes and pulls them down.

Again, I flinch, moving to cover it.

His hand stops mine, and when our eyes meet his are hard with determination. "Don't hide yourself from me, Imogene."

I relent and lean back against the hard door as his fingers gently explore the wound. I refuse to look at it, hating the damaged, burned skin, the red, never healing sore. Silas drops to his knees, and a low curse cuts through the quiet of the room. His fingers explore the edges of the brand.

"It's fine," I tell him, wincing as he touches a sensitive spot. "Hardly any pain left. The scabs are healing—"

"I'll kill him for this." I hear the promise in his words.

If only.

If only Anex wasn't surrounded by armed followers. If only he didn't have Rex guarded twenty-four hours a day. If only we knew how to find Levi and Elon. If only we'd left when we'd had the chance—when Rex asked us to. He knew. He knew and we fought him.

I touch Silas' chin, lifting his gaze upward. "You're not a killer."

His jaw sets. "You don't know what I've done or what I'm capable of, Imogene, especially when a man harms something so important to me."

I see it now, that even in this short time, Silas has changed. That I've changed. We're raw. Lost. Broken.

Desperate.

"I know you're strong, but I also know you're a good man. You care for people, and you can't let him take that away, or allow him to use it against you." I press my hand against his cheek. "We're here to make a difference. To help those who can't help themselves. The Fallen—the pregnant women out there. Someone has to, and if it's not us, then who?"

"You're too good for Serendee," he says, still on his knees. "You're too good for *him*."

He takes my hand, kissing my fingers before moving back to the brand. He kisses the skin around it gently, so soft I barely feel it, except for the siren of goosebumps rising across my flesh. My head falls back, sinking into the touch of the man that showed me a whole new way to view my body—opening me up to something besides what I'd been taught. That it's okay to seek pleasure, to fulfill my desires.

Silas's kisses move from the wound, down my legs, and to my inner thighs. His tongue lathes over the scars put there that forbidden night by Levi. His touch is feather light, soft sucking that sends sparks of heated want between my legs. It's wrong to want this, to risk this, but it's been weeks since I've seen my men—felt their touch. I crave something other than the cold sterility of this place.

The threat of what's to come.

I crave him.

"Silas," I whisper, tugging at his thick hair. "Please."

"Please what?" he asks, breath hot on my pussy. A tremor runs up my spine.

"I want you inside of me." His tongue drags across my core, and I buck against his mouth. "Silas, give me this."

He rises, taking more time than he should, more time than we have, kissing a trail along my neck. I push at the buckle on his pants, reaching for him with needy hands. The feel of him, hot and hard, sends a rush of sticky warmth between my legs. He doesn't hesitate, hooking my leg around his waist and entering me with a thrust.

"Oh," I breathe, loving the invasion—the feel of him thick and wide—pushing at my walls as they clench around him. "I've missed this."

"I missed you." He rocks back, punching in, and I wrap my other leg around him, wanting him deeper. "I dream of you at night. Of this. Being with you, being safe."

My reply comes in a rush of air, panting from the way he makes me feel. Silas is a skilled lover—trained—and the way he touches me, strokes me, guides his cock into my body, sets every nerve on edge.

But none of that is what sends me to the precipice. It's the look in his eye, the way his tongue licks hot against my lips, is the way he sees me—the way no one else in this place can. Silas and I are bonded in this moment, in the fear of being caught, in the struggle of being alone—our closest confidants ostracized.

His thumb grazes over my clit, making my walls clench around him. "Fuck, baby, you feel so good."

Silas stifles his pleasure by biting down on my shoulder, teeth bared, hard and painful against my skin. That pain, so delicious and raw, triggers a shuddering orgasm. Warm and deep, a hard final thrust. We stay this way for a long moment—him inside of me—my body clinging to him inside and out.

He looks down at my shoulder. "I'm sorry—"

"Don't be." That pain is a sharp reminder I can carry with me long after he's gone. I kiss his jaw. "You have to go."

My statement comes out abrupt, but we both know it. Every minute he's here is a risk we're discovered.

Even with the pressure, Silas moves with care, making sure to wipe between my legs, removing any trace he'd claimed me.

"Have you seen him?" I ask, finally speaking his name. It feels even more dangerous than what we just did. "I only get glimpses from the window."

"I saw him." His eyes shift, not meeting mine.

"Is he okay?" A dark laugh rushes out. "Of course not. Anex wouldn't allow it, and Rex—"

"He's still stubborn. Defiant. He took a pretty severe beating. Thankfully, I was able to sneak in and treat him."

"A beating? Why?"

This time his eyes meet mine and there's no mistake. *Me*. He took a beating because of me.

I reach for Silas's shirt, curling the cotton in my fingertips. "Tell him to stop. Tell him that there's nothing he can do to save me. He shouldn't sacrifice himself—"

"Imogene." He smooths down my skirt. "You belong to him. To us. Telling any of us not to sacrifice for you is like asking for our hearts to stop beating. It's impossible."

Warmth fills my chest, but it's also tinged with fear. "No, what's impossible is Anex allowing it. The best thing for all of you, is to forget me."

This was a mistake. Seeing him like this, feeling him, when I know that a future together is impossible. "He's planning on me becoming his mate at the equinox. There will be a ceremony, and he's waiting for me to begin menstruating again so that after the ceremony..."

I can't say it, but I don't need to, Silas knows. What I don't expect is for him to say, "You're not going to have a period, Imogene. Not if I can help it."

A door slams in the hallway, followed by footsteps and voices. Our time is up.

"What are you talking about?"

His voice is barely a whisper. "I've been swapping your supplements. The ones he hopes will make you fertile for a compound that does the opposite. It's not a guarantee, but the herbalists say the mixture will keep you from ovulating."

I blink. "You're why my period hasn't returned?"

He cups my face in his hands, voice a whisper. "I mixed it myself. Something to buy us time."

"Time for what? For them to come for us?" Uneasiness blooms in my chest just thinking about my men on the outside. "They can't, and they shouldn't."

He presses his lips to mine and steps back, moving to the door that leads away from the hallway. "Never underestimate what the four of us can do. Especially when it comes to you."

He slips out, my heart hammering from his kiss and the threat of being caught. I scramble to the counter where he left the delivery, picking up a bottle just as the door opens. Healer Bloom narrows her eyes at me.

"What are you doing in here?"

I keep my hand steady, hoping she can't see the red of my cheeks in the dim light. "There was a delivery from the apothecary. I figured since everyone was busy with Anex's visit…"

Her lips set in a frown. "Make sure you check everything off the list. And put everything in the correct place."

"Yes, ma'am."

She gives me one last glare and exits the room. I exhale, but don't fully breathe until hours later, long after Anex has left, and it's clear that Silas escaped undetected.

6

Levi

Elon never sleeps until the sun rises, and today is no different. He finally succumbs, still drunk, but exhausted. And if the pattern he's kept up the past few weeks maintains, he'll stay this way, until he goes back tonight and repeats the cycle.

He pretends he does it for money, but we both know the truth. It's self-punishment. Correction. Why? It's how they were raised. Those lessons are impossible to break—inside or outside of Serendee.

Probably even more so now that we're out, which is exactly why Anex banished us. He knew how bad it would hurt. How devastating. It's exactly what I would have done, if I'd been the leader.

I shrug on my jacket and step into the hall, quietly locking the door behind me. The hallway smells damp, like mildew and moisture. Like the stale cooking odors behind residents' closed doors. The stairwell is worse, reeking of piss and beer. I hold my breath as I take the steps, not inhaling until I reach outside. The air is better, but clogged with the gust of the idling bus. I long for the clean air of my home, the fresh homegrown food, and my classroom.

I need a purpose, and over the last few days, while Elon succumbs to his demons, I've come up with a plan.

A plan to earn our way back into Anex's good will and Serendee.

A way back to Enlightenment.

Using a few of the dollars Elon won in the fight, I step onto the bus and pay the fare. I take a seat and watch the buildings change from deteriorating, to the crisp, clean façade of Whittmore University. The passengers change, the bus filling up with students on their way to class—on to learning about the secular world. Greed and destruction. Wars and wealth. Science for profit. I shift, leaning forward, squashing the nerves as we approach the long strip of businesses where The Center is located.

For a heartbeat, I consider aborting the plan. Passing by and heading back home, but that lick of desperation tickles my spine and I stand, yanking the cord for the driver to stop. The bus lurches forward, and I stumble down the stairs, expelled into the street. The bus hisses and drives off, leaving me in a cloud of exhaust. Two blocks away, I see two women, wearing pale blue long dresses, their hair long and twisted into tight braids.

Turning quickly, I duck into the alley next to the building and make my way to the back. As much as I'd like to walk in the front door of The Center and demand an audience with Anex, I know I wouldn't make it past the threshold.

But I'm not just any member of Serendee—I'm one of the inner circle. I know the workings of this building and many of the others. I step behind the building and search for the brick with Serendee's logo stamped in the side. I pause, considering the last time I saw this design it was branded into Imogene's flesh. Property. His intention was clear. Imogene belongs to him, the same way this building does.

Using the tips of my fingers, I work the edge of the brick out and peer inside. A flat key rests against the back. I remove it and replace the brick. Standing before the door, I have a brief fear that maybe he changed the locks, but it's quickly replaced with the knowledge that no, Anex wouldn't change his locks. It would never cross his mind that I would return without his blessing. That I would ever go against his will.

Anex may understand me, but he doesn't understand this emotion coursing through my veins—this desperation.

As expected, the key slips in, and I turn it, releasing the bolts. A moment later, I'm inside.

The room is the same as the last time I was here. The table in the center of the room where Imogene bent over and I lashed her backside with a leather strap. Where I became so angry, so lost in my own desires, that I left and Elon came in to finish the job.

Well, this time I will finish what has been started.

I approach the wall and stare at the point where I know a camera is placed and speak aloud, "I know you never want to see me again, and you can send your guards to toss me out, but I think it's in your best interest to come talk to me." I swallow back the fear rising in my throat. "Alone. I'm pretty sure I have something you want."

～

FIVE MINUTES LATER, my stomach drops when the door opens and a guard walks in. His hand is on the butt of his pistol, chin jerking toward the table. "Face the table. Legs spread."

My mind blanks, wondering if this is the end, a bullet to the back of the head. A quick and quiet removal. No one would ever know. Not Elon, who I left without a note or any indicator of where I was going. Not Silas or Rex... not Imogene, who I wanted to see more than anything.

I do as I'm told, placing my hands on the table, legs slightly spread. The guard shifts behind me, hands running down my sides, patting my hips and legs. "He's clear," he says, and it dawns on me that he's just looking for weapons.

Anex thought I came to kill him.

No, this man doesn't know me at all.

Turning, I see Anex in the doorway. He gestures for his guard to leave. Once the door shuts, he looks at me with expectation. The movement is instinctive, I touch my forehead and bow. "Thank you for meeting me."

"I'm not used to taking demands," he says, walking around the table and settling in the only chair. "Especially from the Banished."

All of this is expected. Anex, for all his power and control, can be petty. Especially if he doesn't have the upper hand. Knowing I'm treading on thin ice, I get to the point.

"Things... things did not go as planned," I admit. "You asked us to train Imogene for Rex, in an effort to prepare your son for his position as heir and although we tried..."

His blue eyes watch me carefully. "You became Indulgent."

"Yes."

A smile quirks the corner of his lips. "As much as I want to say that you should have been stronger, that The Way should have provided you with the strength to resist temptation, I believe I unintentionally set the three of you up for failure."

I blink, trying to process his words. "Excuse me?"

This time he laughs. "I knew the Regressive streak was strong with her, but I didn't realize Imogene is a siren. She beckons men into foolish, emotional, *physical* reactions. She is impossible to resist. You fell for it. Elon. Silas. Even Rex, who, to his credit, noticed it sooner than I did. He requested her. My son, who has spent his life in Indulgences, teaching himself how to resist the depravities of the outside world, succumbed to her seduction."

Imogene. Of course, he would blame her for all of this. Not himself, not truly, just her. The Regressive in our midst.

"Then why not Banish her instead of us?"

He leans back in the chair, fingers tented in a contemplative pose. "You were my brightest teacher, Levi. Why do you think so?"

"Because she is a lesson. An example."

"As were you, yes." His eyes hold mine. Swirling anxiety fills the cavity of my chest. "Imogene is the worst kind of Regressive. She came by it naturally—born into it from her mother's betrayal, but she plays the part so well. A lion in sheep's clothing. A toxin in our water. A poison among our innocents. She is dangerous inside these walls and out. Banishing her is an impossibility. Reeducation is a risk, but at least a warning to the other women she may have tainted with her ideas."

"Then what?" I ask, fearful for the woman that opened up my soul.

"Only one person can eradicate the evil inside of her."

His smile tells all.

"You."

"Yes, Levi, me." He licks his bottom lip. "In a few short weeks she will become my mate. I will reclaim her. Filling her with my seed—giving her my blessing and light. She will become whole again. I will save her and bring her personally to Enlightenment."

His plan... It sounds righteous and true. It sounds like the perfect embodiment of The Way. There is nothing I can do but nod, because if I open my mouth, I may scream. But I am here for a purpose. I have a plan, and Anex may have just given me the path back in.

I swallow back the sour taste rising in my throat. "I want back in. I want Elon back in."

"And why would I allow that?"

"Like you said, we fell victim to a powerful and dangerous woman. We were weak. Confused. We lost our Way."

"I didn't come down here to listen to your groveling," he shifts, the metal chair creaking under the movement, "tell me what it is that you think I want to hear."

"You and I both know there is no Redemption for the Fallen. You kept Silas here to train them for your next endeavors. Yes, you need an example for your followers, but not just an example of punishment—you need an example of Redemption. Elon and I can come back as proof that the Fallen can emerge and regain their rightful position." When he doesn't respond, I add, "Hope is a much better motivator than fear.

"Possibly, but who are you to come to me with demands."

"Well, that is where I can get the one thing you've been desiring and is out of your reach. The person you truly want to punish."

His eyebrow raises. "And who is that?"

"Imogene's mother."

7

Imogene

Serendee is, at times, a strange mix of past and present. Anex discusses this in his lectures, how taking from both creates a perfect community. We don't drive cars inside the walls—we walk, or occasionally use horses or wagons. But there is still use for the innovations of the outside world—trucks for delivering product from the farm. Solar powered electricity to keep the buildings running day and night. And thankfully, he believes in washing machines because the amount of laundry we go through at The Center is getting out of hand.

Our detergents and soaps are locally made, and we hang everything on the line. That is my task for today, but when I walk into the laundry room, I stop short. Maria is already there, pulling white sheets from the machine. It's not so much that she's in the room that causes my pause, it's the way her hands flutter up to her belly—her bare belly. She's in a top and skirt similar to the one Margaret wears.

"What—" I clear my throat, drawing my eyes away from the deep v of her cleavage. "What are you doing in here?"

The women do help around the house, but nothing physical.

Mostly sewing or cooking. She shrugs, hands still splayed over her pale stomach. I've known Maria my entire life. The skin on her abdomen has never seen the light of day before.

When she doesn't, I step forward and thrust out my hands. "Let me do that."

"I'm fine."

"You don't need to do such strenuous work." I bend, taking over the chore. "I've got this, you go..."

"Go what?" she snaps, stepping back with the swish of her skirt. "Imogene, you know I need something to do. Sitting around isn't my thing."

She's right. Maria is a hard worker. She was always busy with something in our Domun. And now Anex has taken that away from her too. He's taken her home, her mate, and now her clothes.

Maybe Maria and I aren't so different after all.

I pick up the loaded basket and nod to the container of clothes pins. "You can carry those and hand them to me while I hang the wash."

"Seriously?"

I shoot her a look. "Do you want Healer Bloom lecturing you about overworking?" She shakes her head. "Then take what you can get, Maria. That's all any of us can do."

We walk out the back door, to the grassy area set up with clothes lines. The weather is a perfect pre-fall day. It's a reminder that the clock is ticking—the equinox is coming. The idea makes me tense and I get to work, lifting the first sheet.

Maria stands behind me, one hand trying to hide her stomach, the other holding the clothes pins. I can't help but notice her discomfort with showing so much skin outdoors. I pick up the next sheet and pause. "Here," I hand it to her, "hold that to cover yourself."

She takes the sheet and pulls it to her belly, holding it loosely. "Thank you."

I go back to my chore. "You shouldn't be put in this position in the first place."

A gust of wind blows, whipping my hair around my head. I grab for it, pushing my collar aside in the movement.

Maria gasps. "What happened?"

I frown, fingers brushing over the spot where my neck and shoulder meet. The skin is tender, and my nose wrinkles at the sensitivity. "Oh, nothing," I say quickly, adjusting my collar back. "Just a bruise I got from being clumsy."

She eyes me warily, and I refocus on the laundry and keeping it off the ground. Maria knows me—well, knew me—better than anyone. If anyone can see through my lies it's her.

"Looks painful."

"It's nothing." Just a love bite from my forbidden lover, that's all. "I'd forgotten all about it."

She hums and hands me a clothes pin, watching as I struggle with attaching the corner to the line.

"You're different," Maria says.

I glance down at her belly. "I'm not the only one that's changed." She blanches and clutches the sheet like a shield. "What's with the clothes?"

"Anex decided that Margaret's dress elevated the importance of the womb. That for the baby to experience the most love, it should always be forefront."

"You're pregnant. Exposing your skin doesn't make it more noticeable." My eyes dart to her chest where the real feature is her tits. "And it's not just your belly you're revealing."

"Anex said—"

"Do you hear yourself!" I twist the cotton sheet in my hands, trying to control my annoyance. "Anex said. Anex thinks. Anex wants to see how far he can push you outside your comfort zone and see your tits, Maria. Trust me, that's all."

She blinks. Cheeks red, horrified at my words. Women in Serendee don't talk like this. We don't use words like this, but all I do is smirk and say, "I'm Regressive, remember?"

"This is what I mean." She shakes her head. "You're not the same person I knew—that I grew up with and studied and learned with."

"You're wrong," I say, but then reconsider. "But also right. I am that same girl but... things happened to me after the Ordering. Before really." The examination by Healer Bloom comes to mind, the truth that I know we weren't alone in the room. I think about how much Anex loathes my mother, how betrayed he felt, and how that anger has festered into something deep and complicated.

I think about my training. My men, and how they opened up the world to me.

But I never speak those things, not to Maria, not to anyone.

"You were Chosen. How could you give that up?"

"That word doesn't mean what you think it does," I tell her. "I know it is impossible for you to understand, but I did everything asked of me." Like a beacon, the brand itches below my hip, and I fight to scratch it. It's a constant reminder of who I belong to. How far I was willing to go for approval, for *Enlightenment*.

"Anex builds mazes," I continue. "Complicated labyrinths with only one way out. Every turn leads to the same ending—the one he has determined for you." I look around the grounds, out in the distance to the massive red barn. So peaceful on the outside. Danger and trouble buried underneath. "This is your maze, Maria. It's only going to end up where he decides."

Maria watches me closely, the white sheet pulled to her belly. "You think I don't know that?" she says. "That I don't accept that his decisions will be the best for me and my baby? He is our *leader*, Imogene. Are you saying you don't trust him? That he doesn't know best?"

Maria doesn't know the truth about what he asked me to do, the way he looks at me—touches me—the plans he has that I can't fully comprehend. She hasn't seen the Fallen or known about the people Anex plans to trade to men like chattel. All Maria can see is the path he has created for her. One she—and everyone in Serendee—thinks will lead to Enlightenment.

But in reality, it's a path of doom.

A path none of us can veer off. The walls are too high. Too

narrow. I look at my friend and say, "Whatever you think of me, understand I am here for you and your child."

She nods. "Anex wouldn't have put you here if he thought you a danger to us."

I fight a laugh. Anex put me here for monitoring—for Healer Bloom to make me fertile. For whatever perverse plan he has next. He put me here to keep me away from *them*.

"I'm glad you see that," I say, because even though it's foolish, it does feel comforting for my oldest friend to trust me.

8

Rex

The rattle of the doorknob startles me from a restless sleep. The door opens before I can swing my legs over the side of the bed, the bright light from the hallway, a glare in my eyes.

"What the fuck," I mutter, rubbing my eyes. There are no windows in here, no way to tell what time of day it is down in my father's hidden home for The Fallen. I blink, trying to acclimate to the light and sense movement in the door.

"Jesus, Erik, what happened to knocking?"

"I don't knock in my house; you know that, Son."

I turn my head and see my father standing in the doorway, head nodding to the guard outside to shut the door.

"Of course you don't." I reach for the bottle of water by the side of the bed and take a gulp. "What did I do to earn the honor of a personal visit?"

Anex has something draped over his arm, clothing from the looks of the way it hangs. He tosses it to the end of the bed. One glance, and I can tell it's not for work—at least not the manual labor

I've been doing lately. It's the kind of clothing I wore when I was still the heir.

"Get dressed."

I could fight it. Fight him, especially without the guard here, but my father isn't weak. He's a strong man who could snap my neck if it came down to it. But I'm barely healed from last time, and I know Erik is right outside the door waiting for a reason to come in. I take a deep breath and think of the conversation I had with Silas. Getting the shit beat out of me, staying locked in this cell, none of that is helping Imogene. If anything, it's probably making it worse.

It just makes me so fucking angry.

I step to the corner, to the small toilet installed in the wall. I yank my pajama bottoms down and handle my dick. The stream is loud, filling the tiny room, but not loud enough to cover as my father huffs at the human display.

"Sorry, there's no privacy. The room came this way." God he's such a prick.

I finish up and flush, then kick off the cotton pants, followed by the shirt. I feel Anex's eyes on me as I pull on the pants first—black linen. They gape around the waist, an indicator of how much weight I've lost. My muscle seems more pronounced, but not in a healthy way. Like I'm eating myself from the inside. I grab the shirt and slip my hands in the sleeves, hating how right the expensive linen feels next to my skin. I'm spoiled. Entitled. Chosen.

Or, rather, I was.

I look down at my cracked, raw, hands. They tell the story of the weeks of Banishment. I glance up and catch him watching me.

"You're too thin and your hands..." His nose wrinkles in disgust.

I hold them up, tanned from the sun. "Have a distaste for the working man all of the sudden? The backbone of Serendee?"

He shakes his head, but he barely meets my eye. I wish it was shame he felt, but this man has no humility. No conscious. Not even when it comes to blood.

"What's this about?" I ask, like I don't already know. My father made it clear the day of our fight. He needs my services. He's spent years relying on me bringing in the big fish—the big *bank accounts*—he needs to live his extravagant lifestyle. He needs me to seduce someone.

He's well aware that I know so he doesn't waste time.

"I've got Jasmine West upstairs, the princess of Cobra Tequila. She needs a little nudge. I've got her committed. She's been taking classes down at the center. A week ago, she moved into one of the guest suites. Everything is going according to plan, but she keeps asking for you—making it clear that your involvement is a deal-breaker."

"There has to be someone else that can handle Jasmine."

"Sorry, Son. Whatever you did to her over at Whittmore has her focused on you and, I suspect, your dick. She wants you and only you. Otherwise, there's no way we're getting into her trust fund."

There was a time my father wasn't so blunt about it. So crass. Everything was for the Greater Good, but I guess the scales have fallen and we're not pretending anymore. At least not father and son.

I start to tell him that Jasmine doesn't want my dick. She wants the pretty pictures from the brochures. What the classes and certificates and courses push. Extravagance, plus meaning, plus sex, with an added dash of rebellion against her family. She wants more. *Everything.* And my father and myself have sold her on Serendee truly being utopia.

I start to tell him this, but I don't. My father has forgotten the true product of Serendee. The fantasy. Which means I finally have something: leverage.

"I'll do it—for a price."

"Ah, there he is. My son, the negotiator." He leans against the metal edge of the bed and crosses his arms over his chest. Pride lights his eyes. "What do you want?"

Without hesitation, I make my demand. "I want to see Imogene. In person. Face to face."

Conflict crosses his expression, but it quickly fades. "I can do that, but you have seal this deal for me. I need a million dollars transferred from her trust to our account today."

I run my hands through my hair. "Done."

"You're that confident?"

With Jasmine? "Absolutely."

"You make that happen and then you get to see Imogene." He pushes off the bed and then adds, "On my terms."

He offers his hand, but before I shake it, I say, "Don't try to get something over on me with this. A deal is a deal. I want to see her. Talk to her. No fucking around."

"I'm a man of my word, Rex, you know that." Our eyes lock. "But no fucking around on me either. You do whatever it takes to lock Jasmine in. Understand?"

My father never just wants one thing. Sure, Jasmine's trust fund is the priority, but if he can degrade me in the process? Get me to betray Imogene by being with another woman? Icing on the cake. I should tell him to fuck off, but I reach for his hand and shake it, confirming the arrangement.

Anex has what I want, and I'll do what it takes to make it happen. Even if that means doing what he's taught me to do best: selling myself.

∼

Erik escorts me from my basement cell, through the maze of staircases and hallways in the Main House, to the French doors that lead outside. Jasmine is sprawled on a lounge chair, catching the last rays of warm sun by the pool. From this vantage point, Serendee appears to be a luxurious retreat. Sure, by the time a recruit gets to here, sitting by the edge of the sparkling infinity pool, they have taken the classes and learned the lessons of being part of our community. But the classes are not equal. What the natural born residents of Serendee experience is a different world than that of the chosen plucked from outside the walls—the women and occasional men attached to wealthy portfolios and trust funds.

These people get special treatment from my father and will continue to do so until they no longer suit his needs.

"Don't do anything stupid," Erik says, easing into a position near a massive white column. His gun is hidden, but I have no doubt he can access it quickly. "I'll be watching."

The only stupid thing I did was not forcing Imogene and the others to leave this godforsaken place when we had the chance. I descend the stairs, eyes sweeping over the pool. Jasmine isn't out here alone. My father has other guests, recruits, people he has in various states of fleecing. My gaze lands on two people floating in the far corner of the pool. Two men. One familiar. One not. Silas.

His eyes flit past mine, not making any kind of lingering contact, before locking back on the man he's entertaining. The man is a little older. Hair graying at the temples. He's not bad looking, nearly as handsome as Silas, in a more distinguished way. Men like this... they're usually in some kind of mid-life crisis, seeking meaning in their lives, and my father snaps them up.

My stomach twists as the guy places his hand on my friend's muscular shoulder, fingers spreading over his warm skin. It only coils tighter when Silas gives him a coy, flirty grin in return. I recognize the move. I have a dozen of my own, but the things my father has Silas do... it's different from me fucking a sexy blond.

I don't miss the dark shadows under his eyes. The exhaustion in his limbs. The weight of what he is forced to do for my father is weighing on him. All the grooming and manipulation. What strikes me is that my father has us both out here, selling, trading, degrading ourselves to fill the coffers of Serendee.

Does he need money?

"Rex!" I snap my eyes away from Silas and his target, shifting them over to Jasmine. She's blonde, young, and beautiful. Exactly my father's type. She's in college, so somewhat educated, but barely hanging on, with abysmally low grades. Like many girls at this point in their lives, she's trying to find herself—separate herself from her family identity and make her own. It's so much easier when daddy's bank account is funding the process. Girls like Jasmine are at a crossroads. Finish school and live up to family expectations or take her own path.

Serendee is the latter.

Jasmine stands, revealing her lithe, taunting body in a barely-there bikini. It's not exceptionally warm—and a rush of goosebumps rises across her flesh, hardening her nipples into sharp peaks.

"They said you've been busy." Her lips twist into a pout.

I take her in, the blond, bottled hair. The expensive swimsuit that fits like a second skin, the flashy gold jewelry around her neck and fingers. The skin. The nipples. The mouth.

Six months ago, if I met up with Jasmine or any woman that looked like her, I'd be calculating how fast I could get my dick in her. How hard I could use her before getting access to her bank account. What those lips would look like circling my dick. But now?

Disinterest settles over me.

All I want is my mate back. I want her shy, clear expression. Her fair, natural hair that curls by her ears. I want to bask in nervous movements. Her eagerness to learn. Her loyalty. I want her nipples. Her mouth. Her *everything*.

But most of all, I want the woman who can see Serendee and my father for exactly who he is and still want me.

I push all that want, all the need, deep down to that black ball in my chest and slip into the man my father made me and flash a smile at Jasmine.

Doing this, whatever it takes, is the only shot I may get.

"Sorry, babe," I say, striding over and giving her a kiss on the cheek. "My father has had me occupied."

"The fact he relies on you is proof of how good you are at your job."

Word must not have gotten out to the potential recruits that I've been Banished. It makes more sense why Anex kept me here. He still has use for me beyond backbreaking work. He needs me, just like Silas, to be his whore.

Jasmine pushes up on her tip-toes and presses her lips against my neck. Her tongue darts out, lathing the flesh and it strikes me. I can't do this. I won't betray my mate. I made a promise, and I plan to keep it.

To both her and my father.

I glance across the pool where I see the target resting his chin on his elbows while Silas rubs his shoulders. Our eyes meet over Jasmine's head, and I lift my chin toward the pool house.

"Babe," I say, tilting her chin toward my face. "How about we take this somewhere a little more private?"

She leans into me. "That would be great."

Sliding my hand down her backside, I lead her across the pool deck to the small cottage. Inside, Jasmine gushes, "This is freaking adorable," as she takes in the space. A soft, circular rug fills the main room. The rug is dotted with fuzzy pillows. Twinkling lights hang from the ceiling casting the room in a hazy light. Unlit candles sit on mounted shelves, their lingering scent earthy and warm. I don't know who decorated it, but I suspect Margaret had a hand.

This isn't just a pool house; it's a trap.

Against the back wall is a bar, stocked with wine and alcohol. A box of premium weed is tucked behind the glassware, but I don't want anyone stoned. Not for a decision like this. I need everyone clear—their decisions firm. I flip on the stereo and soft music spills from the hidden speakers, then walk over to the wine rack. "Grab a few glasses out of that cabinet, will you?"

She skips across the tiles, the ties on her bikini bottoms swaying with every step. I select a bottle and Jasmine locates the glasses quickly, bringing them over to me while I turn the corkscrew. "Are you trying to get me drunk?"

"No, but it's been a few long weeks, and I'm happy to see you." The cork gives, and I fill the two glasses, handing her one. I hold up my glass, and she does the same. "To catching up and new beginnings."

The glasses meet, emitting a chime in the small space. She takes a gulp and while I lift the glass to my lips, I barely take a sip. The wine is sweet, but it does nothing to take the bitterness off my tongue.

"Come," I say, linking her fingers with mine and lead her over to the rug. "Tell me what's going on. How did you end up here? The last time we were together, you hadn't made any decisions about Serendee."

To be fair, the last time I saw her there was no talking involved. I didn't really give a shit if she joined up or not. Most of the potential recruits don't, and once my father gets them to the Main House, he hands them over to someone more skilled in this area, like Silas.

Jasmine curls against a pillow, wine in one hand, and beams up at me. "I don't even know where to start. The last few months have been incredible. I've really immersed myself in the programs down at The Center. There's just something about it that feels so right." She reaches out and rests her hand on my thigh. "But you know that, right? I mean, you'd have to when you have someone as smart and powerful as Anex for a father."

I reach for the wine, needing something to do with my mouth other than tell the truth about the man she idolizes. I swallow it down and do the job I promised to do.

"I hear you're trying to decide if this is the life you want or not—long term."

Her fingers play with the linen covering my thigh. "I know it's what I want… it's just that my family doesn't approve. My father and I have been fighting about it. He thinks I'm tossing my life away to join some 'hippie commune.'"

Her eyes roll as she mocks the word with air quotes.

"Well, he's not entirely wrong. I mean, my father loves a drum circle." I flash a grin. "But not everyone understands what it's like to have a higher calling. To have the tug of something bigger than what you're used to. Where we don't worship chasing money, but seek a different way. It's a life away from all the secular nonsense—all the traffic and non-stop connection. Phones and laptops and constant input."

"Yes!" She jerks up, tits threatening to spill out of the top. "It's so much more than just a group of people living together. It's a revolution. It's something I want to be part of."

I reach out and push a lock of hair behind her ear. "You want Enlightenment."

Her eyes lower to my mouth. "More than I've wanted anything before."

I clear my throat. "Let me guess. Your father doesn't like the idea of you relinquishing your secular connection?"

Money.

She smiles, impressed by my bluntness. "No. He thinks it's a scam—a way to steal the Cobra empire." She snorts. "As if my trust fund even makes a dent in his billions."

"My father has no need for another's empire, but what he does demand is absolute commitment. Loyalty and dedication. You're a guest here, but out there—" I jerk my thumb to the land behind the Main House, "—that is where the real Serendee lies. Where the real value is in giving everything up to live this life. The sustainability, the organic food, the fresh air, and peaceful life. Access to that, to Anex's teaching, to the lifestyle afforded to residents, it's expensive. You're not buying in with dollars—you're trading an old life for a new one."

I see the wheels turning in Jasmine's head. She wants this, but she has to give up everything to take it. Her family, her money, her future. That part she understands. What she doesn't know is everything else Anex will take.

The door of the cottage opens, and Silas appears in the gap. He's shirtless, wearing a pair of obscenely tight swim trunks. "Oh sorry, I didn't know the room was occupied."

A shadow moves behind him: his target.

"There's room for everyone," I say, ignoring Jasmine's questioning expression. I rest my hand on top of hers and give it a squeeze, before hopping up. "I just opened a bottle of wine—let me get you a glass."

Silas enters and gestures to the man following him, "This is Robert."

"Jasmine." Her eyes take him in. These two have more in common than looks. Their wealth wafts off of them like a perfume. There's no need for an introduction with me and Silas. We're inner circle. We're known. It's what allows me to do what comes next.

"We were just talking about taking the next step toward Enlightenment. What it's like to be part of this community." I allow my eyes to slide from Silas to Robert. "Anex doesn't believe in coincidences. He calls those opportunities. I have to think you showing up means that you were both sent by The Way."

"Very perceptive," Silas says. "So, you're saying you'd like us to join you?"

"Please." I open a drawer and pull out a box of matches. "How about lighting the candles?"

Robert takes them and the scent of sulfur fills the air as he strikes the match against the graphite. I grab the bottle of wine and turn my back to Jasmine and Robert.

Silas leans toward me. "I can't believe he let you out."

"He needed something from me," I whisper, glancing over my shoulder. Robert smiles at something Jasmine says. Good, they're distracted. "And I made a deal."

His eyebrows rise. "For?"

I hold his gaze, but don't speak her name. Understanding lights in his eyes.

"I have to lock Jasmine in. But if we play this right, we can kill two birds with one stone." I fill the glass. "I can't cheat on her, Silas. She's my mate. I made a promise, and I won't let him destroy that."

He nods, pushing the second glass closer. "I understand." He inhales. "Remember that weekend your father sent us to the hotel for my sixteenth birthday?"

God yes. That weekend taught me a lot about myself. About all four of us. It bonded us forever. It's what made me able to trust them with Imogene, to train her to be my optimum mate. That weekend allowed me to open myself to the possibility of more.

"We play it like that."

He rests his hand on my forearm, squeezing it with his strong hand. To get out of this—*with her*—we have no choice, but to work together.

9

Silas

"The path to Enlightenment is about releasing Resistance," I say, handing the glass of wine to Robert. He takes a sip before setting it off the rug, on the tile floor. Like Rex, mine is left mostly untouched. It may be counterintuitive, but we both need to be stone cold sober for what comes next.

My best friend and I join the tight, intimate circle. I'm only wearing swim shorts, but the room is warm. But before he sits, Rex unbuttons his shirt and tosses it on one of the pillows. His thinness shocks me—weeks of deprivation—but it doesn't take away from his overt masculinity. Rex is a big man, not as bulky as Elon, but a commanding presence. I understand why women and men are attracted to him. It's not just looks, although that's part of it. It's his charisma. His dominance. Even after the degradation Anex has put him through, he hasn't lost it.

While he leans back on the pillows, stretching his legs to the middle of the space, I cross my legs and sit where I can see everyone.

One thing I've learned in all my training, eye contact is important.

Robert and Jasmine relax, although I can feel the spark of energy running through them. Once we're settled, the candles are flickering warmth around us, I continue, "You both seem to be at the same point in your journey, standing on a cliff trying to decide if you're going to jump or turn back around."

Jasmine nods, licking her lips, and glances at Robert, whose eyes slide down to the swell of her breasts.

"To make that jump, you have to release all of those hang ups from the secular world. The conventions and norms that keep people from taking those first steps toward understanding The Way." I reach out and take Rex's hand, stroking along his thumb. "Here's the thing. The people that were raised here, who live here, they do not go through this process. They were born into this world pure, unburdened by the sins of the outside world. To take this step toward enlightenment, you must shed it. All of it. You must rid yourself of everything tying you to that world. Everything." I lean over and kiss Rex. His mouth warm and receptive. I pull back and look at Jasmine and Robert. "Are you ready?"

"Yes," Jasmine says, without hesitation.

"Me too," Robert says. I'd had him locked in for a while. It's different for him. He's handing over his own money. Sure, his family may get suspicious, but he's an adult. And right now, I can tell he wants to dive in head—or dick—first.

Jasmine rises to her knees, inching closer. "I want it. All of it. Show me."

I sense Rex tensing next to me as she reaches for him. This is where things get complicated. I understand his desire to stay true to Imogene, and I'll help him achieve that. I intercept Jasmine's hand, and I give her a soft look and an even softer kiss on her shoulder. "You and Robert need to experience this together. Take this journey as one." I turn back to Rex, licking open his mouth, begging for his tongue. "Jump off the cliff."

They need a little nudge, so I run my hand down the front of my too tight swim shorts and stroke my cock. Every eye in the room watches me do it, watches me swell in my hand. It doesn't take much. I'm already turned on by the heat of Rex's body next to mine. Jasmine responds by facing Robert and tugging at the strings behind her neck. Her top falls, revealing her tits, and Robert's eyes lock on. He's a fucking goner and doesn't skip a beat, dipping his head and capturing one of Jasmine's nipples in his mouth.

The room fills with her moan, and Rex's hand slides behind the back of my neck, drawing me closer. Our bodies meet, and it's familiar. I love this man, and he loves me. We love the same woman, and this is how we get her.

With my tongue in his mouth and his warm skin pressed against mine, I flash back to the first time we kissed. Anex set us up in a fancy hotel suite for Rex's birthday. He'd just started introducing us to the secular world. It was overwhelming. Bright and shiny. Decadent.

The suite was awesome. Cable. Booze. Greasy pizza and piles of junk food. All the stuff off limits at home. The first night was just for fun. We were all alone, living it up, but Anex had told us about the surprise for the next night. The *entertainment*. He'd hired prostitutes from a nearby brothel to pop each one of us off. He explained that we were men, and we couldn't lose our virginity in Serendee. The girls and boys were kept completely separate. He left us with an all-access pass to the porn channels and a stack of condoms.

It was a night of experimentation. Learning what our bodies like —what they respond to. Although I understand now that it was something else. It was the start of our training—in truth, Anex was already breaking down our boundaries. It's the night that opened Elon and Rex up to using their charm and sexuality to lure recruits into the Center. It confused and conflicted Levi into devout dedication—something Anex manipulated. And it was the test Anex needed to use my looks, my body, and my nature to keep the community in line.

We never spoke of that night, but it bonded us. In every aspect of our lives. And I understand exactly why he needs me to take the lead now.

I glance over at Jasmine and Robert. She has her hand wrapped around his cock, and they look fully engrossed in one another. It's the charm of the cottage, the music and candles, the soft lighting and comfort. It's warm in here, making our skin damp with sweat, enticing. The room is designed to draw out our senses, and it seems to be doing its job.

I turn back to Rex, and I know we could probably end this here, but if Anex found out, if he's *watching*, it'll give him the excuse to back out of the deal.

I rest my hand on his abdomen, feeling the hard muscle dip. There's no mistaking his erection pushing at those thin linen pants. He's gone weeks without release. His body not used for pleasure, but for service and solitude. His skin still carries the faded tint of healing bruises. I dip my fingers underneath the waistband, brushing over the soft hair that trails under his navel. Before I get far, his hand stills mine.

"No?" I ask, looking up at him.

He caresses my cheek and says quietly, "You give too much of yourself to everyone here, Silas. And everyone takes too fucking much." He holds my gaze, fingers moving under my chin, not allowing me to drop it. "For once, let me take care of you."

I'm stunned by the sincerity of it. In the sincerity in *him*. Rex is my best friend, but I know he's a spoiled, entitled, brat. This is part of the change in him. The change Imogene has created. When I don't respond with anything other than a nod, he takes charge, pushing me to my back. He positions himself between my knees, his Adam's apple bobbing roughly. I watch him as he hooks his fingers in my shorts, freeing my erection. His eyes never leave me as he abruptly stands, dropping his pants, and climbing back on top of me.

"I'll make this good for both of us," he says, licking my ear. The heat of his breath on my skin elicits a shiver but then he slides his hand between our bodies and grips both of our cocks in one of his large hands.

"Fucking hell," I choke out, feeling warmth spiral down to my balls.

Slowly, he jacks us together, applying friction with every stroke. His mouth finds mine, his stubble rough, kissing me hard. I feel the need behind his movements. This isn't just a means to an end; we're both desperate for affection from someone that actually understands who and what we are. We're desperate for someone that cares.

With the next upstroke, I feel the pre-cum slide down my tip, mingling with his own slippery fluid. It eases the friction into something sweeter, slicker. My balls tingle and my breath comes in jerky bursts. I've sucked a lot of cock in my life. Eaten pussy. Groomed and manipulated, but no one has ever taken care of me like this.

My hand covers his. "I'm gonna come."

"Not yet," he says, eyes shifting over to Jasmine and Robert. She's sitting on his face while he eats her with abandon. Her head hangs lazily to the side, and she pinches her nipples. Our work here is done, I know it. He knows it. But one look into his crystal blue eyes, tells me he's not finished.

He releases us, our cocks springing apart. A moment later he's working his way down my body, fingers skimming my overheated flesh. He stops with his mouth inches away from my cock. Lower down, he's gripping his shaft, rubbing slowly.

I swallow and ask, "Have you—"

"No." He cuts me off, cheeks a faint pink. "How hard can it be? Dicks aren't complicated."

I laugh and he smiles, cutting through a little of the tension— mostly from the sound of Robert's grunts from the other side of the rug. I focus on Rex, on his mouth, on the pink of his tongue and block out everything else.

It's not hard to do once his lips graze my cockhead.

Fuck.

It feels so good when he closes his lips around me. Skin prickling, balls aching, blood thumping in my veins. He wraps his hand around the base and takes me in, warm and hot, then sucks.

My cock pulses, and he groans, signaling that he's not hating this at all. He's still working his cock, jerking his length with controlled strokes. His eyes fog over, and he focuses all of his attention on me. My hips rise, fucking upward, he never flinches, taking everything I give him—all the way to the back of his throat.

That's when I feel the climax seize my balls, and I push him back.

His broad shoulders tense and a heartbeat later, the rush of cum spurts between us—his and mine—as we both grunt through the release. It pools hot and sticky on my abs and chest.

I blink at him hovering over me, chest heaving, at the mess spilled on my body and feel the first sense of calm in weeks. He grabs his shirt and wipes us down.

"Thank you," I say, rising up on my elbows. I know it took a lot for him to do this for me. For us. For *Imogene*.

"God, that was hot." We both look over and see Jasmine slick in sheen of sweat. Robert lies spread eagle on the floor, cock flaccid against his thigh. He's lost in some kind of post orgasmic haze. "That," she says, pointing at the two of us, "is all I want. That. I can just feel it rolling off of you."

"Feel what?" I ask.

She grins. "Enlightenment."

10

Elon

"I'm not sure about this." I stare at the small brick house. The bungalow is tucked in a transitional space between commercial and residential property in the small town of Thistle Cove. There's nothing interesting about it. The awning over the front porch is rusted and needs a fresh coat of paint. There are no signs announcing what goes on inside. If it's a residence or a business. Just big numbers with the street address—the nine hung askew. The only sign of life is the wreath made of sunflowers on the door.

I didn't go in last time we were here. Silas and Rex went in. I stayed outside to keep watch. It wasn't my idea to come today. That's on Levi. He's the one pushing us to meet Camille Montgomery. Imogene's mother.

"We have to do something," Levi says.

"*This* seems extreme."

He looks from me to the house. Camille works in that house, helping former cult members move on with their lives. It's the word cult that trips me up. I'm not dumb, I know Anex is up to shady and nefarious shit. I know he uses his charm and charisma to manipulate, but cult? I'm not even sure what that word means. It was never in our vocabulary other than defensively. We were told our entire lives that Serendee is a community. Not a cult. And the people who say so are trying to destroy what we've worked so hard to build.

People like Camille.

It's been an hour since the bus dropped us off at the stop across the street from the house. I look over at Levi, taking in how tired and lost he seems. Even so, I don't hold back. "I'll tell you what I told her," I say, remembering the day I took her to the library, and we covertly tracked her mother down on the internet. Imogene had been conflicted—scared. Levi glances at me. "I told her by searching for her mother we were crossing a line. That it would change everything."

I'd been right, more tragically right than I'd even realized.

"Everything's already changed, Elon," he says, running his hand through his red hair. His eyes never leave the house. "We're broke. Basically homeless."

"I make money."

"Getting the shit beat out of you," he snaps, but there's not much energy to it. "We need help."

He's right. We can't keep going on like this. My body aches. I probably have a concussion. Levi has an edge—a nervous energy that I've never witnessed before. He needs *something*, a focus, and maybe this is it. What I don't admit to him—to myself, is that I feel wrong coming to Camille empty handed. Without her daughter.

Fuck. I need to man up.

"Let's do it." I rise to my feet. Levi follows, hands shoved in his pockets. We wait for a truck to pass, then cross the street. I've just stepped on the brick pathway leading to the porch when the front door opens.

"Hold up." I pause, grabbing Levi's elbow, and jerk my chin to the door.

A figure steps out, shadowed by the awning on the porch. It's not until they step out into the daylight that I see that it's a woman.

And she's holding a shotgun.

Her voice carries, calm and collected, across the yard. "You have fifteen seconds to explain why you're on my property."

"Whoa." I hold up both hands. "We don't mean harm—"

"I know who you are and who sent you." She's far enough out now that I see her short blond hair. Her eyes, her bone structure, the tight, sassy, set of her jaw. This has to be Camille Montgomery. Imogene's mother. "You need to turn around and go back to your master. Tell him that if he keeps sending his boys around, I will retaliate."

Boys. Rex and Silas.

Next to me, Levi swallows. "No one sent us. We came on our own."

Her gun falters, half an inch before she levels it again. "Where's my daughter?"

"Rex was going to bring her to you." I take a breath and slowly lower my hands. "But Anex..."

"Timothy stopped it, didn't he?"

I blink at the use of Anex's name. "Yes."

"And what? You're here to finish me off?" Her eyes are wild and that gun, it's still pointed at us. "Shut me down? Teach me a lesson?"

Hearing the pain in this woman's voice, the *anger*, it shakes me to my bones. Why? Because I feel the same way. Levi and I look at one another and the grimace on his face says he does too.

"We're here," I say, hating the clench in my chest, "because we need your help."

∾

Camille checks us for weapons before allowing us inside, forcing us to grip the railing of the porch while she pats us down. Her hands are firm—diligent, checking inside our boots. We must pass her inspection, because she grunts, and opens the screen door with a screech.

I'm anxiously following her in. Not because I'm afraid, but because I get the sense that she is. And scared people do impulsive things.

The inside of the house is much nicer than the outside, although it's clear it isn't used for a home. The front living room has a defined reception area, with a small desk. A rack on the wall is filled with pamphlets that have titles like, "*What Makes a Cult?*" or "*Releasing Your Mind.*" I avert my eyes, not liking the way the titles make me feel, but I notice Levi lingers, gaze glued to the literature.

I turn, and see that the adjacent dining room has chairs in a circle—like it's set up for a meeting. Still, it's got a warm feel to it, welcoming—you know when you're not being held at gunpoint.

As I assess our surroundings, I keep one eye on Camille. The shotgun is in her hand, but at least she now has the barrel directed down to the floor. I take the opportunity to introduce myself.

"Ms. Montgomery," I say, thrusting out my hand, "my name is—"

"Elon. And you're Levi. I remember you, and your parents." Her eyes roam over us. "Although you've grown since the last time I saw you."

I rub my chin, feeling my beard. "Yeah, I guess we have."

She taps the barrel of the gun on the hardwoods. "I need you to understand that I will protect myself and this program." Her jaw tightens. "I will not allow him to enter this world. Is that clear?"

Him.

Anex.

"Yes, ma'am," Levi says. "We're not here to hurt you."

"Maybe not intentionally," she says, but gestures for us to follow her. We walk down the hallway toward the back of the house. We pass the kitchen and enter a sitting room.

She points to a couch, and Levi and I take a seat. She leans the gun against the fireplace, and it's not until she's sitting across from us, pushing her hair out of her eyes, that I have a striking memory of this woman in Serendee. She'd been on the stage with Anex during one of his talks, and her expression had been clear and pure. Enlightened.

What and how had everything gone so wrong between her and Anex?

"What happened?" she asks. "Rex told me that he was going to convince her to leave Serendee. I said I would take her. Happily." She looks down at her hands. "To be honest, when she never showed, I assumed she changed her mind, or that Rex was probably sent here on a recon mission for his father. Are you telling me something else happened?"

"She didn't choose Anex. He, unfortunately, has chosen her," I admit. It's hard to know where to begin. I'm not sure exactly what Rex and Silas told her—or what she assumes about Imogene's life. It's clear Camille is a smart woman, and it's probably better not to withhold information. "Things escalated over the last few weeks—months really. Ever since Imogene and Rex were Ordered."

"To marry," she says, then clarifies with an eyeroll, "to *mate*."

"Yes," I reply. "She was instantly in over her head. Being Ordered to Rex wasn't like being paired with an ordinary resident of Serendee."

"He's 'Chosen' and that put Imogene in the spotlight—again." She uses finger quotes around the word chosen. "I'm well aware of Timothy's bullshit hierarchy."

A laugh bubbles from my chest. Levi frowns at me, but I don't care. I raise an eyebrow at the woman. "You're ballsy."

"Yeah, well Timothy tried his hardest to break me down, and he almost did it." She frowns. "He's punishing Imogene for my betrayal, isn't he?"

"Partially," Levi admits. "He definitely is focused on her. He's convinced that she's got bad blood—Regressive."

"God, these stupid terms." She looks between us. "You know he made all of these up one night after too many tequila shots, right? Regressive. The Way. Enlightenment. He added to them as needed—when someone stepped out of his ever-changing line."

"Fallen," I add, the word making me feel dirty.

"Correction," Levi whispers.

She studies him for a long moment, then says, "Exactly."

I lean forward, resting my elbows on my knees. "Rex has been disillusioned with Serendee and his father's methods for a while. He's suspicious of his mother's death. Judgmental of the hypocrisy between the Chosen and the rest of the community. Falling for Imogene has only amplified that."

Camille straightens. "What do you mean 'falling' for her?"

Levi and I share a look, we're not about to admit to the unconventional relationship we have, not when we've just gotten our foot in the door. But she can know the truth about Rex.

"Rex loves her," Levi says. "He wants to protect her—at any cost."

"Then why isn't she here? Why didn't he get her out?"

It's Levi that answers. "The truth is that Imogene wasn't ready to leave on her own. She was committed to Serendee, to following The Way and finding Enlightenment. She'd been chosen for a special group and was very excited about it."

"What kind of group?" Camille asks, warily.

"A women's group, run by Anex's spiritual wife—"

"You're fucking with me."

"No," I say. "Anex has additional wives now. One in particular, Margaret, has the most sway. She invited Imogene to an exclusive group that involved offering damaging collateral."

Her eyebrow rises. "You mean leverage. Blackmail."

Levi nods. "Yes."

"The final part was a ritual." Bile rises in my throat. "A branding."

Camille's face pales. "He branded my daughter?"

"With his initials," I admit. Then, knowing she needs to hear the rest. I place my hand on my body, pointing to the location. "Right here."

A tremor wracks through her body, so violent that I start to reach for her. She jerks back, giving me a cold look of warning, and I give her space. "This is on me. I never should have left her with that monster."

"You couldn't have known he was going to go this far," Levi says. Of course, the problem is that I did know. Anex told me his plans for

Imogene, and he didn't warn me about this. "His focus on Imogene is... it's different."

"The night we found out about the branding, is the night Rex decided she would leave. He was livid. He knew why his father marked his mate. He was claiming her as his own," I explain, aware that every word I say is making it worse. "He was going to force her to leave—to come to you. But Anex called a last-minute meeting—it was late, the music sounded, and we knew that not showing up would tip him off. It felt safer to go and leave after."

Camille's eyes are ringed in red when she guesses, "But that never happened."

"He called us out in front of the entire community. He read Imogene's collateral, proof that she'd been Regressive. That we had broken rules. He banished me and Levi—tossing us out of Serendee, and forced Imogene, Rex, and Silas into Re-education."

"That's not all he wants from her, is it?" she asks.

"Anex wants her to be his next spiritual wife," Levi says quietly. "They'll be mated at the equinox."

"If I could get her out, I would've done it years ago." Her hands fist at her sides. "Why are you here? Just to hurt me? To pick at old wounds? To show me how, after all this time, he still has control over me?"

"We're here because we have nowhere else to go. No one else understands what we've been through." But it's more than that. "You understand Anex—Timothy Wray—what he is capable of. We need someone as desperate to get Imogene out as we are."

"You care for her?" she asks, blinking as though she's seeing us for the first time.

"Rex and Silas are our brothers," Levi says. "Imogene... she's important to us. We won't leave them behind."

"How? How do we get them out?"

"First," Levi says, running his hands over his thighs, "we have to get inside Serendee."

"That's not going to happen," she snaps.

Levi tilts his head. "It will if Anex thinks we've got something he wants."

I frown. His eyes shift to Camille and recognition hits the two of us at the same time.

"Camille—" I whisper, but she cuts me off.

"Me." Her expression is impassive as she repeats, "He wants me."

"You're the one that got away. The only thing he wants. The failure he needs to redeem." His voice seems steadier. More confident and I realize Levi had this plan all along. It's why we're here. "The only way we're getting them out is if we trade them for you."

11

Imogene

"Imogene."

"Shoot." The sound of my name makes me skip a stitch and the needle stabs in my finger.

"Sorry to startle you," Margaret says. She's standing in the doorway of the common room where me and several of the pregnant women have spent the afternoon sewing baby clothes. "But I need you to come with me."

Her voice is light—unassuming—but my chest clenches regardless. I feel like all I do is try to keep a low profile, stay off the radar of anyone with connections to Anex. I should know better. This is his world, and I'm nothing but a planet caught in his orbit.

"Of course," I say, trying to keep the blood beading at the tip of my finger from spilling on the white cotton dress I'd been working on. Maria, who is sitting next to me, takes it without a word.

"Thank you." I stand, giving her an appreciative grin.

I'm met with silence and a blank expression. We've spoken very little since hanging laundry together. There's nothing much to say. She thinks I'm Regressive.

She's not wrong.

The other women watch this exchange closely, and I ignore them as I walk past them to Margaret. When I reach her, I ask, "Do I need to change?"

Her eyes flick down to my basic gray dress. It's in sharp contrast to her and the other pregnant women, with their growing bellies, and swollen breasts, bared for all to see. I've been trying to acclimate to this change—to the revelation of skin and intimacy—but it's so far removed from the way we were raised, that it's impossible.

How is this okay, but my behavior is deemed Regressive?

"You're fine." She takes a step back. "We shouldn't waste time anyway. He's waiting."

He.

My pulse beats, the urge to run overwhelming. But just over her shoulder, standing by the exit, is one of Anex's guards. There is no running.

"Do you know what this is about?" I ask as we exit the center and start up the road toward the Main House. As much as I dread this, the fresh air feels nice, and the stretch in my legs. I've been trapped in that building for weeks.

"Nothing bad." She gives me a small smile. "In fact, I think you're going to be pleasantly surprised."

That information does nothing to allay my fears, instead sending a chill of warning up my spine. The feeling doesn't decrease as we walk up the steps and wind through the maze of staircases and hallways. It's hard to believe that this was my home a few months ago.

"You know," she says, pausing in the hallway I know leads to Anex's private rooms, "you're caught in the darkness of this journey right now, Imogene. The bad days leading to the good. The narrow part of the path. You've already been accepted. Chosen and Marked. Anex isn't the bad guy here. He's waiting for you to see the way out, but only you can do that." She takes my hand. "Stop fighting him. It'll make everything fall into alignment."

Margaret didn't grow up here. She wasn't raised in a Donum or told to conform. Her dress and autonomy prove this. She probably thinks that she convinced him to let her wear these clothes. To plaster on makeup and become sexually free. But no one manipulates Anex. She's just the vehicle he's using to change our world.

"You realize," the words spill from me impulsively, "that you think you're different. That his affection for you will be enough to protect you. But it won't. He'll turn on you just as fast as he turned on his own son. On Elon, Levi, and Rex." Her eyes narrow as I speak the truth. "On his real wife, Beatrice."

"Beatrice was a fool," she snaps, her façade slipping. "Just like your mother."

"No. You're a fool. The rest of us were born into this disaster. You chose it, Margaret. You're the one who is blinded by the man behind that door."

"That man is a god. He is the only one that can bring any of us peace. As you're about to find out now." Without another word, she squares her shoulders and opens the door.

My eyes go straight to Anex's chair, but it's empty. The space next to it isn't. My stomach caves, and my breath catches in my throat.

Rex.

His eyes pin to mine when he sees me, raking down my body in a long, assessing gaze.

"What..." I ask, unable to finish the thought. It's good to see him. Even though he looks thin and tired, that same commanding presence defines him. I glance at Margaret. "What's going on?"

"He earned it," she says, stepping back.

When I look back at Rex he's striding forward. The gap vanishes, and he scoops me against him. I sink against him. The man I once feared, that took everything from me, is now one of the few things to bring me solace.

I feel the difference in his body. The thinning of his arms and the lost bulk in his body.

He earned it.

I pull back, getting a good look at his face. His cheeks are hollow, and there's faint bruising near his temple. "What did you do?" I ask quietly.

"What I had to," he admits, but there's no shadow of guilt in his piercing eyes. "I needed to see you. To make sure you're okay."

"I'm fine." It's not entirely true, but physically, yes, I'm solid. For now.

His hand runs up my neck, settling on my jaw. "I should've—"

"Stop. Whatever time we have together, it's not enough to go into should'ves."

He frowns, gaze darting between my eyes and my mouth. Fingers on one hand digging into my hip. There's a hesitation there, but that is not who my mate is—he takes what he wants, and I know for certain he wants me. I push up on my toes and brush my lips against his, reminding him of who we are.

That's all it takes, that one small, heated brush, flesh against flesh for him to snap back into himself. His tongue seeks mine, strong and coaxing. Rex roughly pulls me against him, and for the first time, the balance between us is even. He needs me as much as I need him.

That's the moment our armor falls away and I know for absolute certain that this man is different than the one I was Ordered to. There's no façade here. No farce. No mind games or manipulation.

There's only us.

Until, there isn't.

"Ah, the lover's reunion." Anex's voice carries from across the room. My spine tenses, habit and self-preservation propelling me to bow and honor my leader. Rex doesn't allow it, hands cupping my cheeks as he continues to kiss me. He groans regretfully against my mouth, before stepping back. "Don't stop on my account, Son."

Rex turns, his hand dropping to hold mine. "You told me we'd have time—*alone*."

"That was when I was under the assumption that everyone was playing by the rules." Rex's fingers twitch against mine, and his shoulders stiffen, the armor setting back in place. "I've allowed this meeting because Rex fulfilled a promise to me. Which," he addresses his son with his eyebrow raised, impressed, "well done. I've never had someone hand over her entire fortune to me so quickly. Whatever you did to her must have been magnificent."

There's an implication in his words—that Rex had done something to convince a recruit to hand over her fortune. I'm not stupid. I'm well aware of what Rex and the others are required to do to fill the coffers of Serendee. He'd made a promise to me, that he wouldn't sleep with another woman, but none of us have autonomy right now. It's nothing but a constant state of survival.

If Anex wanted a reaction from me, he doesn't get one, and continues, shifting his blue eyes to me. "Unfortunately, I can't say the same for Imogene who continues her Regressive ways."

"I—" I swallow past the lump in my throat, "I don't know what you're talking about."

Anex crosses the room, passing us, and approaching Margaret who is standing near the door. He kisses her on the cheek, lifting a hand to her full breast, and squeezing it gently. He then bends, pressing another soft kiss to her belly. Once I would have thought this was sweet—a loving father expressing his delight for a new child, but now I know better. It's a display of power. That Margaret, her body and the child inside, belongs to him. Just like we all do.

He faces us and says, "Security caught Silas going into the Childcare center—entering the back door carrying a box from the apothecary. Once this was confirmed, Healer Bloom conducted a complete inventory of our supplies and discovered you'd been taking supplements not prescribed to you. In fact, they have the opposite, desired effect."

The blood rushes down my body, leaving my head woozy and light. As if he can tell, Rex's hand drops mine and circles my waist.

"That's Silas' issue," he says, pulling me to his side. "Not Imogene's. She couldn't have known."

Anex shakes his head. "You think I'm stupid."

"No," I blurt. All that does is turn his gaze from his son onto me. My knees shake at his attention, increasing as he walks over.

"Oh, Imogene. I'd like to say my son and his friends corrupted you, but we both know it's the other way around." His hands snap out, one grabbing for my collar, the other clasping my skull.

"Get your filthy hands off her!" Rex lunges, but the tell-tale sound of a gun racking forces him still. Erik, the guard is across the room, the gun leveled at him, a hair's breath away from shooting.

"Rex," I whisper, terror squeezing my vocal chords. "Don't."

He grimaces and swears under his breath. Anex cuts his eyes between us, then wrenches my head and neck apart. "Care to tell me where you got this little bruise?" His eyes narrow. "Careful, Imogene, I'll know if you're lying."

"It was an accident," I reply quietly. "While I was doing chores."

"It looks like a love bite." He releases me, fingers trailing down my neck. "If you haven't seen Silas, been intimate with him, then where did you get this? Are there other men trying to claim you?"

That last question is a trick. He knows there are no other men that can get access to me. He wants me to report Silas for breaking the rules. I can't—*won't*.

"I understand. You don't want to betray one of your lovers." The corners of his mouth turn down. "Well, I'll save you, Imogene. One of your housemates saw the mark directly after his intrusion."

It had to be Maria. The hurt from knowing she went to Anex about me... it burns in my gut.

"Do you deny it?"

I can't speak, but I manage to shake my head.

"For the violation of meeting with another member of the Fallen, for going against medical policy, and most of all," his jaw tenses, "betraying my trust, you'll receive Correction."

"Hell no, she won't." Rex moves toward his father, uncaring that the gun tracks his every move. "That's not happening."

"There is no alternative, Son. She willingly violated the rules of Serendee."

"*Your* rules! No one voted on these. There were no agreements. It's your unilateral command."

"Do you think you're shocking when you say things like that? That you've revealed a dark secret of this place?" he asks. He walks over to the mahogany chest pushed against the wall, opens a drawer, and removes something. He turns. "Serendee is under my will, Rex. It has been since the day I purchased the land. Since I created the bylaws that we adhere to. The residents of this community have chosen to follow my path. My way." He walks back over, the dark object clenched in his hand. I can't see what it is. "It pains me that you are choosing the opposite. That you, your friend, and this girl have all decided to work against me."

"We will never be on your side, Anex," Rex declares. "Never again. Just let us go. We don't need money, or anything more than the clothes on our back. Banish us—all three of us—and you'll never have to worry about us again."

"I would if I could." His father stops before us. "But letting you go would be the easy way out, and finding Enlightenment isn't easy. It's arduous. Exhausting. Painstaking. I will not release you from finding your way."

His eyes are on me as he says this, and as it is every time Anex has blessed me with his attention, I'm caught in his vortex. Except this time, I don't feel the desire to appease him. I feel the urge to run, because the way he looks at me, the small curl to his lips, it's the look of a predator and I'm nothing but prey.

"Sit," he says simply, nodding at a hardback chair.

"Anex." My voice is a whisper.

His hand rises and I see the object. A paddle. Slightly larger than a hairbrush, with silver rivets embedded across the back. "Come here, Imogene, and prepare to receive your Correction."

Rex vibrates next to me. "If you touch a hair on my mate's body, I will end you."

Anex sighs, deep and exasperated. "I appreciate your bravado, Son, but you don't have the upper hand here. You never do. When will you learn that?" He waves over the guard. "I'd have you remove him, but he needs to see this. See what happens when they break the rules." His eyes go to the gun. "Keep him in line."

"Yes, sir." Erik's eyes never leave Rex, as if he knows that all my mate needs is a split second.

"Imogene, come," Anex commands. "Or I'll be forced to make you." His head tilts. "Or is that what you want? Is that what gets you wet? Binding you up? Forcing you?"

"Stop!" Rex roars. "I swear to God."

Anex snorts. "There is only one God here, and I've already made up my mind. Imogene will be punished, and you'll watch." He jerks his head to another guard stationed at the door. "As will a selected audience."

"Punish me instead," Rex blurts. "Leave her alone."

Annex's eyes narrow. "I'm sure you'd like that, but no. That's not how this works."

The guard opens the door and a small group files in. I know the majority of them—the women, at least. They were all part of the secret group I'd joined. My eyes meet Kayla's—the woman I'd personally held down while she was branded, talking her through the pain. The scent of burning flesh, singed into my nostrils. The scent I will always associate with guilt and regret.

But she doesn't look regretful. No. She and the others surrounded Anex like a harem in their flowy dresses and painted eyes. I would have been one of those women—should've been.

The urge to run across the room, grab Kayla by the shoulders and shout, *'Can you see how easy it is for him to turn on you?'* That the brand doesn't protect you, it makes you a target? They're Collateral. I know for certain it will be used against them. Not if, but when.

"Fuck," Rex swears, and my eyes are drawn back to the door.

One last person walks through. His hands are bound in front of him, tied at the wrist. A watchful black-clad guard stands nearby. My heart cracks in two, because I'd hoped he would leave him out of this and focus his punishment on me alone, but no, Anex is always two steps ahead.

Silas.

"Everyone, take a seat," Anex says, gesturing to the area around his chair. They file in, curious looks on every face—everyone but Silas, whose skin is pale.

Rex's eyes dart around the room, at the guards and the new witnesses. To Silas and then to me. They finally land on his father. The tension trembles between them, or maybe that's just the fear spiking up my spine.

"May I approach?" Rex asks.

"With caution." That simply means Erik never lowers his weapon.

Rex moves toward his father, and he speaks, voice so low that no one in the room can hear. No one but me. "You can't Correct her like this. Not when you want her for your own." He swallows painfully at the admission his father plans on keeping me for himself. "You'll see those scars every time you're with her, a constant reminder of this event. The humiliation and defeat."

"Marks of her journey," he counters. "That she deserves."

Rex continues as if his father hasn't spoken. "More than that, she'll hate you. She'll poison any future children you have with her into hating you too—and she'll have the proof she needs to convince them."

The thought of losing more children seems to make Anex consider the argument. He rests a hand on Rex's shoulder. "You make a good point. I've trained you so well, Son. I can sense the leadership that runs through you. My blood. My power." He presses the paddle into Rex's hand. "You do it."

"What?" The device falls to the ground like it's made of fire. "No."

Rex has done many things to me. Hurt me in many ways, but he's never Corrected me. Levi, of course. Elon, when I needed it, but not Rex. This kind of behavior goes against his values—the ones that make him such a threat to his father.

"Do it," Anex says, eyes darting to the paddle on the carpet. "That way, when I see these scars on her body, I'll remember the strife and trouble it took to get her to a place of Redemption. And I'll remember that you helped."

"You're fucking deranged, you know that, right?"

He shrugs, the gesture small and innocent. "There's a long history of people calling genius insanity. I'm willing to join their club."

They stare at one another for a long beat, a power struggle that ends with one of them Correcting me. In a slow, sweeping movement, Rex bends, swiping the paddle off the floor.

I witness the whole thing, the entire exchange where it becomes strikingly clear that I *will* be Corrected. I have no choice in that. My mate has just managed to negotiate who inflicts the pain.

Anex crosses the room, heading over to his chair to surround himself with the small group of spectators.

"I'm sorry," Rex says quietly as he turns to me.

I lift my chin and clear the tremble from my throat. "Let's get this over with."

12

Rex

I hate everything about this.

The knowing, smug expression on my father's face. He has me right where he wants me—controlled, demeaned, and inflicting pain on my mate.

I loathe the guilt deep in Silas' eyes as he watches this scene unfold.

I hate the fact that Jasmine and Robert have been brought in the room to watch this sideshow. Can they tell this is all part of the same manipulation tactic I used on them? Trading bodies and souls? Exploiting intimacy. Bile rises to the back of my throat from awareness. I deserve this for what I've done, but Imogene...

She looks at me with those wide doe eyes, and my heart skips a beat.

I may deserve all of it, but she doesn't.

She's a pawn in this game between me and my father. A prized toy we're squabbling over like two boys on the playground. It's wrong, so fucking wrong, but there's no out for either of us. I cursed her the moment I picked her for my mate, but she was doomed long before that because of her mother's betrayal.

"I know some of you may find this excessive, or even barbaric," Anex says, from his throne. "But such is the resolve of The Way. It doesn't adhere to the laws of man—the moralistic and ethical. It's harsh and unyielding." His tone has shifted, lowering to that mesmerizing tenor that lulls the most Regressive into compliance. "Enlightenment comes in many forms. Imogene has expressed in her logs that she feels closest to her higher self when in a state of Correction. What Rex is giving her is a gift."

His justifications—his lies—they make the hard ball of rage inside of me send a spark of energy through my limbs.

Margaret is on one side of my father, Jasmine on the other. That's who he's addressing—Jasmine. He has plans for her now that her money is locked in place. From the corner of my eye, I see him stroke her hair, doling out affection and praise.

The look on Jasmine's face when our eyes meet? Pity.

I grip the paddle and take a deep breath.

Anex clears his throat and nods to the chair in the middle of the room. It has a high back, made of solid, carved wood. I remember it being in my childhood home—placed at the head of the dining room table. My father's first throne, back when he was only the leader of my family, not an entire community. Before he eliminated his biggest threat: my mother.

"Undress," he commands Imogene once we're positioned near the chair. Her hands move to the high neck of her dress, to the first of the long row of tiny buttons. A tremor runs through her fingertips, shaking uncontrollably.

"Here." I step forward, placing the paddle on the seat of the chair. "Let me help."

She nods, words seemingly caught in her throat. I keep my eyes on hers, finding a strength there to get through this moment. The tedious nature of the task, the small, slippery buttons, the slow reveal of her pale skin underneath.

Soft.

Perfect.

Mine.

"We'll get through this, okay?" I tell her once her dress sags from her shoulders. "You and me, no one else."

It's a dumb thing to say. We're in a room full of spectators. Captives, like Silas. My father. His followers. But when I look at her, at her beautiful face, I feel it: me and her. Us.

The dress drops, sliding down her narrow hips, hitting the floor. Reaching for the hem of undergarments, I lift her top, exposing her to the room. My eyes fall to her nipples, watching as they harden. I run my fingers down her sides, resting them on the waistband of her shorts. I pause, unable to push them off—unwilling to show her perfect body to these vultures lying in wait.

Her hands cover mine, urging me to finish what we've started. She shimmies the shorts over her hips, and they fall with the dress, pooled around her feet. My gaze falls to the brand, still scabby after all this time. Painful and slow-healing. Every act from my father sends a message, and that brand is the loudest. His initials, bold but hidden. His ownership.

I press my thumb into the soft skin just above it and clarity strikes. He had to brand her because he knows that deep down, she'll never belong to him. Not like she belongs to me. To Silas, Elon, and Levi.

That thought allows the anger and rage, all the frustration and dark thoughts to vanish for a moment, another emotion taking hold. It's unfamiliar and pure. It's pure instinct—maybe, fuck, maybe it's the ever elusive Enlightenment. Whatever it is, it propels me to take her face in my hands and brush my thumb over her full lips, whispering, "I love you."

The smallest, brightest, most life-affirming smile tugs at her lips. "I love you too."

Before I can process it, act on it, she inhales deeply and then turns to face the chair, bending, hands flat on the arms. She's offering her body to me, under duress, but offering it all the same. It's wrong, but my cock twitches at the sight of her soft, supple flesh and all I want to do is—

"I love your initiative, Imogene, but you won't be bent over for this. Sit in the chair, sweetheart."

I blink, my father's voice snapping me back to the moment.

She rights herself, hands moving to cover her breasts and pussy. Her forehead creased in confusion. I feel the same.

"What are you asking me to do?" A thought flickers in my mind. "You want me to beat her face? That's foolish even for you."

"Of course not." He waves this off as if it's a ridiculous thought. As if I'm the sadistic lunatic. "Her breasts. A lash for every Regressive act."

Next to me, Imogene's arm flattens across her tits.

I start to ask why, but I know the answer. Imogene does get a thrill from spanking. She and Levi have been experimenting with that more and more. My father isn't willing to go over existing territory. He wants to push her further. Degrade her more. Expose her to the room—face and body.

"How many is that?" I try my hardest to keep my voice even.

Anex licks his lips and holds up a hand. One finger ticking off at a time. "*Meeting* with Silas. *Altering* her supplements. *Spreading* Regressive thoughts to the other women in the Center. *Lying* about it when given the opportunity to confess. *Defying* her leader."

Five. There are five in all.

"Rex," he says. "Do it right."

The threat is implied. Do it right, or the consequences will be far worse. Reaching around Imogene, I grab the paddle off the chair. Schooling my face in the hard, controlled expression my father raised me to wear in situations like this, I command, "Sit." She does, dropping her arm, revealing her breasts without being told. I brush a strand of hair off her cheek. "Good girl."

In our world, women's bodies are hidden under thick cotton, high collars, and complicated buttons. In the secular world, I've had my share of tits. I've sucked, fucked, bitten, and come on many. But

Imogene's are the first I've revered; that I've wanted to cherish. I take them in now, full and round, nipples a dark peaked pink.

I say a silent prayer that she doesn't hate me when this is over.

The first slap comes without warning. A hard strike to the soft side of her breast, driving it into the other. She cries out, eyes instantly watering, cheeks turning red.

Her hands grip the arms of the chair.

"One," Anex says from his throne. "Don't hold back."

I switch hands, elbow back, slamming the paddle against the other breast. Welts rise from the raised surface. Her teeth bear down on her bottom lip and a fat tear slides down her cheek. The sight of it triggers something inside of me, and I lower the paddle. "Imogene—"

"Keep going." She cuts me off, her eyes forged of steel. Lifting her chin she whispers, "That's two."

Again, I paddle her, my grip wavering, catching her nipple with the rivets. She yelps but swallows it quickly, pale throat bobbing dramatically. It's after that third strike that I see it. My eyes draw up to hers, then back down. Her hips shift, the slightest squirm.

My balls twitch in response.

Licking my bottom lip, I slap her again, just the tips and hitting both of her nipples at the same time. Imogene groans, head falling back. Her fingers tighten around the arm of the chair, but I realize now it's not out of the urge to run—it's to stop from touching herself.

Sweat gathers on the back of my neck and my cock thickens, the urge to bury myself in this girl—my mate—dire. But I know better than to let my father see what is transpiring between us.

I grip the paddle, thinking of how I want to do this, how I want to please my mate. How far I can take this—how far can I push her? Because that's the truth about Imogene, she's looking for that line and she hasn't found it yet.

I reach out, rearing back, striking her hard, twice. She screams, unable to hold it back, but I drop the paddle, my hands snatching out for her nipples. Her eyes widen at my forcefulness—at going off script—and I twist them, sharp and hard, driving another scream from her. Her legs fall apart, and I see the slick wetness between them.

I grab her by the throat and lift her from the chair like a goddamn rag doll.

A slow clap fills the room, followed by my father's voice. "Bravo, Son. Gave her exactly what she deserved—and a little more." He chuckles. "You pretend you're different from me, but we know the truth, don't we?"

I don't take the bait. I just say, "I'm going with her."

He doesn't fight me, just waves us off. The show is over. He's moving on, and when I grab Imogene by the waist, holding her up as we pass by him and his shiny group, I see Jasmine's hand on his lap, stroking an obvious erection.

Well, I guess she will fit in here perfectly, after all.

Silas is the last person we pass, still bound and guarded. Our eyes lock, his red-rimmed and worried. Something deep transpires between us. Something I'm not ready to accept.

In a small sitting room. One where Anex entertains members of the inner circle. Female members. There's only one way out and I shut it behind us.

"Rex." My name comes out as a moan, and she sags against my side, body rubbing against mine.

"Hold on, baby," I say, kissing her neck. "I'll take care of it."

She's impatient—grinding her pussy against my thigh. I feel the warmth through my pants. Her fingers twist in my shirt and she looks up at me, tears streaming down her face.

Not out of fear or humiliation. Out of want.

Reaching between her legs, I groan at the slippery heat. "God, Imogene."

She bucks against my palm, her pussy seeking friction. Something primal comes over me, the urge to satisfy my mate. I slam her into the wall, using the surface to hold upright. Crashing into her body, tongue thrusting inside her mouth, two fingers sinking deep in her pussy.

She cries out, teeth rattling. I fuck into her, seeking the quick release she so desperately needs. The walls of her pussy are tight, clamping around my fingers. I add in a third, stretching her.

"Let go, Imogene," I tell her, licking her tongue. "You're safe here. You're a good girl. You're such a good, good, girl."

Her eyes open, meeting mine. I grab her thigh, lifting her leg, and hook it over my waist. The shift in angle is what triggers the release. I feel every wave of it, in her straightening spine, the clench of her pussy, the vibrating groan deep in her chest. Her head falls to the side, the tension finally easing. I hold her up, hold her *to* me, and lift her in my arms. Crossing the room, my hand thrusts out to brace us as I lower us to the couch and settle her in my lap.

"I don't know what's wrong with me," she says quietly. With the urgency past, I take a moment to assess her wounds. Her tits look rough, with red welts rising, nipples looking raw and sore. "The more it hurts, the more I want."

"It's a kink, baby." I press a gentle kiss against the swell of her breast. "Silas taught you about that?"

She nods, chest slowly rising and falling at the feel of my lips. "He told me, but that in there… it went somewhere different."

"Exhibitionism. Punishment. Degradation." I ghost my palms over her nipples, barely touching them. "My father primed you for this kind of desire, Imogene. The corrections and deprivation. The need for approval. He's a goddamn son of a bitch."

"That makes it worse. He's everywhere, Rex. In my mind and body."

My heart feels heavy, weighed down by the trauma of what we just went through. How sex and intimacy is always part of a game—a manipulation.

"I went too far," I tell her. "I lost myself in the moment. It was wrong."

She shifts in my lap, her crotch heavy against my cock. "You gave me what I wanted."

"You only want it because he's created that desire in you." I grab her face, forcing her to look at me. "He may have created this, but you get to own it." My thumb catches a tear. I fucking hate seeing her cry. "I get to be the one that helps you through it. Not him."

Her lips blaze across my cheek. "And I get to help you."

She rises to her knees, hands grabbing at my waist, creating room to push down my pants. My shirt goes next and then she's back on me, pussy warming my swollen dick. Her pale hair curtains around us and I take her tits in my hands, carefully squeezing them together, lathing my tongue over her nipples. I want her to feel the good in my touch—not just the pain. There's a place for both of those but right now, in this brief respite from my father's insanity, I want her to feel cared for.

She looks up, eyebrows furrowed.

"What?" I ask.

"Why are you being so sweet?"

Fair. We've had our share of hostile encounters. I'd forced my cock in her mouth. The way I took her virginity. My drunken late-night fucks.

"You deserve to be cherished," I confess. "Treated like a queen. It's okay to want it hard, but it's also okay to let someone take care of you." I slide my hand behind her neck, pulling our foreheads together. "Let me take care of my mate."

"Can I take care of you, too?" she asks.

"Fuck yes."

Imogene's hand falls between us, gripping my cock. I feel huge against the spread of her fingers, desperate because I fight the urge to come the second she touches me. She jacks me, thumb grazing over the sticky tip, and it becomes hard to breathe.

"Baby, that feels so good." My eyes are cast down, watching her work me, watching those perfect tits sway between us. I look up and capture her mouth with mine. "I want to be inside. Feel you around me. It's been so fucking long."

Lifting again, she rests a hand on my shoulder and angles herself with the tip of my cock, pressing me to her entrance. My balls quiver, it's been so long since I've had this woman. Felt her skin, smelled her scent, had her this close and I don't want it to go too fast, but I also know that door is going to open at any minute and reality's going to come rushing back in.

Imogene sets the pace, lowering herself, taking me in, inch by inch. With my eyes closed, my hands hold onto her hips, reveling in the feel of her, how her walls hug me tight. We sit like that for a long moment, just feeling one another. I open my eyes and find her watching me.

"What's wrong?"

"Did you mean it?" she asks. "What you said in there."

That I love her.

"I meant it." Fuck yes, I meant it.

"How do you know? Are you sure it wasn't just the moment? The stress of the situation?" She frowns. "It's okay if that's what happened. I won't get upset."

I rest my hand on her lower back, pulling her as close as possible, which is pretty fucking close since my cock is buried inside of her. "We're connected, Imogene. Physically and emotionally. Hard against soft, lost against broken." I move my hips, barely, softly. "He can drive us apart, force us to hurt one another, banish and abuse." Moving faster now, but with restraint, I kiss her breast, licking a hot trail to her neck. "He can do whatever he wants, but ultimately, we're bonded. We're mates. We've probably been so since that day on the cliff, two messed up kids, traumatized from losing our mothers."

She shifts against me, arms linked around my neck. Nose to nose, I stare into her eyes, willing her to believe me. I didn't agree to a mate because I wanted love. But I found it anyway. In this beautiful girl writhing on top of me.

The room fills with the sound of our breath, the slip-slide of our bodies, the whisper of our voices. I tell her again. "I love you," warm on her ear, for only her to hear. And when I fill her with my seed, hot cum, buried deep inside, I vow anew to get her out of here.

Sagging onto me, bodies still connected, she looks up and says, "Silas…"

I shake my head. There's only one reason my father left us alone.

He had business to attend to. Silas is already gone. My father will not abide by his betrayal.

Next, he'll come for me. This time together? It's another game, a way to lull me into thinking I have the slightest thread of control. That if I work with him, we can come to an agreement, but I know my father. He's biding his time before he banishes me for good. All that will be left is the prize he truly wants.

I'm selfish enough not to let him have her.

13

Levi

The squeal and hiss of the city bus outside jolts me awake—but it's not like I was sleeping very deeply. The noises are different here. Mechanical. Loud. *Secular.* The bus came by several times overnight, along with the constant passing of cars. The lights flashing in the window a constant reminder that I'm not home. That I've been Banished.

It's more than the distractions though. My brain won't shut off, not with so much at stake. I keep going over my plan again and again, looking for loopholes. Mistakes.

The springs in the bed next to mine creak, straining from Elon's weight. The upstairs of Camille's bungalow has spare rooms. Twin beds in each bland, nondescript room. The drawers are filled with extra clothing—clearly for people with no possessions—people on the run.

We're refugees.

Dressing in a worn T-shirt and loose sweatpants that I find in the drawer, I leave Elon to get more rest. It's the first full night's sleep he's had since being Banished. The first night without a fight down at the bar, trying to scrounge together enough money for us to survive. I wonder if they noticed. I wonder if the people in Serendee notice us being gone. Are we missed? Or are we just a reminder of what could happen to anyone that breaks the rules.

Halfway down the stairs, I hear a voice—two voices. Camille and another woman. I pause, unsure if I should interrupt. Slowly, I take one more step and peer around the corner.

"I feel so helpless. Like, if I could just talk to her—get her out of that place—and make her listen, she'd see how crazy all of this is."

The two women are in the former dining room, sitting on two of the chairs that form the circle. A teapot and two cups sit on the coffee table. Camille's forehead has a deep, concerned crease slashed through the normally smooth skin. "I'm not going to tell you that you shouldn't feel this way. You should. Your sister has been behind the walls of Serendee for months now. She's in a dangerous position."

"We've just always been so close. How could she push me away like this?"

I study the woman, trying to get a better view. She looks to be in her mid-thirties. Dressed in secular clothes, a V-neck sweater and jeans. Gold bracelets wrist and a smart watch circle her wrist. Her eyes are red-rimmed, tears building in the corners. There's something vaguely familiar about them. I've probably met her sister, perhaps taught her in my courses.

"Gabi," Camille says, reaching behind her to a box of tissues. She snatches out a few and hands them to the other woman. "You have to understand, none of this is about you. Or anyone else. Her erratic behavior is the result of the methods conducted in that place. The residents of Serendee are under deep control. Sleep, diet, and sensory deprivation are part of the tactics. Fear that they may lose favor with the leader of the group."

"I've watched some of his videos. Early on, Kayla was trying to talk me into taking courses with her." She dabs at the corner of her eyes with the tissue. "How is this guy appealing? I mean, he's attractive, but otherwise I don't get it. Listening to him talk about all this stuff, Enlightenment and The Way and all that bullshit just... well, it sounds like bullshit."

Camille laughs. "It *is* bullshit, and Timothy slings it with perfection." The way she uses Anex's birth name so casually is unnerving. No one calls him that. He's said over and over that he is no longer that person. Calling him Timothy Wray is with intention—one Camille wields like a sword. "You're right though. He's handsome. That gets people in the door, especially women. But he has this knack for finding a weak spot. A hollow place inside of people that they desperately want filled." She takes a sip of her tea. "What is Kayla's weak spot?"

Kayla. My thoughts sort, flipping through the files in my mind, ultimately landing on the right one. Kayla Montclair. Priority recruit due to her status of being the heir to a publishing empire. She's a newer recruit. Heir to the Montclair Publishing fortune.

"She was engaged," Gabi says, "and was in the middle of planning a very extravagant wedding. Then she found out he was cheating on her. The entire situation was very public and humiliating. After that she started immersing herself into a lot of self-help programs, which we had access to because of the publishing house. Yoga retreats. Health and wellness workshops. At first it seemed good that she was throwing herself into the business. My father was ecstatic. She was able to test products, go to seminars, get free courses. It was obvious she was really seeking 'something,' you know."

"That's the kind of thing Timothy is good at. Spotting that 'something' no one else can."

"Slowly she just drifted away. Her language sounded like nonsense. All these fake terms. She started losing weight and looked like she hadn't slept in a month. Then, one day I went by her apartment, and it was clear she'd abandoned it. Left all her clothes and possessions." Her eyebrows rise. "Everything, but the bank accounts."

Camille doesn't seem surprised by any of this and confirms that by saying, "As horrifying as it sounds, all of this is right out of the Serendee playbook. She's not the first to be taken in by this man. He's good. Very, very good. And once he has them locked behind the walls there's little chance of them leaving, especially on their own."

"So, what do we do? How do we save Kayla?"

Camille squares her shoulders. "We gather evidence. Keep trying to make contact. Don't push. Play by her rules. I'll connect you to our private investigator who has been helping us gather information for years."

"Okay, I can do that."

"Most of all though, you have something different from the others that have come through here. Influence. Your family is connected. For the first time, we may be able to get people to listen."

"I've tried. The police couldn't do anything. Said she was there on her own free-will."

"We have to go higher than the local police and see if we can find someone else in a similar situation. Politicians. The county prosecutor. Maybe the attorney general. Whoever your family knows that can dig into the dirty secrets of Serendee."

A strange feeling spreads across my chest at the idea of really exposing the innerworkings of Serendee. I watch as Gabi frowns. "What kind of dirty secrets are you talking about?"

"You and I know the real focus is getting the victims of this con man out of his control, but, as you know, that's nearly impossible to prove." Camille grabs a file from the seat next to hers. She opens it and starts flipping through papers. "The way we're going to take him down isn't about kidnapping or holding people against their will. It's through boring, stupid stuff like tax fraud, embezzlement, running illegal businesses." She pauses, eyes flicking from the paper to Gabi's face. "Then we expose him for the monster he really is: Human trafficking."

The words linger in the air. The real dark and dirty secret of Serendee. The Fallen. Those sent to Re-education. Corrections.

I look down at my hands, clean and smooth. The scars, the *blood*, from the pain I inflicted are still there even if you can't see them.

"I get the feeling Timothy is going after bigger and bigger marks —people with extreme wealth, like your sister. The government may not care about people, but they sure as fuck care about money. Especially money they want to get their grubby hands on—taxes."

"But why? Isn't the whole point of Serendee that it's self-sustaining?"

"Once upon a time, maybe. But those days are long gone. Serendee is there to feed Timothy's insatiable ego, and he's going to need money and influence to do it." She reaches out and takes the woman's hand. "We're close, Gabi. I've been trying to find a way to bring this man down for years, and for the first time I'm hopeful."

"I just want my sister back."

"That's all I want, too."

I step back up the staircase as the women say goodbye, considering the exchange. Camille's program is more than just helping victims and families of so-called cults. She's not just focused on saving individuals. She's determined to bring Anex and Serendee down. I don't even fully understand all of the terms she just used. *Tax fraud, embezzlement, illegal businesses.* Taxes are something Anex taught us is an absurd government overreach, something we were Better than. The people of Serendee shun the ideas of the outside world, the laws, and regulations.

The other ones... Anex has the right to manage, control, and determine the use of all monies coming in and out for the betterment of the community. It's part of our fundamental beliefs not to get tied down in these secular rules. We don't abide by any philosophy but our own.

Camille knows that. She helped define it. And the fact she's willing to use this against Anex means she's more dangerous than I anticipated.

∽

Holding the key in my hand, I pause when I notice the apartment door is ajar. I'd left Camille's house an hour before, prepared to clean out the few things we'd left. It isn't much, but when you have nothing, it matters.

Turns out I may be too late and that the manager beat me to it when we didn't pay next week's rent—due yesterday.

It only takes a heartbeat to realize it isn't the manager.

I see the guard first, standing stiffly next to the refrigerator. Unmoving, his eyes sweep over me. Across the room, Anex ligers by the window, fingers parting the metal blinds as he looks down on the street below.

"Anex," I say, already bowing. When he turns, he waits for me to go through the motions, touching my forehead, giving him honor. "I didn't know you were coming." I didn't know I was coming. "How…"

The question trails off.

"I followed you from the house."

Ah, right. Has he been watching us the entire time?

My neck warms. "I can explain."

"No need." He waves his hand and assesses the chairs, nose wrinkled, trying to determine which is cleaner. He picks the one at the small kitchen table. "Camille's been working out of that little dump for years now. I figured you'd end up there." He looks around at the cobwebby corners of the room. "Even if it's a dump, it's less dumpy than this."

The criticism of my temporary home rankles me. He kicked us out with nothing. Literally nothing to make our way and he's judging where we landed? I swallow my ire and circle back.

"You've known about Camille's program."

"Of course. I've been tracking her since the day she left." He gestures to the chair opposite of his and I sit, back rigid against the hard seat. "I knew she wouldn't go far—not with Imogene still with us. She's a betrayer, but it hurt leaving her daughter behind." He crosses his legs, resting his hands on his thighs. "To be honest, I thought she'd get over her silly tantrum and return. She was weaker than I realized, so Regressive it ate away at her very soul."

Weak isn't how I would describe Camille, but I wisely keep my mouth shut. Anex isn't finished. "What did you tell her when you and Elon showed up on her doorstep?"

"The truth," I respond without hesitation. "Anything less would have made her suspicious. She was suspicious, but our story smoothed that out. She's happy to help two fellow outcasts."

I try to keep the pain out of my voice. Speaking of this so lightly—it digs deep under my flesh. Serendee is my home. Anex my leader, but things are different now. I am on uneven ground. I have to do everything I can to level the field.

I must answer correctly because Anex simply nods and asks, "How is Camille?"

"She hates you." I flash him a grin. "And you're right, she's completely lost to The Way. But she's also conniving. She's aware that there's no way to get to you—at least by normal means."

"She's never had the power to touch me."

So arrogant. How had I never seen that before? That his confidence and false sense of identity will be what brings him ruin. Yet here I am, telling him. "You need to know she's rallying the families of the people you've brought in recently—the *wealthy* families."

"Interesting." His eyes flick over to the guard, and he scratches his chin. "Did she say how?"

I shake my head. "She's hoping to use their influence."

"Bad press? Politicians? Government bureaucracy. How pathetic." His voice rises an octave as he stands. "She's going to use the system to take *me* down? What? Uncle Fucking Sam? What a goddamn hypocrite."

My hands grip the edge of my seat, body frozen as he rants. I've seen many sides of Anex. Thoughtful. Wise. Intelligent. All powerful and judicious. But this anger, it comes in a flash and sets my nerves on edge.

"She's culpable, you know that? Her name is on so many things—all of the early ideals of Serendee. She made promises to me. Oaths. I wonder how she'd like me to expose her to the world for being a lying, betraying, cock-teasing bitch?" He swings his arm around, catching the top of the chair and slinging it across the room. It clatters against the floor before toppling into the wall. "Fuck!" He spins. "No, fuck *her*."

The outburst is intense. Wild and erratic. I slide my eyes in the direction of the guard, but he hasn't moved an inch. I take a deep breath and swallow past the lump in my throat. "Although she wants revenge, I think the one thing she wants more than that, is to see her daughter."

"That," he snaps, head whipping around, "will never happen."

"No, I would assume not, but," I weigh my words carefully, "what if there's another way to handle all of this?"

"I would have killed her already if that was an option."

The lightness in the way he says it chills me to the core. "Although that's one way to do it, I'm not talking about killing Camille."

Anex snaps his fingers and the guard bolts forward, picking up the chair and placing it back at the table. He sits, running his hands through his hair, regaining composure. "Explain."

"Serendee operates quietly. We keep to ourselves, living in our small, walled-in community. We're self-sustaining. We don't need outsiders, but that's one of the things that makes people uncomfortable. It seems like we're keeping secrets." I run my hand down my thigh. "We do have secrets, but they're locked up and hidden under barns. We may need to open the doors a little to ease some suspicion."

"Impossible. We can't have the secular world gawking at us. At our women. I've always promised they would be safe, and I'm not going back on that because of a threat."

"How about we open the doors to one person. To one event."

"What are you talking about, Levi?"

"I think, no, I feel," I touch my chest, "The Way is speaking to me, telling me that you should invite Camille to the equinox."

"The equinox."

"To her daughter's mating ceremony."

"To *our* mating ceremony." He grins. "As a gift, to Imogene."

"Yes. No secrets. No hiding. Fully transparent."

"I like it. I like it a lot." His eyebrow rises. "And you actually think you can get Camille to come?"

"I do."

"If you pull this off, I'll grant you and Elon status back in Serendee."

"As part of the inner circle," I include, feeling the sweat spread across my lower back. "Full standing."

His smile never falters, but the corner of his eye twitches, and I think maybe I've pushed it too far. Overplayed my hand. But I've spent a lifetime studying under this man. I know his strengths and weaknesses. I know his ego. And right now, I know he'll do anything to get Camille Montgomery under his thumb. Even reinstating me and Elon back in the fold.

"I'll accept your proposal," he says, leaning forward. "I can see now that when I assigned you, Elon, and Silas to train Imogene you weren't as strong as I'd hoped. You were taken by the allure of that girl's innocent, tight, pussy." He laughs, as if he deeply understands where things went sideways. "But, understand, once Camille is behind the walls, once she's come voluntarily, she and her daughter are mine to deal with."

14

Elon

Camille looks over her shoulder when I walk into the kitchen, giving me a tight smile. "I hate tea," she says without any context, then dumps two cups into the sink. "But it seems to put people at ease." She opens a cabinet door, revealing rows of mugs. "Coffee?"

"Sure." I don't miss the way her forehead rises as she pours me a cup and slides it across the island. "What?"

"I thought drinks like coffee were off limits. You know, anything addictive." She pours herself a large cup and takes a large gulp, as if making a point. "Or did he change those rules?"

"I wasn't raised like normal people in Serendee—one of the perks of being best friends with Anex's son."

She glances down at my scabbed knuckles. One had torn overnight, leaving a spot of blood on the sheets. "Where'd you get that?"

"There's a bar on the other side of Whittmore's campus. They have paid fights in the basement." I sip my coffee, feeling burn on my tongue. "We had to earn money somehow."

"Right. Limited education. No real job experience. No paperwork." Hearing it sounds so pathetic. She looks me up and down. "You're a big guy. What did you do for Timothy?"

I try not to squirm. It's been a long time since I've been around a woman like Camille. A mother. I left my own home at twelve and moved into the Donum like everyone else. At least until Anex brought us to the Main House to be with Rex. "He saw my size and ability. I worked in security. Protected Rex, mostly."

"He decided," she says. "You had no choice."

I open my mouth to reprimand her. To remind her that it isn't just Anex that makes these decisions, but it's The Way, the gut feeling he gets about the people in our community. But I stop myself. Those beliefs are lies.

"No," I confess, probably for the first time, "I didn't have a choice."

"Who are you, Elon?" She rests her elbows on the countertop, leaning forward slightly. It's unnerving looking at her—so similar to Imogene. My heart contracts. "If Anex wasn't there to decide for you, who would you be?"

"I don't know." I stare down at the hand holding my coffee mug, looking at those worn, torn, knuckles and think. I try to remember who I was, who I wanted to be, but there's little space between who I am, who Anex created me to be, and any organic truth. I close my eyes, and a memory returns. I'm back to when I was a kid—bigger than the rest—and I'd spin the others on the merry-go-round at the playground. That was the first time I saw Imogene, wide-eyed and bossy.

I'd told her about this memory after she was Ordered to Rex and later, I kissed her for the first time.

Those moments unearth something in me, something long buried, away from Anex and his greedy control.

Across the table Camille watches me, and a flood of emotion runs through me. It's her daughter I'm thinking of. Her daughter that technically belongs to another man—my best friend. Camille has been tolerant of us, but knowing how we share Imogene?

There's no way she'd accept that.

Except the truth is on my tongue and heat builds in my cheeks. Approval from this woman suddenly means everything. I open my mouth to speak, but the front door opens, and my courage slams shut, just like the door.

"There's no reason to talk about 'what if's.'" I rise, carrying my cup to the sink. I wash it quickly, feeling my hands burn under the hot water. "All we can do is accept reality."

15

Imogene

Just when I thought this mansion of horrors couldn't get any more disturbing, Rex and I were taken to a room in Anex's wing that made the rest of the Main House seem like high level accommodations—*including* the basement cells.

The guard came for us not long after Rex and I dressed. He gave me his shirt, eyes worrying over my tender and swollen breasts, while he pulled on his pants. By gunpoint we were led back through Anex's room. It was empty. No Anex. No Inner Circle. No Silas.

I wanted to ask about him, but I knew better than to express concern. Anex was determined to destroy the things I loved. I wouldn't give him more ammunition.

"What the hell is this?" Rex had asked, feet planted to the floor. The room in front of us is divided into two, a clear, thick wall separating the space. Everything was pure white. White walls, white bed, white chair, white carpet. Two white toilets and sinks sat in each corner. Rex's eyes grew wide. "Hell no!"

Erik shoved Rex into one side and secured the door. He jerked his gun at me, and I entered on my own volition. The instant the door closed I felt the air grow thin. I slammed my palms against the glass door. "Is there enough oxygen in here? Is this how it ends? With Anex suffocating us."

"Please, Imogene. Acting out isn't going to make this better for anyone."

I turned and saw Margaret standing outside the door, hand cradling her belly. "Let us out!"

"This is your room for the foreseeable future." I looked over and saw Rex sitting on the end of the bed, eyes vacant. "Your father designed this room knowing that one day he may need to keep you close, the both of you."

"He built this room a year ago," Rex said, forehead creasing. "Before the Order."

"Your father is all knowing, Rex. Led by The Way," Margaret says. "I don't know why you're surprised."

"He planned this," Rex said, pieces clicking into place. "From the beginning. He never was going to let me have you as a mate. He set up the training with Elon, Levi, and Silas. He got me to fall for you. Got us to *all fall* for you so that we'd make mistakes. He knew I'd get possessive, blind with obsession and want. And that would make me, and the guys, trip up and fall right in his trap." He ran his hands through his hair and looked up at Margaret. "The whole plan was to keep Imogene for himself, but he couldn't just pluck a girl out of Serendee and make her his mate. That would raise questions, so he had me do it instead. The catch is that he didn't expect her to be so goddamn stubborn. So defiant." He laughs darkly. "So *Regressive*."

"You'll stay here," Margaret repeated, ignoring Rex's moment of clarity. "Where your every movement can be watched. Every piece of food you consume. Every supplement. Every bodily function will be monitored."

"Everything?" I asked, eyes shifting to the toilets.

"Everything, Imogene. You've lost the right to privacy, to autonomy, to everything. Anex is fully in control now. It's how it has to be. It's The Way."

"For how long?"

Her expression softened, and there was a flicker of something in her eyes that chilled me to the bone. Something dark and lost. "Until the equinox, of course."

Fear climbed up my spine. "The equinox?"

"The day you will finally be mated."

That conversation had been days ago, at least three, I assume, but the days are getting shorter. The sunlight fading sooner. I can measure this through our window. It's high, out of reach, but it does provide some awareness of the time of day. This is especially true in the morning because the window faces east, and the bright stream of sunlight makes it hard to sleep.

Which stinks, because sleeping the day away, dreaming of being somewhere else, would make everything more bearable. The light has been glaring in my eyes for at least an hour when I give up and swing my legs over the side of the bed. Across from me, on the other side of that clear divider, Rex is already up. Well, up and down. Rex is in the middle of one of his impressively long sets of push-ups.

My eyes follow the taut muscles that run the length of his back, the way they pull against his skin as he rises and falls. There's a brutality to his movements, the distinct impression he's punishing himself.

He does this every morning. Push-ups. Sit ups. Balancing exercises. At first, I thought it was just his regular routine, but then I realized that there was something else going on.

He's distracting himself from my visits from Margaret.

The unlocking of the door draws my attention away from his muscular form. Like clockwork, Margaret arrives, holding two trays of food in her hands. "Rise and shine, sweet Imogene." She says this every day, cheerful and unrelenting. The exact opposite of how I feel.

Rex flips on his back and begins the sit-up phase of his routine, eyes focused on the wall. Margaret slides his tray through the small opening at the base of the wall, then carries mine into my section.

The food smells good. Eggs and bacon, homemade biscuits. Everything sourced from Serendee. Anex hasn't been limiting either of our meals. A quick glance tells me Rex has an appropriately larger portion than I do, but one thing is for certain, our leader is allowing me more calories. Margaret explained that the first day she delivered food.

"Anex is a genius, but like all men, the female body is something of a mystery. I explained that by reducing your intake he could be inadvertently stopping your menstruation."

So, right. He's letting me eat again so I can be fertile. For the equinox.

"Here's your supplements," she says, resting the tray on the end of the bed and handing me a small cup of pills, followed by a cup of water. She watches as I take each one, swallowing and showing her the inside of my mouth to confirm. "Good girl. Now, time to check."

Every time she mentions the "check" my cheeks burn hot. "There's no need. Nothing has changed."

Margaret shakes her head. "We go through this every morning, Imogene. You know I need to look for myself."

"Why? So you can humiliate me?" My eyes snap over to Rex who hasn't missed a crunch. "I'm not bleeding. I promise, I'll let you know if and when it happens."

She frowns, a flicker of empathy crossing her face. "Is that what this is about? Your feelings of insecurity, like you're less of a woman because you're not having your period?"

"What?" I stare at her like she's lost her mind. For the record, she has. She lost it the second she stepped into Serendee and fell into Anex's trap. Again, I glance across the room at the man who made me realize I'm more than the parameters that Serendee has placed around me. Rex. Silas. Levi. Elon. They taught me to be a real woman. Rex never stops his movements but his head tilts slightly, and I know he's listening. "Unlike you, I don't feel less female without falling into Anex's antiquated version of womanhood. I don't need to bleed to feel complete."

I yank up the hem of my dress and pull down my pristine white panties. I toss them at her and she catches them in her hand. If my rant affected her, she shows no sign of it, not when she checks the crotch of the panties for signs of menstruation, or when she fishes a clean pair out of her skirt pocket and hands them to me.

"It'll be best for you," her eyes flick to Rex's back, "for all of us, Imogene, if you stop being a petty bitch and remember your place."

"I'm a captive no matter what I do, so if I want to be a petty bitch, I will." I cross my arms over my chest. "What happens if my period doesn't start before the equinox? What if it doesn't happen at all? Does he keep me locked away forever?"

"It will happen because Anex wills it. It is The Way, Imogene. When will you realize this is out of your hands?"

I refuse to answer, and she stares at me, unblinking. I do the same, refusing to back down. I know I can't beat Anex. I know my life is fucked. But holding my own against this woman, this manipulator, feels good.

At least for a minute.

~

The rest of the morning falls into a routine. Rex has the grace to look away as I tug on the clean panties and use the toilet. I do the same for him, although it's futile. When Rex urinates, I'm reminded of horses at the stable. Does a man's bladder always hold so much? Is that what I sound like?

We've each been given two sets of clothes. Mine are thin dresses. While Rex floods the earth with his heavy stream, I start to lift my dress over my head when I notice he quiets. I sense something, turning my head. He's watching.

"Will you show me?"

It's an ask. Not a demand. He's careful with his words, careful not to sound like Margaret. It's a subtle change. I know what he wants. He's asked me every day. Always my decision. I turn around fully and remove the dress.

"It looks better." I know he's lying because his forehead stretches upward when he sees my breasts.

I glance down at the mottled flesh, a mixture of yellow and purple. I make a face. "Thank you for saying so, but you and I both know I look awful."

He shakes his head and presses his hand flat against the clear divider. "You're beautiful."

"Stop." I reach for my dress. "I'm not beautiful."

"Don't cover yourself. Not yet." His voice is deep, impossible to say no to, and I find myself standing in front of him, exposed. His gaze rakes over me. "Jesus, Imogene. I know you don't believe me, but you're the prettiest, sexiest, thing I've seen." His other hand shifts to the front of his pants and I see his erection straining at the fabric. "I'd tear down this wall to get to you, if I could, to kiss those bruises away and make new ones if you'd let me."

My heart pounds and I press my palm against his, the plastic in between. "I'd let you," I confess. "I'd let you do anything you wanted to me."

The muscle in the back of his jaw tenses and releases. "He's doing this to dehumanize us to one another. To force us to see one another in our most base moments, so we're unattractive and unappealing. And maybe with anyone else it would work, but every moment with you just makes me want you more." Below his waist, his hand moves, tugging down his pants and exposing his hard erection. His hand wraps around his shaft and he tugs upward, Adam's apple bobbing as he reaches the tip. "All I ever fucking want with you, Imogene, is more."

Heat unspools in my belly, a hot coil wound inside. The warmth flickers out from there spreading first to my arms and legs, then to my nipples and between my thighs. I understand what Rex is saying because I feel it too. After the time here together, I only love him more.

"Touch yourself, baby," he says, leaning his forehead against the surface. I run my hand down my body, over my tender breasts and stomach, down between my legs. He licks his lips and nods. "That's it. That's my girl."

His words spur me on, fingers sliding between my slippery folds. My breath hitches and I press against the glass. Our bodies are separated, but our movements fall into sync. The push-pull, the shuddering want. Keeping my eyes wide, I take in the long line of muscle on his forearm, that tenses as it draws up and down his cock.

Rex's shoulders quiver, his eyes meeting mine. "I love you."

"I love you, too," I say back, feeling it bloom in my chest, feeling it *explode* between my legs. I'm all alone in that room when the orgasm comes. Alone as Rex's guttural groan bounces off the cold, oppressive, walls. Alone when we're both finished, nothing left but the greasy print of our bodies on the glass.

We spend the day that way. Eating our now cold breakfast. Telling small stories to pass the time. Fall asleep. Alone, but together, satiated but sacrificed, until the streaming light from the window wakes me the next day. A twinge in my belly draws me to my side, and my eyes meet Rex's as he lowers himself to the floor to start his workout. His mouth lifts in the smallest smile.

I rise, tossing my legs over the side of the bed, feet on the cold floor, warmth between my legs. Blinking, I look down and see the spread, dark and red, like a flower blooming across the bottom half of my night dress.

Movement across the room draws my gaze, and I see Rex, pressed against the divider, eyes wide and focused on the red.

My period.

The Way has spoken.

Rex is mid-pushup when Margaret arrives. He hasn't spoken since he saw my bloody panties, the closeness of the day before gone. Just like any hope I'd had of getting out of this.

"Rise and Shine," Margaret calls, giving me the worst sort of déjà vu. I've already changed. My soiled panties are wadded in a ball. I don't hesitate to hand them to her without a word.

She sets the trays down and looks at the balled-up cotton. Her lips are turned down, but she unfolds them, revealing the dark stain. "I knew it would come. Just in time."

Up and down. Up and down. Rex never stops, even though his muscles are quivering from exhaustion.

"What now?" I ask, bracing myself for the sharp pain of another cramp. I haven't missed these.

"You'll go into Preparations."

"Already?" Every Ordered female goes into Preparations three days before the Mating Ceremony. It's a secret, mystical time. I used to crave knowing what happened, to be one of those women elevated to the next step, but after everything I've been through, after the branding, the idea sends a tremor of fear along my nerves.

Nothing good comes from being Chosen in this world.

"I told you, Imogene, your bleeding came just in time. It's a sign from The Way. The equinox is in three days."

It takes everything in me not to slap the grin off her face.

I'm using every ounce of energy trying not to cry.

Her hand stretches out. "We should go."

"Wait." I glance at Rex. Sweat drips down his temple. He stares forward, never glancing my way. Why won't he look at me? I just need to see his eyes. To feel their warmth. To know he still loves me.

Otherwise, how do I survive?

"Imogene, everything changes now. All of this," her hand waves around the cell, "all of this vanishes. Your bleeding is proof that you're worthy. That Anex was right to have persevered. It means you are no longer Fallen. The Reeducation worked."

I drag my eyes away from Rex and look at this woman, wondering if I ever sounded this delusional.

"Everything," she continues, "goes back to the way it was supposed to be."

"How was it supposed to be?"

She grins. "We'll be true sisters. Spiritual sisters, bonded together with Anex in union."

Warm, prickly heat coats my body. My armpits and neck. Bile thrusts up my throat and I bend, arm across my stomach, trying to hold back the gag.

"I know it's a lot to take in," she says, placing a hand on my back, "but it's right. You have to understand that."

I understand nothing, other than the fact that my fate was sealed long before my awareness kicked in. Nothing will change the course of Anex's will. My mind slips away, along with the urge to fight or rebel. It's done nothing but make things worse all along.

Maybe Margaret is right.

This is The Way.

And there's nothing I can do about it.

16

Elon

The envelope arrives on a Monday. Tucked between the stack of mail Camille carries into the kitchen. I recognize the paper right away. Handmade from recycled materials.

"Stop." The words are harsh. Blunt. "Give me that."

Camille's eyebrow raises. "What are you talking about?"

"It's from Serendee," Levi says, striding into the room. "The paper. It's unique."

Every muscle in Camille's body tenses, but she doesn't relinquish the envelope. She just stares at it, long and hard, until she asks, "Did you give them this address?"

Levi shakes his head.

"No," I reply. "But it's not unlikely that he's had an eye on you this whole time, you know that, right?"

I've felt his eyes on us since we arrived. Nothing I can confirm. Just a sense. It could just be paranoia from years of living under his rule, but it feels like more.

"There have been threats over the years from a variety of groups that don't like us helping the families of their victims." My jaw tics at the word "victim." "You realize Serendee isn't the only cult out there? It's not even the only one in this region." She grabs a knife and wedges the tip into the corner of the flap. The sound of tearing paper fills the kitchen. Levi and I watch as she pulls out a single card. It's handwritten, the curling cursive writing printed across the paper. Camille's eyes flick over the words and she says, "It's an invitation."

"To what?" I ask, heart thudding in my chest. Something is off. Weird. Wrong.

"To a ceremony." She tosses the card on the table, turned so we can read it. I see, not only her name listed, but mine and Levi's as well. My eyes jump to read what it says, but Camille beats me to it. "In two days, Anex is Mating with my daughter and he wants all of us to come."

~

Camille doesn't say much after reading the invitation. Just excusing herself and taking the stairs to the second floor. A moment later a door clicks shut.

I, too, feel the need to move. And I run upstairs, grabbing the bag Levi picked up at the apartment, and head back to the front door.

"Where are you going?" Levi asks, hot on my heels.

"Out." I clear the steps, but stop when I feel his hand on my shoulder.

"Elon, wait."

I spin, glaring at my friend. "I can't sit around here and just do fucking nothing while all of this is going on, Levi. I can't log all my feelings into a journal, or meditate to the fucking Way, hoping everything will work out."

"So what then?" I don't miss the hurt in his eyes at every jab I make about his values. "What the hell are you going to do?"

"Not what I want," I say, hitching the bag over my shoulder. "But the only thing I can. I'm going to go hit something."

Or someone. Hopefully one of those frat boy pricks down at the bar. It always feels nice to hear the smack of my fist against their pretty faces.

I pass the bus stop and head north. It's not the best part of town. Seedy hotels and abandoned buildings. Drug dealers lurk in the shadows. I'm familiar with the area because of Serendee's drug trade. It's not the neighborhood anyone chooses to live in, not anymore.

"You're not taking the bus?"

"I need to blow off some steam first." Goddamn Anex. Goddamn him. It's bad enough that he's doing this to Imogene. To *our* girl. But to invite Camille? Us? He's relentless and evil. The absolute worst. And if I know him as well as I think I do, it's a fucking trap.

That thought lingers and I stop short, turning to face Levi who is still only a few feet away. He stops too, wariness in his narrowed gaze.

"What?"

"You set this up, didn't you?" I ask, slowly walking toward him. "The invitation?"

"We agreed to use Camille as bait. I just cast the line. Anex bit, just like we thought."

"Using Camille to get Anex to work with us is one thing. Walking into the lion's den," I shake my head, "to witness that—you went too far."

"I did what I had to do, Elon. You knew it would have to be drastic."

I search his face. His body language. Look at the way he's standing. His shoulders and hands. His feet. All the tells I'd been taught to assess someone on the spot. But Levi is also trained, and he gives me nothing. Finally, I go with the truth. "You've handled all of this well. Too well, Levi. The Banishment. The Shunning." I start walking again, to the corner, I wait for the light to change, letting him catch up. "Your entire life was wrapped up in Serendee. In achieving Enlightenment and Anex's approval. Way more than me and Rex."

Something's off and I've felt it for days. I was just too preoccupied with my own pain to address it.

The light changes and I cross the road, passing an old boarded up building. People lurk in the old alcoves, men and women—*girls*—slumped against the walls, in skirts too short for this kind of weather. I keep my eyes open, instincts on point. The last thing we need is to get caught up in trouble down here.

"How many times have you talked to him?" I ask, terrified of the answer.

"Twice," he answers quickly. "Once at the center, hoping to establish contact. Then again at the apartment. He was waiting for me."

This time when I stop, my arm snaps out and I grab him by the collar, twisting until my knuckles bear against his throat. "And what? You just offered the three of us up on a platter? Happy witnesses to the abomination of the century?"

He doesn't fight me, just swallows thickly. "I had to do something. We need a way back in."

"I don't want back in!" My fingers twist. I'm hurting him and I don't care.

"For them," he wheezes. "For *her*."

My grip loosens. "What are you talking about?"

"I've gone over it a million times. All night. All day. While you were out beating the shit out of college boys, I was coming up with a plan. A plan that gets us back into Serendee. That's why we needed Camille—the one thing Anex is willing to compromise for."

"We take one step on that property, and he'll never let us go again." I drop him entirely. Disgusted. "He definitely won't let Camille leave again. That's not a compromise, that's a goddamn trap."

"It'll work. I convinced him that this will make him look good—transparent. That there are people investigating him, and he needs to look above board. If he has nothing to hide, then don't hide it. He's going to let us walk in, and then when it's over, we're walking away with our family."

I want to think this is a good idea, but I can't. There are too many obstacles. Too many guards and guns and hidden, secret cells underneath that mansion. But I also know that he's right. This may be our only chance. Walking in on his terms.

"If you're lying to me, Levi, I swear I will end you. I don't care if we've been friends for twenty years, or everything we've gone through. I will destroy you if this is just another way to fuck with my head."

His eyes dart over my shoulder. "Elon."

"Don't talk to me unless you're going to tell me every step of your plan. All of it. Up front. No secrets."

"Elon," he says again, eyes shifting from mine to behind me. I exhale and turn, prepared to fend off a junkie or a hooker. I'm not wrong. There's a prostitute in the alley behind us, with a man. His hand is wrapped tight around her arm and she's fighting him as he drags her farther away from the main road.

"Let go," she hisses, stumbling over her heels. "I can't just—"

"You'll do what I want," he barks, shoving her against the brick wall. "And if it's good enough, then I'll think about paying."

I don't get there before he yanks at her top, the strap snapping in two, but I do get a hand around his throat before he takes it farther.

"She said she didn't want to go with you."

He fights against me. "Fuck you."

"Get her out of here," I grunt at Levi.

I hear her heels on the pavement, the sound fading as she gets further away. I laugh. "You got me on the wrong day, brother. I've been looking for someone's ass to kick."

"You're going to kick my ass over a whore?" He scoffs. "Trust me dude. No piece of ass is worth it."

Once, I'd felt the same way. Women were objects to be toyed with. To be used. But then Imogene came into our lives, and fuck, I treated her exactly the same and now all I have is regrets and the pain of losing her.

"Women should be treated with honor," I growl, my fist balled and elbow lifted. I slam my fist into his jaw, hearing the snap I'd been craving all day. I go for another—

"Elon!" My name echoes off the brick.

I ignore him, knowing he's going to try to make me stop.

"Elon, you need to see something," he says, voice firm. "Then you can finish kicking this guy's ass."

I shift my gaze long enough to see Levi and the girl at the end of the alley. He's removed his jacket and slung it over her bare shoulder. The way she looks at him is... familiar. Slowly, I release the guy and say, "Beat it and don't you fucking come down here again."

He doesn't ask why, just scrambles away, running the opposite direction down the alley.

The scabs tore off my knuckles and I wipe them on my pants. Getting closer I narrow my eyes at the girl. I remember her from the cells under the Main House. How Anex groomed her to work out on the streets. Silas and Imogene had taken care of her. Her name pushes past the adrenaline. "Charlotte, right?"

She nods, hands are trembling like a leaf as she wipes away a line of mascara dripping down her cheek. "I was on the way back from the store and that guy just came out of nowhere and grabbed me."

"So he wasn't a client?"

Her mouth turns down. "I don't have clients. We *recruit* from there."

Her wet eyes slide over to a building that isn't boarded up. The windows are still intact, the front steps clean. An uneasy feeling rolls over me. "Recruit?"

"It's Anex's new program." Her expression brightens when she says his name. Fuck.

"Is he up there now?"

"No. He only comes once a week." Her hands twist together. "Please don't tell him this happened. I know it's my fault. That I should do better, but I just... I want to see him."

"And he won't if he finds out about any problems." Understanding flickers across Levi's face. He mutters, "Jesus."

"I'm trying so hard to follow The Way. To be the good girl he wants." She grabs my forearm. "But you can go up and explain. Explain that it wasn't my fault, right?"

My gaze meets Levi's. "Yeah, we're happy to clear things up."

And find out exactly who's running this sex trafficking business. Maybe I'll still get to beat the crap out of someone today after all.

We enter the building—an old hotel—and it's cleaner than

expected. We pass a reception desk, manned by another vaguely familiar face, and follow Charlotte into a spotless elevator. The doors open on the top floor, and she steps out, heels sinking into a new emerald green carpet. She stops at a door.

"Thank you so much," she says, turning to us. "I've been working so hard, and The Way must have sensed my need."

Levi nods. "Because it sent us to protect you."

"Yes!" She smiles. "And because you're the only two that he'll listen to."

She opens the door and before we even cross the threshold, we see him, her handler:

Silas.

17

Silas

"Charlotte." Her cheeks are stained, makeup a mess. I'm already off the couch when I realize that underneath the unfamiliar, too-large, jacket the strap of her dress is torn. "What the hell happened?"

"It's okay," she says, letting me inspect her. There are no real injuries, just some irritated skin near her shoulder. And the tears. "Some guy got rough with me, but they were there."

"They?" I tilt my head, realizing that we're not alone. Instinct propels me to reach for the gun at my back, fingers coiled around the handle. I shove Charlotte behind me, extending the weapon.

Except, the men in the doorway aren't a threat. At first, I think I'm hallucinating. It wouldn't be the first time since I got here. Whatever is in the pills Anex makes me take every day sends me on fucked-up trips until they work their way through my system. But my hallucinations don't touch me and right now the figure closest to me grabs me, pushes the gun aside like a gnat, and pulls me into a tight hug.

"Elon?" I ask, but I feel him. Smell him. An anchor in the storm.

"Yeah man. It's us."

Us. I see Levi over his shoulder, and he tugs Elon back, pulling me into an embrace. I squeeze him tight, wanting to feel his warmth and strength. His existence.

He releases me, and I turn, setting the gun on the table. Tears burn at my eyes, relief at seeing them. I wipe them away and ignore the way Elon's studying me when I turn back around. "Charlotte, honey, why don't you go clean up? Take a shower. Eat something."

"Okay." She turns to the guys. "Thank you, again."

Elon looks like he wants to say a million things. Throw her over his shoulder and drag her out of here to safety, but he must realize how precarious this situation is, and lets her go with a nod.

Once the door shuts behind her and the lock engages, I return to the couch and sit, sinking into the cushion like a thousand-pound weight rests on my shoulders. The guys don't wait for an invitation, they each take an armchair.

"Fuck," I start, pushing my fingers through my hair, "it's good to see you. I've been worried."

Worried is an understatement.

"We're okay," Levi says. "Managing."

Elon runs his thumb over his knuckles. They're raw, bloodied recently, but I also note the yellowing bruise by his eye. I've spent years taking care of his post-fight wounds. I know a fresh injury when I see it. I can't help but ask, "You sure about that?"

"Yeah," Elon replies, noticing my attention. He drops his hands to his sides, out of view. "Tell us what's going on?"

"What is this place?" Levi adds.

I rub my eyes. They burn from exhaustion. Sleep is elusive. Ever since I was forced to watch Rex Correct Imogene. Watching him punish her for *my* crimes.

"*This* is what Anex has been preparing me for my whole life." I laugh, although it comes out more of a choke. "I think he always knew that the four of us weren't enough to build the membership of Serendee the way he wanted. Our process was too slow." I look at Elon. "You and Rex flirting your way into rich girl's pants, giving them just enough to draw them down to The Center. Once there Levi would educate—indoctrinate. And then once they're good and hooked, I'd seal the deal by providing them with the best orgasms of their life." I'm not telling them anything they don't know. "Anex needed something more streamlined. Faster. A broader approach and he created this: a new kind of recruitment center."

"A whorehouse," Elon clarifies.

"Anex knows that the way to a man's wallet is through a woman's pussy. Or a man's cock. Whichever applies." I wave my hands. "And apparently my fate is to orchestrate it all."

Levi's eyebrows raise. "You're a pimp."

It hurts to hear him say it. I sag back against the cushion. "Basically. I mean, haven't I always been to a degree? Haven't we all?"

"Well, I don't—" Levi starts.

Holding up my hand I cut him off. "We all are, Levi. We all use our bodies one way or the other. Elon's brawn. Rex's charm. Your brain. And yeah, my... everything."

Levi frowns, but for once doesn't argue. He looks around the room. "So, this is why he's needed to lock in the bigger fish lately. He needed money to expand."

"Yes, and that's also what made him realize that he could be making more money, smaller, but more consistent. And he's been cultivating his workers for a while: the Fallen."

Elon shares a look with Levi. "This setup also eliminates nosy family coming around wondering where their family and bank accounts went."

Levi nods thoughtfully. "I knew he had big ideas, but this is more than I imagined."

"This place has thirty-six rooms. Right now, only twelve are finished. I'm responsible for four females and three males that are working their way through Re-education by fucking prospective recruits that come in looking for a little Enlightenment."

"Jesus," Elon mutters. "And if they don't want it?"

"We keep their 'introductory fee' and they can come back as often as they want—each time a little pricier."

"And if they do want more than sex?" Levi asks. "Then what happens?"

"They're given one-on-one time with an educator." I look him up and down. "Basically, someone like you."

"And everyone is just going along with this?" Elon's jaw tenses. "No one has pushed back?"

The accusation makes a direct hit. No matter, I have one of my own to toss back. "I did what I had to do because my number one priority was Imogene. Rex was locked up, and while my movements were limited, I did what I could."

Unfortunately, while I was busy doing everything I could to protect her—Anex was planning this.

Elon's eyes soften at her name. "Did you? Protect her?"

"I tried." Guilt hardens in my gut. "I tried. She was held in a secure location, but I managed to get in once and see her. I was able to adjust some of her supplements to push things off as long as possible, but in the end my defiance only made it worse on her and Rex."

"What does that mean?" Levi asks.

"It means Anex is a monster, does it have to be more than that? You know it. I know it, but that's about it. He's got everyone wrapped around his finger." I stand, gesturing to the door Charlotte walked out of. "And if not that, wrapped around his goddamn dick. These people are a herd of lost sheep, and he assigned me to be their fucking shepherd."

The more I speak, the more rattled I become. Every word out of my mouth is Regressive. Every word could get me in more trouble, but what's worse than this? I cross the room, reaching for the bottle of pills on the counter. I open the top and shake out two. Hallucinating is better than this. I control the accusations there. The dark, accusing looks in my friends' eyes.

"Whatever those are," Elon says, "put them the fuck down. You're coming with us."

"No." I close my hand around the pills, making a fist. "Didn't you hear what I said? I'm their shepherd. I'm the only one watching out for these people. I make sure they eat. I force them to sleep. I clean their wounds and keep them as healthy as possible. I'm not leaving them."

"We have a plan, Silas," Levi says. That statement elicits a frown from Elon. "Come with us, and we'll come back for them. Every one. I promise."

"How far do you think we'd actually get, brother?" I lift the cuff of my pants, revealing the black band around my ankle. "He'll track me and whatever plan you've got worked up will be over before it's started."

Elon rises, shooting Levi a look loaded with meaning. I don't know what, but he runs his hand through his hair, a sign of agitation. "We're going to take him down, Silas. Levi has a plan and it's coming up fast. Two days."

We're conditioned to know the big dates in Serendee. There's no mistaking which one is coming up. "The equinox."

"We're not letting him have her." Elon's words are calm but forceful. "She doesn't belong to him. She belongs to us. And we'll do whatever it takes to get her out."

"Good," I reply. "Once you have her out and safe, then you can come back for us."

Levi thrusts out his hand, and I shake it. Followed by Elon and something unwinds in my chest. I have no idea if they'll be successful, but I'm doubtful. What I know is that if they make a move, nothing will ever be the same. One way or the other, there's no coming back.

No matter the consequences, I'm ready for the end.

18

Imogene

After leaving the cell I shared with Rex, I'm taken to a different wing in the Main House, this one on the ground floor. Panic shadows me with every step. Margaret says she's taking me to Preparations, but she's also the one that lured me out into the dead of night, marking me with Anex's brand. She took my Collateral and handed it over to be revealed to the whole community.

She's complicit, and I don't trust her.

Down the hall, I see the black clad guards that are stationed at the double doors leading to the wing, these men—boys from the hunch of their shoulders—are new. "Are there more guards now?" I ask, the question slipping out.

"Recent events have made Anex increase his measures of security."

I'd never even noticed the guards until I became one of the Chosen. I'd lived a blissful, ignorant life of what really made Serendee prosper. But the veil has been removed and now it's all I can see.

"They seem young," I note.

"A special group selected from the donums."

Okay, that *is* new.

Halfway down the hall, Margaret touches my arm, drawing me to a stop. "Imogene, I know the last few weeks have been a challenge."

I snort. "That's an understatement."

"I know it's been a challenge," she repeats, "but now that Anex has accepted your Reeducation, it's time to release the anger and hostility you've been carrying." Her thumb runs gently over my arm. "This is your second chance. Make the most of it."

She doesn't wait for a response, heading for the doors. The guards open them and step aside, allowing us to enter. I cross the threshold, but stop instantly, taking in the wing. It's not like the rest of the house, a maze of hallways and closed doors. This area is large with glass walls and ceilings. The air is humid, and green leafy trees grow in every corner. A circular clear pool is in the center of the space.

"What is this?" I ask, stunned at the sight. How can Serendee have so many unknown rooms? Every day it's like a new layer of this place is stripped away and something new is revealed.

"Anex calls it the Cleansing Room. It's to be used before important ceremonies, or in times of transition."

Laughter across the room catches my attention, and I see a group I knew in the donum—the other girls Ordered the same day I was. They're all wearing white robes embroidered with flowers along the hem.

Maria is among them, her pregnancy now showing and pushing against the fabric of her robe. It hurts to look at her, knowing she's the one that betrayed me to Anex by telling him about the love mark Silas left on my neck.

I hesitate. "I don't think they'll want to be with me."

"Everyone that enters this room comes at Anex's request. This is a place of repurification. Where Regressions are washed away, and your body and soul are realigned for Enlightenment." She touches my face gently. "You are Chosen, Imogene. You are special. They will accept you because it is Anex's will."

Not one word of that makes me feel better.

"Come," Margaret says. "It's time to start your Preparation and I have a surprise."

She gestures toward a small room off the solarium and a line of women in dark gray dresses file out. I spot Clarissa, my house mother from the donum. She gives me a small smile when she sees me and walks over.

"Clarissa will attend to your needs during your Preparations." Margaret smiles warmly. "I thought it may be nice to have a familiar face during this."

I relax, marginally. At least she's not Healer Bloom, or Margaret herself. Clarissa may believe in The Way and everything that comes from the journey to Enlightenment, but at least she's not a monster.

At least, I don't think she is.

~

"We lift these women to The Way. Asking for cleansing and purification of every cell in their bodies, their spirit, and nature. Return them to completeness in preparation for their service to Serendee."

Margaret stands at the end of a narrow, tiled, passage—shower heads mounted to the ceiling. Quickly, I learn that the cleansing part of this is literal. We'd stripped and had our foreheads anointed with oil. Then we filed into the shower room, where we receive Margaret's blessing, bare as the day we were born, skin gooseflesh from the cool air.

With her hand on a lever, her words echo off the floors and walls.

"May the powers that guide us to Enlightenment be with each and every one of these women as they prepare themselves for their mate."

She flips the handle and a hard, hot, stream falls from the showerheads, pounding painfully into our skin as if it's trying to strip off a layer of flesh.

Then we're scrubbed down by our attendant. I can't help but notice the way Clarissa's eyes linger on the brand, her touch careful as she makes sure not to tug on the last few scabs.

She's not the only one that notices the mark, curious eyes watching as my skin turns pink. As abruptly as it started, the water stops, and we're shuffled out of the shower and wrapped in thick towels.

From there it's mostly hair removal—trimming, plucking, shaving, waxing. By the time it's over I'd almost wish for another branding. At least that was fast.

It's dark when we're brought to an outdoor patio. There's a firepit in the middle, the heat of the blaze hot on my overworked and sensitive skin. Scrubbed, plucked, and robbed, we take a seat on one of the soft pillows and receive a cup of tea. Everyone looks relaxed and at peace. Holding the warm cup between my fingers, I feel nothing but anxiety. The last time I was with a group of women like this, I was held down and branded.

A woman, Nadine, who was one of our health and body teachers in school draws our attention. She's in her educator's dress, dark blue with cream trim.

"Seeing you all here today is like coming full circle," she says, the flames dancing across her face. "I remember teaching you the fundamentals of hygiene and how to manage your cycles and document your caloric intake for your food logs. Together we learned how to care for your bodies while honoring The Way. All the pieces of developing into a young woman in Serendee." I remember other lessons too—about graciously receiving Corrections for any transgressions. "And now you are about to be mated, and you need to learn about that, too."

Every girl leans forward, eager to learn the secrets of men from this woman.

"Men are simple," she begins. "They have the ability to be brilliant—Enlightened—but they are easily distracted by needs and desires woven into their biological nature. They are ruled by their bodies. It's what's kept them alive and evolving since the beginning of time. That instinct, that drive for creation, is what built Serendee. But it must be harnessed. Regressive thoughts are always seeking to take over. That's why Anex leads these men. He is there to keep them on the path. To help them follow The Way. But Anex cannot do it alone."

"He needs us," a girl near me murmurs.

"Yes," Nadine says with a serious expression. "Our leader needs you to do your part to keep your men healthy, happy, and productive. For the Betterment of Serendee." She walks around the fire pit, making eye contact with each one of us. I remember her doing this in school. Back then it always felt personal. Now it just feels intimidating. "They will need to be fed, which I assume you are already doing. They will need you to use your ears—to *listen*. Communication is good, but our roles are specific in Serendee. Anex's commands are what keeps our community running smoothly. He doesn't need your input on duties and jobs. He needs you to run interference with those needs and desires."

Everyone here has lived with their Ordered for months now. It's doubtful that anyone is unclear about what she is speaking of. It's not forbidden to lay with your Ordered, not after the ceremony declaring intentions. My fingers reach instinctively for the leather bracelet that I'd worn after Rex and I went through the process. It's gone. Stripped from me like everything else.

A girl across the firepit named Deena looks at Maria, eyes darting down to her belly. "What was it like?"

Maria blushes, but she's unable to pretend otherwise, the evidence of fornication pressing at her abdomen.

"It was fast," she admits with a shy smile. "Hurt a little, but you get used to it."

"Did it feel good?" one of the girls asks.

"It didn't feel bad."

"Then it sounds like he didn't do it right," someone whispers, loud. Too loud.

Nadine shoots her a glare. "Maria's pleasure isn't a priority."

"Why are you asking me?" Maria says cheeks dark red. "Imogene is the one with experience of having been with *four* men."

Every eye in the room swings to me, and I busy myself by taking a sip of tea. It's bitter, but warm, and I take another drink. Maria's outburst about me isn't new information. They were all there when my Collateral was exposed for the entire community to hear. When Anex lied about instructing me to train with Rex's friends to prepare myself to be a better mate. He hadn't been specific though, just that what I'd done had been enough to send me to Reeducation.

Nadine's eyes narrow. "Stories from the Fallen shouldn't be used as an example."

"Telling her story is part of the purification process. She must purge her past Regressions," Margaret says, eyes twinkling in the firelight. "Tell us, Imogene, what was it like to allow four Regressive men to have their way with you? To let them defile you in any way they want outside the sanctity of Anex's Order."

My gaze holds Margaret's, fully aware of what she's trying to do to me. She's always trying to break me down. Tear me to nothing so that I'll relent and become the passive mate Anex wants so badly. She wants me to tarnish the memory of my men, betray them in front of the masses to belittle what we had.

I lift my chin. "No."

"No?"

"No. I'm not going to tell you about my relationships."

Margaret's eyebrow raises. "I remember you coming to me, eyes red from crying all night after being forced to your knees by Rex."

I remember that day, too. Clear as crystal. Rex had forced me to suck his cock at the club. I'd been humiliated. Naïve. Margaret had been an ally then—or pretended to be. She'd soothed my sore eyes and talked me through the pain. She gave me advice. Clearly all of that was a set up. Everything is a set up—probably including this.

"Rex is—*was*—my Ordered. I was only pleasing my future mate."

"What about the desires you have during Corrections? When you found pleasure while being strapped by Levi? Or when Levi couldn't finish the job, he sent Elon in to finish it."

I see the jaw drop on a girl across from me, and the person sitting closest to me shifts away. I inhale in an attempt to steady myself. I look around the room at the innocent, naïve women who have no idea what they are getting into. No more than I did.

"Fine, you want to know? I'll tell you." I straighten my back. My tongue feels loose and I'm tired of hiding who I've become. "At first, it was a challenge, because the men assigned to train me were raised as the Chosen. Part of Serendee led by a man who believes all this nonsense Nadine is spewing. About serving men and meeting their needs and desires to keep their Regressive thoughts in line." I roll my eyes. "Men are horny, plain and simple. They want to get their cocks into something warm all the time. They want to get their cock into *you* all the time."

"Imogene!" Maria gasps, but I'm too busy thinking about Rex hurting me that first time. And how Silas took the time to take care of me and educate me about all of this confusing stuff. How to enjoy it. I think about that first kiss with Elon and the relief he gave me after Corrections with Levi. And Levi... well, he showed me a side I didn't know existed.

"Having a man worship you is fantastic. Having *four* men worship me was fucking outstanding." Around the fire, wide eyed girls listen to my every word. Even though I know I should stop, I can't seem to do it. "For the record, that is what it's called. Fucking. They fuck you with their cocks, burying it deep into your pussy. If you're lucky it's big and thick and yeah, it hurts like hell the first time, but after that..." God, I miss them. We didn't get enough time together before we'd been torn apart. "...it's good. Complicated and really, really good."

"*Imogene*," Nadine says, "I think that's enough."

"Agreed." I stand, done with this little circle of truth. "I hope your men treat you right." Blood rushes to my head as I step forward and my eyes swim. The teacup falls to the floor, shattering into a million pieces. "Wha—?" I ask, but the words get lost. The faces around me blur, and the last thing I remember is reaching out to steady myself and the world turning black.

OPEN YOUR EYES.

My brain sends the message, but my eyes won't open.

Open your eyes.

I follow the command, but I'm too tired. I just want to sleep—longer—deeper. I try to curl into myself, snuggle against the soft sheets, but nothing gives.

Open your eyes, Imogene.

Struggling, I get my eyes open into small slits. Warm light makes flickering shadows against the walls. My eyelids drop shut, as if they're pulled down by weights, but I'm more awake now.

"Where am I?"

I open my eyes again, taking in the room. I'm no longer in the solarium. This place is small. The ceiling is low. I crane my neck, spotting a portrait over the bed. The light shimmers off the ornate, gold frame. Slowly my brain starts to work, the image coming into focus. Anex sitting in his lecture chair.

Suddenly, I know exactly where I am: Beatrice House. This is where I took my oath for the women's group. I'm in Anex's former bedroom that he shared with his wife—Rex's mother.

Fear jolts up my spine, igniting my body to move. I jerk up. Or try. Nothing moves but my neck. I know instinctively it's not from sleep or drowsiness. From the sharp digging in my wrist and ankles, I know I've been bound.

"Careful." The voice comes from beside me. A hand brushes the hair off my forehead. Anex comes into view. "You don't want to hurt yourself."

"What is this?" I ask, voice gravely.

"This is for your own protection," he says. His hand is still on my face, thumb grazing my cheek. "You're a danger to yourself, Imogene. Physically and spiritually."

"So you tied me up? You…" I try to think back. I was sitting around the fire. Ranting about fucking men. My teacup shattering and the bitter taste on my tongue. "You drugged me."

"There was little chance you wouldn't act out at the preparation ceremony, but it was important for the other women to believe you'd been Reeducated. The plan, all along, was to slip you a sedative in your tea, to keep you from any outbursts. Unfortunately, it must not have been enough because the reaction was delayed."

My head swims. From the drugs and the deep sleep. From the horror of my life.

He sighs, fingers trailing down my neck. "I hated doing it, but it's the only way. The regression streak is so strong in you. Every attempt has made it worse. Corrections. Training. Reeducation… defiance runs deep in your soul."

"Then let me go. I'll never come back." I swallow as his fingers inch lower, down to the plane of my chest. "I promise."

He smiles sympathetically. "I wish I could, but The Way won't allow it. I've been led to you. Originally, I thought you were for Rex, but I realized quickly that I'd made a terrible mistake by allowing those boys to take your virtue. It should have been mine."

Tears spring to my eyes. Anger and fear. Hatred for this monster standing over me.

"Anex—" His fingers push at the collar of my robe, spreading it apart, exposing my skin to the cool air of the room. "Please don't…"

"Your Preparation is almost complete. There's just one more layer of purification we must complete." I wince as his hands ghost over my breasts, barely touching. It's almost worse than if he'd touched me. "Once this process is over, you'll be ready for the ceremony, and ready to be mine. *Forever*."

My body turns rigid as he unties the knot of my robe, arms and legs paralyzed. My stomach rolls as he touches the brand on my lower hip.

"You look perfect wearing my mark." His fingers drag downward, and I push through the fear, clamping my thighs together. "Don't be afraid. All of this is part of a larger plan."

He makes a gesture, and it's then I realize we're not alone. Two figures move from the shadowy corners of the room. They're cloaked, hoods pulled low over their heads. The same cloaks we wear at our women's group. These are two of my *sisters*. I look to the one on my right.

"Don't let him do this to me! Help!"

One hands him a rectangular, carved wooden box. Anex ignores my protests and opens the lid, lifting an object from inside. Holding it up, the candlelight passes through the thick crystal. It's large, cylindrical in shape, honed and rounded at the top. There's no doubt what the object is for and where he's planning on using it.

"Anex, no." Again, I look to the cloaked women. "Please help me."

"Bless this crystal of purification. Accept this as the call to release all negative and Regressive energies bound inside Imogene. Penetrate the dark rebellion and replace it with the path to Enlightenment."

One of the women pours a clear, thick liquid into Anex's open palm. He coats the sides and tip of the crystal, leaving it in a thick sheen.

Sweat rises on my skin and whatever he says next is covered by the hard beating of my pulse. He runs the tip of the crystal between my breasts, across the tips of my nipples and down my lower body. My thighs press tighter, as far as my bound legs will allow it, and fear ratchets through my body. The women's hands pull apart my thighs.

"I'm still having my cycle," I argue, neck straining.

"It's good that you're bleeding. It's like your body knew that you needed to purge the foul toxins." He nods and one of his partners reaches between my legs and pulls out the tampon holding back my flow. Anex stands at the end of the bed, staring down at me, eyes fixed between my legs.

"Perfect," he says, licking his lips. "Absolutely perfect."

He presses the tip against my entrance.

"You don't have to do this," I tell him. "I'll be with you. I'll go through the ceremony. I won't fight. I'll forget about Rex and Levi and Elon and Silas. I'll be the spiritual wife you want."

"I know you will." My body fights against him, muscles tight and resistant. "Relax, or it'll tear you apart. Don't make me hurt you, because I will. Nothing can stop the path of The Way, especially not a dirty little whore that I can just as easily toss on the streets as welcome into my bed." He wedges the tip in a bit more, lips turned up in a small, l twisted smile. "Nothing will stop me from getting what I want."

Our gazes lock and something in me slips away. This is my leader. My guide. He's raised me and now he's Chosen me—yet here I am, fighting him every step, instead of embracing the honor.

To what end? The abuse of the other men in my life? The Banishment and Shunning? The loss of my friends from the donum? My educators and mentors?

This is not just my second chance. It's my *only* chance.

I exhale, forcing my muscles to release—allowing the crystal to enter my body. Allowing the final step of purification to begin. Allowing Anex what rightfully belongs to him.

Everything.

19

Levi

"Are either of you expecting a package?"

Camille stands in the doorway of the kitchen. She hasn't said more than three sentences to us since the invitation came in the mail. Not while Elon and I discussed plans for getting Imogene away from Anex. Or how to get out in one piece ourselves.

"No," I answer for the two of us.

She carries the large box to the table, setting it down. Leaning over I see that it's addressed to the '*Residents of 238 Arbor Street.*'

The Serendee logo is stamped in the top corner.

Camille opens a drawer and pulls out a knife. Elon's shoulders tense. This woman... we still don't know her well. And we know for certain that she doesn't trust us. We watch as she presses the point of the knife to the center of the package, slicing through the tape.

Elon leans closer, looking into the box with a wary eye, like he's expecting a snake to jump out or something. She pushes past the tissue paper and frowns.

"Un-freaking-believable," Camille mutters, pushing the box toward me.

It's not a snake. It's clothing.

"There's a note," Elon says, reaching inside. It's a simple card, again stamped with Serendee's logo—the same logo branded into Imogene's hip. *"A little something to make you feel more comfortable at tomorrow's ceremony. A car will arrive to pick you up at 11 AM."*

I dole out the items. Basic black for me and Elon; a shirt and pants. Camille's is a dress, made from a bright blue fabric. She stares down at it and says, "He has to control everything, doesn't he?"

"To be fair," I say, folding my shirt into a square, "we would have looked very out of place in Secular clothing."

Her eyes cut to me, and I expect anger. Instead, I see sadness.

"I don't know if I can do this."

"Do what?" Elon asks.

"Go through with this plan. Put on this dress and play puppet to an evil man."

Elon stares at our host, jaw set. "It's a little late to back out now, but if you can't, I guess we—"

"This may be your only chance," I cut in. We need her to attend, or Elon and I won't make it past the gates. "Do you want to wait another eight years for an opportunity to get her out?"

I leave the rest unspoken. If Imogene stays in Serendee for another eight years she'll spend that either locked up with the Fallen or as Anex's mate. She'll never get away from him, which also means, we'll never get to see her again.

Camille has proven herself to be resilient and tough. Determined. But now she stands in front of us, twisting her fingers in the dress.

She looks nervous.

"Are you worried about Anex?" I ask. "Because other than petty control methods like the clothing, he won't try anything on a day like this. He'll want everything to go over perfectly."

"It's not Anex I'm worried about," she admits. "I'm kind of eager to face him again after all this time."

Elon glances at me and says, "If you're concerned about seeing Imogene, don't be. She'll be happy to see you."

"Are you sure?" she asks. "Don't pretend that Anex hasn't tainted her view of me."

"I won't." He meets her eye to eye. "He did do that. You were an example to all of us—"

"Which is why his invitation is a big deal," I cut in. "He's trying to prove he's not keeping your child from you or holding grudges."

Camille sighs and sits at the table. "You know, I tried to get her to come with me, but she wouldn't, and maybe that makes me a bad mother for leaving anyway."

"I don't think he gave you much of a choice," Elon says.

"I had a choice. Be his new wife, take the place of his dead wife—my best friend—or run. I chose to run—even if that meant leaving Imogene behind." She looks up, eyes shiny, looking more vulnerable than I've seen her before. "She has to resent me for that."

"I was with Imogene when we located the information about your whereabouts and this program. She wasn't angry. She was scared. She knew that if Anex found out that she'd found you—how she'd found you—there would be severe consequences," Elon explains. "I got the information for her, because I knew then that she was going to need you one day. I just didn't know when or under what circumstances. She's not going to resent you—she's going to be thankful that you're here."

She sniffs quietly, then stands, grabbing her dress out of the box. "It's going to be a long day tomorrow. I think I need some time to prepare myself." She looks between us. "Is there anything you need me to do?"

"Just be ready," Elon says. "It's going to be a long day."

Neither of us speak until she's upstairs, then Elon turns to me and asks, "Do you think we can really pull this off? Get Imogene and Rex out while saving ourselves?"

I want to tell him with confidence that we will, but there are a lot of balls in the air with this one. My plan with Elon. My plan with Anex. Our plans with Camille. It's ever evolving—constantly moving—but my goal is singularly focused:

Getting back to Imogene.

THE CAR RIDE to Serendee is quiet. There's something about an armed guard that makes conversation seem prohibited. Add in the fact that there are no pockets in our clothes, no way to discreetly hide a weapon. We're managed, contained, restrained, all without putting a finger on us.

Anex is always one step ahead.

Unfortunately, for him, he kicked out one of the more powerful people in his inner circle. Due to Elon's position in security he's aware of hidden weapon caches all over Serendee. "Anex's paranoia will be his doom," he'd told me, when we started laying out the idea. "He was terrified of an ambush or raid by the feds. Expected it, really. So unless he moved them—"

"He may have," I countered. One step ahead. "He should have."

"I agree," he admitted, "but he didn't monitor where the caches were located. Not all of them."

Then he drew a map.

From there the plan is vague. Get to the weapons. Get to Imogene and Rex. Get everyone out alive. I don't like it, but we're walking into a familiar world that follows only their own rules. Rules that change on the whim of a narcissistic leader.

"Look," Elon says, breaking the silence. The car drives toward the front gate—a driveway never used. Residents either walk to town on the path or vehicles are taken out the back entrance, carrying products. The gate has always been purely ornamental. But today it's wide open and not flanked by guards. Instead, two young women and two men stand at the entrance, each dressed in fall colors, holding a basket of flowers. They wave as we pass. "What the fuck?"

Anex agreed to transparency, at least a sense of it, and I guess this welcome group is part of it.

The car stops near a field near the front of the property, and we're escorted down the drive. There are no vehicles inside Serendee—it's one of the primary tenants. Elon instantly shifts into security mode—eyes peeled, looking for threats. Between us Camille's breath comes out short and uneven.

"Are you okay?" I ask, reaching out to steady her arm when she stumbles over an uneven spot in the road.

"It's just super weird being back here." Her hand presses against her chest. "So many memories."

"Take a deep breath," I say, trying to channel Silas. "I'm nervous too, but what we're doing here is the right thing." She nods, following my instructions and inhaling. Silas would distract her, and I point to the Main House in the distance. "Anex has expanded a lot since you left. That's his house."

"A mansion?" She snorts. "God, if Timothy isn't a predictable, pretentious, asshole, I don't know what he is."

The open way she slanders Anex still feels alarming—blasphemous—but there's no time to process my emotions on this. The conversation between us doesn't really ease the tension, but it gets her moving. We pass the donums, the housing area, the community center, and the new childcare facility. In the distance are the fields and barn. On the open field is where the ceremony will be held. A small tent is set to the side and that is where our escort guides us.

I realize then we aren't the only guests from outside Serendee.

Everyone is wearing identical clothing—they must have been sent outfits as well. I scan the area and recognize a woman. She'd been at Camille's house that morning—Kayla's sister: Gabi.

She and Camille do not acknowledge one another. Maybe they don't see one another but my skin starts to itch. Something feels off—like maybe I'm not the only one with a plan today.

"Anyone know what's supposed to happen here?" This comes from an older man. Probably someone's father. Did he really allow in family members? The ones pushing for contact with their loved ones?

"Some kind of ceremony," Gabi says. "Celebrating the equinox, I guess?"

Her voice is even. Calm. Too calm for someone so desperate to see her sister.

"Yes, the residents of Serendee celebrate each of the seasons." Every eye in the tent swings in my direction. "It's a way to thank the earth for a bountiful harvest." Elon shifts next to me. "Part of the event will be what people outside the community refer to as a wedding. Couples will be bound and blessed."

"A group wedding?" the guy asks.

I shrug. "It's just a way for everyone to celebrate efficiently. Everything in Serendee is shared resources. We already have the music, food, and guests." I point to the small group in the tent. "Why not knock out more than one celebration at once."

Camille gives me a curious look—probably wondering why I'm defending the ceremony. I'm just trying to keep things moving forward. The last thing we—or these people—need is to get kicked out before it even begins.

The flaps open, held out by two other smiling residents. These I recognize. They're Anex's guards. They've just dropped the black clothing for the day and their weapons are obscured by the loose fabric. Elon's eyes narrow, and his hand taps his lower back, confirming that, yes, they're armed. No way Anex allows visitors in without protection.

Before I can react further, he walks in the room, Margaret a step behind.

Bowing on instinct, I elbow Elon halfway down. We're here to grovel. To prove we want back in. That we can be trusted. Anex has to know we mean it, even if Camille thinks we don't. The truth is that in my soul, I'm still conflicted. When Anex's eyes drift over me that aching need for approval surges in my chest.

But he's not interested in me or Elon. He briefly nods and greets the outsiders, but then leaves Margaret to entertain the guests. Anex doesn't stop moving until he's a foot from Camille. He smiles warmly, offering his hand. "Camille."

Her throat bobs with a thick swallow, but she doesn't reach out to touch him. "Timothy."

His name rings in the quiet tent—Margaret's eyes darting over. Even Elon stiffens, but Anex, ever charming, just clasps his hands in front of his body and says, "I've always thought you looked lovely in blue."

Hence him picking it out for her to wear. Not for her—for *him*.

"Margaret, dear," he calls, beckoning her with his hand. She comes dutifully. Camille is focused on Margaret's stomach. "I'd like you to meet my old friend—"

"And partner," Camille adds.

"Yes, and partner, Camille Montgomery. Imogene's mother."

Margaret leans against Anex, belly jutting out. She grins wide, showing her perfect, straight teeth. "It's wonderful to meet you. Imogene has become such a dear friend of mine—more like a sister."

Something dark washes over Camille's face, but she pulls it back, ignores Margaret, and turns her attention back to Anex.

"Can I see her?"

Although she's addressing Anex, she asks the question loud enough for the others to hear. The slight tensing in his jaw reveals that he's aware of the entire room watching. All the other guests, the families there to check up on their loved ones, the people noticing their bank accounts dwindling.

"Of course," his teeth grit. "After the ceremony. There's not enough time now."

"I'm her mother, and I'd like to wish her good luck on this special day." She reaches under the collar of her dress and pulls a necklace. "I'd like to give her this—it was my grandmother's."

"I love that," Gabi says from across the room. "My mother gave me something similar and it means so much to me."

A grin is plastered to Anex's mouth. "It's a lovely gesture but—"

"Unfortunately," Margaret interjects, accentuating. "Our time is limited. We must go."

Camille's eyebrow raises, her gaze affixed to Anex's. An energy flickers in the room. Margaret may be his spiritual wife, but Camille... she's something more.

"Please, Timothy," Camille says quietly. "I'd be in your debt."

This time he doesn't bristle at the use of his given name and a spark appears in his eyes. The connection between these two is unmistakable. I'm not the only one that notices, and their gaze breaks contact, and he looks around the room at the watching crowd.

"I'm sure we can spare five minutes so a mother and daughter can reconnect." His head tilts slightly toward Margaret. "Don't you think, sweetheart?

There's no other answer than "yes" and Margaret knows it. This woman thought she understood how to be with this man, and her time on the outside gave her the impression she could be his equal. There is no equal to Anex.

Except maybe the woman standing next to me.

"Thank you," Camille says, doing her best to be gracious.

He gestures and one guard steps forward while the other opens the flaps. Fresh air breezes in and I realize how warm and stuffy it is in here. Anex pauses before leaving. "Levi, I'd like you to escort Camille to Imogene's Preparation tent."

Me, I almost ask, but I catch myself and see the command for what it is. A loyalty test.

"I would be honored."

"Elon and Richard," he points to one of the guards at the flap, "will escort the rest of you to the ceremony. There's music, drinks, and delicious food; all grown and prepared right here in Serendee. Take time to enjoy everything our community has to offer and maybe a little more understanding of why your family has embraced our lifestyle."

"And afterwards I'll get to see my sister?" Gabi asks.

"She'll be eager to see you," Anex replies before dipping outside.

My gaze meets Elon's. Separating isn't part of the plan, but we knew there was no way to control the variables once we got here. Richard ushers the group out of the tent toward the main festivities. Elon hesitates at the entry and turns to me. "Get to her. No matter what."

"No matter what," I repeat.

Camille looks up at me. "What does that mean?"

"It means the task we came to accomplish—it's started." I lead her into the crowd, heart pounding as loud as the drums in the distance. "All we can do now is focus on getting Imogene safely out of Serendee."

She asks no more questions, just sticks close to my side. To the untrained eye, it would seem like Anex let us loose in the community alone, but I know better. I take her hand and drag her around a group of children playing a game, moving quickly.

Stumbling at our pace, she looks down at our hands. "What are you doing?"

"Getting away from the guard."

"Guard?" she asks, frowning.

"He's armed." I nod at a man searching for us. "So are half of these other men, and they're watching us closely."

"I shouldn't be surprised, but I always am."

Leading her toward the large Preparation tent, I take her to the backside of the structure. I stop before going further.

"Would you like me to go first?" I can tell by her expression that her anxiety has returned. "It should be okay, but me going through that door might be less of a surprise than your sudden appearance."

Camille takes hold of my arm and gives it a soft squeeze. "Thank you, Levi."

"I haven't done anything yet."

"You got me this far, and that's more than I've been able to do in years of trying."

I lift the bottom of the tent, and duck under, entering a room filled with women. They're all dressed in sheer, embroidered dresses, but not one of them interests me. I scan the room, passing a blur of faces until my eyes settle on her.

My heart nearly cracks in two.

A ripple runs though the space, the women spotting me. Imogene looks up, eyes glassy. I frown, wondering if she's sick.

"Is she drugged?" Camille asks from behind me.

Her cheeks are hollow. Her skin is paler than before. Her hair is clean but limp. Every effort has been made to make this girl beautiful for her Mating, but something is wrong. I stride across the room, not caring who sees me and kneel at her feet. "Imogene, what has he done to you?"

"Levi?" she asks, blinking away the fog. "Is that you?"

"Yes." I drop to my knees. "I'm here."

Her hands cup my face, soft and cool. She pinches my skin. "For real?"

"Definitely real."

"But why? Why are you here? How?"

I kiss her fingers. "You know why, Little Lamb."

"You shouldn't have come back," her gaze drops. "It's too late. I've already been through the Preparations."

Preparations. Even I don't know exactly what that means other than they spend time together before the ceremony. But knowing what I know now and the lost look on her face, fear blooms in my chest.

"It's not too late." I force her eyes to mine. "Whatever oil they've anointed you with, or blessings they've given—those things don't matter outside these walls."

Suddenly it hits me—why she's so lost. He got to her. The Reeducation, the punishments, the isolation and whatever else he threw at her—he got to her. Her mind is muddled. I understand this. I feel the tug to embrace the familiar. It's nearly impossible to ignore. But the sadness coming off of her is real. As is the unsettling, distant, look on her face.

This isn't the Imogene I've come to love, the spitfire, rebellious, fierce woman.

This is the Imogene Anex has created, and it'll take work to draw her back out again.

Brushing back a stand of hair, I ask, "Imogene, where's Rex?"

"I don't know. I haven't seen him since we were in the white room together."

The white room.

"I don't know where Silas is either," she continues, "but I don't think it's good. He tried to help me, and we were punished."

"It's okay, Silas is—"

I sense the movement of a body behind me, and her eyes lift over my shoulder. Imogene's jaw drops, words lost on her tongue. She looks back to me and whispers, "Levi, who is that?"

I stand, giving Camille room.

"Imogene." The strong confident woman that escaped this place stands tall beside me. "Oh, honey, it's me."

Her head tilts, like she's trying to process everything going on. "Mom?"

The reunion is interrupted, a high-pitched sound pierces the air outside the tent. Our eyes meet in confusion. "What was that?" she asks.

Faint pops sound in the distance, then grow louder and closer, until a large explosion shakes the ground around us.

Without thinking, the name escapes my lips. "Elon."

20

Imogene

I'd been lost since the night before. My mind is slipping somewhere safe—away from the madness and hurt. Somewhere I had to reconcile my truth.

Anex was never letting me go.

I was going to become his Mate.

And I would be required to perform all duties demanded of that position.

My life had always been leading to this—I realize that now. My mother's betrayal, Anex's hurt and obsession, my objectification. I can still feel the intrusion deep in my core—the promise of what's to come.

What I didn't expect was Levi. My mother *or* the bombs.

"Imogene!" Levi's arm comes around my shoulder, lifting me up. "It's time."

"Time?" I ask, feeling two steps behind. "Time for what?"

"To get you out of here." Another explosion rocks the ground. Cries come from the other women in the tent. Some have already run. A few are curled on the floor. Panic seizes the room in everyone but the man holding me.

"You did this?" I ask, my eyes shifting to my mother, who doesn't seem startled by the explosions. "And you?"

"We'll talk about it later," Camille says. "Right now, we need to get out of here while we can."

Levi pulls me out of the tent. The air is thick with sulfur and the sound of screams. Fear ripples through the crowd, releasing in panicked screams and feral cries. Whatever celebrations have been going on have stopped, everything altered by the attack.

"This is Elon?" I ask, gripping Levi's fingers as someone tries to wedge between us, stepping on the hem of my dress. His answer is lost in the sound of screams, but I believe it. Elon isn't the kind of man that just stops. He'll fight to get to his family—to me and Rex.

I jerk Levi to a stop. "We need to find Rex."

Levi turns, looking down at me. "You're the priority."

I yank my hand from his. "I won't leave without him."

"Do you even know where he is?" A woman, blood dripping down her temple, slams into me. Before I can react, she's gone, leaving a smear across the bodice of my gown. "What the hell is the white room?"

I tell him what I can, fear choking my throat. A room in Anex's private quarters, the last place I saw him three days ago. "How do you know he's still there?"

"We have to try, Levi."

Camille stands nearby, shifting on her feet. Smoke rises behind her, the stage on fire. My *world* on fire.

"We have to go," she says. "This is about to get nasty."

"Take her," Levi tells my mother. "Get her to safety. I'll go find Rex."

"Alone?" I ask. "No—"

"It's the only way it's happening, Imogene." He jerks his chin. "Go with your mother."

"But—"

He grabs for me. "Go with her. You can trust her. She got Elon and

I in here today." He lifts my hand to his mouth and kisses the back. "I love you, Imogene."

My heart swells. "I love you, too."

He's swallowed by the chaos, and I feel like my heart goes with him. Lifting my skirt, I start toward the path, the easiest way out of the walls, but Camille's hand comes down on my arm. "I know another way."

"There is no other way!"

The fact that I say this during this type of crisis means everything. Anex had us trapped. No way out.

"There is. Follow me."

I don't know this woman. I don't trust her. I barely remember her, but the set of her jaw is familiar. A mirror to my own when I'm determined. We head the opposite way, up an incline on the backside of Serendee. A screech cuts through the madness and a loud voice echoes over the crowd, amplified by a megaphone.

"Everyone, remain calm! Get to the ground! Follow orders, and no one will be hurt!"

That's when I see them. Men and women pouring into the field. They're wearing black vests, letters imprinted across the chest. Helmets and guns held in the air.

Thwap, thwap, thwap... I look up and see a helicopter circling above. The sound of the wings competes with my thudding heartbeat.

"We have you surrounded! Get to the ground!"

"What is this?" I ask, paralyzed. "Who are these people?"

Gunfire blazes across the field, and I see people fall, one after the other, tumbling down. Fear grips me, my spine rigid and unmoving. I want to run to help while also wanting to run away.

Camille grabs me and drags me away to a wall covered in thick ivy. She drops my hand, frantically pushing through the foliage. She stops suddenly, hand clasped around something hidden and yanks back. An old creaky, wooden, door falls open.

On the other side is a vehicle. Black and shiny. A man in a blue tie and mirrored sunglasses opens the car door and roughly pushes us inside. We're moving before the door even shuts.

"Did Elon do this?" I ask, trying to reconcile everything I saw. Everything I heard and smelled.

"No," she says, looking out the back window as Serendee fades away. "I did."

∼

UNLIKE MANY IN SERENDEE, I've spent time outside the walls. I worked in the Center recruiting new members. Elon took me clothes shopping in an upscale boutique. I've eaten in expensive restaurants and met up with Rex in a bar. I've even gone to a fraternity party, drank too much, and had sex in a closet. But I've never been here: The police station.

"You're not in trouble, Imogene." The woman that repeatedly tells me this has short reddish hair and thick glasses that make her eyes look too large. Her badge says Agent McNair, and I don't like her. "We just need you to talk to us about Timothy Wray."

Timothy Wray. Anex. The man who groomed me, branded me, violated me. My leader. I can't bring myself to say any of this. One thing he instilled in all of us is that the government is not to be trusted.

"I just want to go home."

"There is no home," Agent McNair replies. "Not until this shakes out. The entire compound is considered a crime scene."

"She means with me." I look up at Camille—my mother—who hasn't left my side. She's the one that did this, invited these people into our home. "Imogene is my daughter, she'll come home with me."

I wish that statement brought me something other than fear.

"Where is Levi?" I ask. "Rex and Elon? Where are they?"

We're in a small room with a window covered with blinds. The bottom left side is askew, giving me a small view of the outside room. It's been nothing but a steady stream of people since I arrived. Each person is dressed in the clothing of Serendee. Each one as lost as I feel. Unmoored by the events of the night.

"I'm not at liberty to discuss the whereabouts of anyone from the compound."

"Stop calling it that!" I hiss. "It's not a compound—it's a community." I narrow my eyes at Camille. "It's not fair to all those people, and you know that."

I wanted to escape Anex—to live my life in peace—but I never wanted to hurt the people that lived there. Whatever happened tonight isn't what any of us wanted.

"What I know is that you're tired, traumatized, and need rest." She gives the agent a hard look. "Can we leave, or should I call my attorney?"

"Look," the agent says, sighing as if she feels as exhausted as I do. Doubtful. "Although the majority of your friends aren't in jail. They're being held in a safe space until we can work this out."

"I don't care about the majority of my friends. I want to know about three in particular. Elon, Levi, and Rex."

She flips through a pad of paper on the table. "You just listed three of Wray's highest confidants."

"You don't know anything," I bite.

"Which is why I need your help, Imogene. I just need you to answer a few more questions. Did you see evidence of illegal drug sales in and out of Serendee? What about sex trafficking?" She looks down at my dirty white gown. "Were you a witness to Timothy Wray's involvement in either of these activities?"

"She's a victim," Camille says, slamming her fist on the table so hard the agent's phone skips across the surface. "And she needs rest, food, and possibly medical care. We'll come back when she's had all of those, with our attorney. In the meantime, I think you have plenty of others to interrogate."

I blink up at this woman—my mother. I have never heard anyone speak with such clear conviction. Especially not a woman. There's no twisting of words or manipulations.

"We're leaving."

"One last thing—" She looks to me. "Do you know if Timothy Wray had other property outside the compound? Like another house? Business property? Close connections in another city?"

"Just the Center in town. Otherwise, we never left." I frown. "Why?"

"Because Timothy Wray and a few others in his circle managed to escape tonight. If you have any idea where they are, you need to tell us now."

I shake my head. "I have no idea."

Camille gestures for me to rise, and I follow, because I want to be anywhere but here. Also, Levi told me to go with her.

The outer room is filled with men and women in uniform, and I feel foolish in my gown—as if it marks me for being one of Anex's loyal followers. I only raise my head when I sense someone's approach. My heart stops. A cop leads three men, all of their hands bound at the wrists. Levi's red hair jumps out at me first, followed by Elon's broad shoulders, and then Rex's ice blue eyes.

They turn without seeing me, down another hall.

"Where are they taking them? Why are they handcuffed?" I ask, turning to Camille in a panic.

"You heard Agent McNair. They're Timothy's closet allies. They'll be questioned extensively."

"And then?"

"I don't know, but it's not your concern. You're away from them now. You never have to see any of those monsters again."

Monsters.

I start to argue, to tell her that they aren't monsters. They're *my* men. I love them, but it feels dangerous to say. Numb all over, I follow Camille out of the police station wondering if I've traded one nightmare for the other.

21

Imogene

We don't actually go to Camille's. Apologizing, she makes a detour, swinging into the hospital parking lot.

"Do we have to do this now?" I ask, arms crossed over my chest. "There's nothing wrong with me."

"I know," Camille says, "but the police want to gather as much evidence as possible."

"So you're saying my body is evidence?"

She frowns. "No. I just..." She looks out the window of the car, unable to meet my eye. "I just want to make sure we get him, Imogene, and that means we can't cut corners."

A social worker meets us inside, along with another female agent. My head spins. It's been hours since I'd slept or eaten. I'm worried about the guys—how long would they be at the station? Are they really in trouble. No one has answers. Just demands.

"Imogene, when you're comfortable, I need you to remove your dress."

I stiffen at the request. I know what my body looks like under the fabric. Bruised and scarred, some self-inflicted, others not. I hesitate, glancing over at Camille, both wanting her to see what she left me to endure and not wanting her to know.

"A little help?" I ask, gesturing to the row of buttons down the back of my dress. It's filthy, covered in dirt and grime from my escape—the hem frayed and torn. Camille moves to assist me, her fingers shaking as she works. This is awkward for her, too, but she's not the one who everyone's eyes pin to as the fabric drops revealing my Anex approved undergarments.

Freak.

The insults thrown at me walking from the Center to Serendee come rushing back. I'd always fought it. I never believed it but now, as I remove the tank and shorts, exposing myself to the room, I know it's true.

We *are* freaks.

It's in the clothes, the conformity, the secrets. It's in the lingering bruises inside and out. It's in the scars etched into my body.

It's in the brand.

"Jesus," the social worker utters when she sees it. Her eyes widen after the words slip out, aware of her error. She swallows. "Did they do that to you?"

"Yes." I ghost my fingers over it. It's mostly healed now, the scabs are gone, but the raised new skin looks angry and sensitive. "It was part of an initiation."

"So you just let them do this to you."

Let them.

"I wasn't aware that they would be burning my flesh. I just thought it was a place for the women in the community to support one another."

The officer circles me, taking photos of every mark, gesturing to the nurse to use a ruler to measure each one. She lowers the camera and nods to my chest. "What happened?"

For the first time heat rises on my skin. *What happened?* Something I can't explain. Something personal.

"Anex ordered that I receive a punishment."

Her eyebrow rises. "For?"

I shake my head, hands trembling. I won't tell them what for. Or who. Or anything else. Camille seems to sense my limit and steps forward. "Take the evidence. Do your tests, but she's not answering anymore questions."

I give her a small, thankful smile, but she doesn't notice. Her eyes are also roaming my body. At the marks on my wrists. On my inner thighs. On my ribs pressing against my skin. When she finally meets my gaze she says quietly, "I'm sorry, Imogene. I had no idea."

"Of course, you didn't," I say, loathing the guilt I hear in her tone. What I can't say is that every mark, bruise, and scar is evidence of my worth. Of my journey. Of my attempts at Enlightenment.

And right now, I can't decide if I'm proud of them or not.

∽

The knock is firm, three raps followed by, "Imogene, dinner's ready."

Three times a day Camille knocks on my door, announcing a meal. Breakfast, lunch, and dinner. I haven't come down yet. The thought of food is like ash on my tongue.

I call out the same words I've repeated over and over, "I'm not hungry."

Usually she leaves, her heavy footsteps on the hardwoods going down the hall, but today I sense her loitering outside the door, her shadow shifting back and forth. There are only four people I care about entering this room, and so far, I've heard nothing about them.

This time she doesn't leave, instead turning the knob and stepping inside. I want to be embarrassed that she finds me curled up in a ball, wearing the same outfit I changed into when I arrived four days ago. I should be humiliated about my dirty hair, and dry skin, and the fact I haven't moved from this bed other than to use the bathroom.

I mean, I *am,* but... I also can't muster the energy to care.

"Do you have any news?" I ask, looking over my shoulder.

"They still haven't found Timothy." A tray of food is clutched between her hands. There are two bowls, both steaming with the scent of something spicy. My stomach clenches, but I push the feeling aside. "They think he may have fled the country with a few of his guards and his pregnant wife."

Margaret.

"I'm not interested in Anex." I swallow back the bitterness on my tongue. "Have they released Rex, Elon, and Levi?"

"Not yet."

"Silas?"

"No." She clears her throat and adds, "But even if they did, I don't think it's wise for you to see them again."

I roll over, facing her. "What did you say?"

"Imogene," she rests the tray on the desk and pulls out the chair. "I know it is difficult to be away from the people you considered your friends—"

"They're my family."

"Of course." Her voice is calm, annoyingly soothing, like one of the bulls down in the pasture you don't want to spook. "This family... it isn't real. The people you think you care for; they are either manipulating you or have been manipulated themselves."

"I know what's real, Camille. And what I feel for those men isn't manipulation."

Her lips make a tight, thin, line. "You were arranged to marry Rex, correct?"

"Yes but—"

"A decision made by Anex—not on your own?"

"That's not—"

"What it *isn't* is love. Taking away your freedom to choose. Destroying your autonomy. All of that is manipulation and coercion. It's brainwashing and look how much danger it put you in!"

I swing my legs over the side of the bed, planting my feet on the floor for the first time all day. Swaying, dizzy from a headrush and low blood sugar, I grip the headboard. "Those men are the ones that opened my eyes to the truth of Serendee and Anex's devious ways.

They brought me into the light—showed me what existed outside those walls. Don't you dare question their motives."

"They hurt you, Imogene!" Her eyes dart to my wrists. "I've seen the scars." She chokes on her next words. "I've seen your body. Love doesn't look like that."

I yank the shirt sleeve down. "My body is none of your business, but if you need to know the truth, I did that to myself. They... they saved me from him, and that's what made him turn on me—on *us*."

Her eyes meet mine, searching for something, then soften. "He felt threatened by you."

I nod. "Yes. He split us apart. Locked me and Rex away. Banished Elon and Levi. And I don't even know where Silas is." I inhale, holding back a sob. "I'm so scared for him."

Camille's hand grabs mine and I'm too tired to fight back. "I know, but you're safe now. I'm here for you."

I yank my hand back. "Are you? Because you left before. They didn't."

She recoils, stunned, like she's been slapped. Good. "I know I fucked up. Big time. Things were—"

"I know how they were. That's what I'm saying. Anex is the devil —he forces us into impossible decisions. *You* had to leave. I believe that. But if I'm not going to judge you then you need to realize that you can't judge us. Rex is not his father. Nor are the others. I love them. I *need* them, and until they're back with me, you and I have nothing to talk about."

A cold silence settles between us. I've been manipulated my whole life and I'm not going to let it happen again.

Camille sighs and says, "I'll talk to Agent McNair about Levi and Elon, tell them their part in helping me infiltrate the compound. But Rex... I'm not sure what I can do. He's Timothy's son—"

"And as much of a victim as any of us." I lift my chin. "He's also Beatrice's son. She was your best friend, wasn't she?"

She hesitates, her forehead creased like she's deep in thought. Finally, she says, "I'll do what I can for those boys—but if I do, you have to promise that you'll eat something." She slides the tray closer. "Just get your strength back."

I'd like to argue, but I'm exhausted, and I know she's right. Starving myself isn't helping anyone. I need to be strong for them.

"What can you do?" I ask, lifting the spoon.

"Maybe more than I realized."

～

The bed sinks next to me, familiar warmth sliding under the covers and against my skin. I sink into the dream, holding onto it like threads of gossamer. A hand slides across my stomach and warmth tickles the back of my neck. Silas always makes me feel safe. Loved.

"I've missed you," I tell him. Pressing against the curve of his body.

"I missed you, too. So much." It's the feel of a kiss on my neck, warm, then cool, that forces the thread to part. I'm awake, in the room at Camille's. Except I'm not alone—the body behind me is very real. I turn and find Silas curled into me.

"Oh my God." It's not the first time this week I'd been confused about reality. "This isn't a dream?"

His fingers trace the line of my jaw. "I fucking hope not."

Licking my lips apart until our tongues meet, he kisses me to prove it. I feel the heat of him through my limbs, electric and real.

Yeah, I think, definitely real.

"Where did you come from?" I ask, body glued to his. "How did you get here?"

"Your mom. I could have waited until morning, but—"

"No!" I kiss him. His mouth, his nose, his forehead. "Never wait." He laughs, but it sounds tired. His arms wind around my body. "So, my mom found you?"

He nods against my shoulder, chin scratchy with stubble. "Yes, me and the others were at the hotel. Anex sent us a message days ago that there had been some trouble and to lock the doors and wait. We had no idea about the raid at Serendee until your mom showed up with the FBI."

"She came with the FBI?"

"Yeah. She came in first and," he runs his hand through his hair, "honestly, I was kind of out of it. It was easier to stay fucked up than deal with everything going on. But she told me that you were here, and the guys are being detained. I thought she may have me arrested too, but she didn't. She actually made the Feds go easy on us."

I don't have to ask why. Even with my mother's bias about Serendee, she understands the circumstances Silas has been living in are not of his making. "Because you're victims."

Of sex trafficking, I don't add.

His eyes darken. "I don't know about that, Little Lamb."

"What he made you do—me do. That wasn't with our consent. Not really. That was stripped away from us a long time ago." I've seen Silas work and I've felt Silas' love. Although I know his mind is a mess over it all, these are two different things.

"I thought we would go to the police station but instead we spent the day in the hospital undergoing an exam and then the FBI came—asked a lot of questions."

"So many questions," I agree, laughing lightly. I touch his cheek. "Are you okay? Physically?"

He nods. "All my tests came back clean, but I wasn't working—not like that. Some of the girls… they've got infections. Hopefully nothing worse. The medications and supplements Anex had me give them… I don't know. I'm not a healer, but I don't think they're effective."

"Did Mom bring them back here?"

"A few stayed in the hospital overnight, and I think she has some other friends in her network that took the girls in." He exhales and tightens his arms around me. "I'm just happy to be with you."

He's skinny, but so am I. His eyes are tired, but so are mine. This is who we've become but we recognize it in one another.

"Does Camille know you're in here?" I ask.

"She didn't stop me." That's progress. Maybe I got through to her.

"I told the police everything I could to get the guys released. I don't know if it's going to work, but I tried."

"I know you did." I kiss him again and watch his eyes flutter shut. "Sleep and we'll figure out what we're going to do in the morning."

His breathing evens out and I find myself drifting off to the rise and fall of his chest. I've got one of my men back, but I won't rest until the other three are also home.

22

Silas

I wake in the bed alone, daylight waning outside the window. I slept all day. Or more than one day? My brain is foggy. The sleep was so good.

The bed next to me is cool, making me wonder how long Imogene's been gone. Across the room I hear movement behind the bathroom door.

"Come in," she says when I tap on the door.

I walk in on her standing in front of the mirror, naked, hair long and wet, and dripping over her shoulders. Gorgeous, but battle worn. Her body showing the markings of a soldier.

For the first time in weeks, my cock thickens at the sight.

Stepping behind her, I press into her backside, I'm caught by her scent, by her soft skin and lick a trail up her neck. I've missed the way she tastes. Imogene exhales at my attention, then pins my eyes in the mirror.

"How did you sleep?" she asks.

"Like the dead." I brush aside her hair to kiss her shoulder. The move exposes her breast and my stomach drops. *Fuck*. It's been weeks, but the skin is still discolored from the punishment Rex was forced to dole out. Sliding my hand between her side and her arm, I ghost my fingers over the flesh. "I'm so sorry I couldn't save you that day. That punishment belonged to me."

"He did punish you. There was plenty to go around for all of us."

I touch her gently, running my knuckles over the side of her breast. "I hate this."

"I hate that I don't know the difference between what I like and what Anex has groomed me to like."

I nod, resting my chin on her shoulder. I understand. "It's so fucking hard."

"The lessons, and instruction, and Corrections, all the stuff he taught us muddles up the mind and body."

Because even though all I want to do is take care of her, seeing those bruises makes my dick hard. And taking care of women is what I do. I calm, I sooth, and yeah, I manipulate, usually resulting in my own pleasure along with whatever job Anex has me doing.

But it's not like that with Imogene. I know that. I want her because I love her. Because she's mine.

She takes my hand, placing my palm over her breast. Hers rests on top and she encourages me to squeeze. "I like it when it hurts. It feels right. Like I don't deserve something good without going through something painful to get it."

I press a kiss under her ear. "What if it's not about deserving and just what your body likes? Pain or pleasure."

There's something holding her back, a tension in her limbs, the shallow rise and fall of her chest. "Did he do something?"

"There was a cleansing."

I've heard this before—actually, I've applied some of the methods with the recruits as they come into Serendee, purifying them for their new life.

"Before the ceremony?" I ask, dropping my hands to wrap them around her waist.

"Yes. The Preparation. They said a blessing and anointed us with oil, then sprayed us in the showers." I nod at her description, but she isn't finished. "We were all sitting around the fire, getting a lesson on how to please our men."

I snort and that draws out a smile. "You probably could've taught that lesson."

"Oh, they wanted one, but... they put something in my tea, and I woke up the next day bound to Anex's bed."

My grip tightens around her waist, holding her tight. "They drugged you?"

"Yes." Tears build at the corner of her eyes, and she looks down. "Anex wanted a special cleansing for me because I'm so... dirty."

"Hey," I lift her chin and force her eyes to meet mine in the mirror. "You're not dirty. You're perfect."

She shakes her head. "What *he* did made me feel dirty. The way he used me as an example. The way he made the women hold me down when he forced—"

"Imogene," I ask quietly, "did he rape you?"

"I don't know. There was this crystal..." she doesn't finish, instead crumbles in front of me, sobs ratcheting though her body. It's all the answer I need. He may not have used his body, but still forced his will on her. I turn her, pull her into my chest and hold her. "It hurt."

"He'll never hurt you again," I assure her, holding back the mounting rage.

"You can't promise that."

She's right. A normal man couldn't, but this one? The one holding the woman he loves in her arms while she falls apart—so convinced she's damaged and dirty that she doesn't even recognize assault when it happens to her.

This man can make the promise. Because I know for certain that I'm going to kill him.

∼

"What did you say this was?" I take another bite into the

rectangle. It's both hard and soft, the red fruit substance in the middle hot enough to burn my tongue.

Imogene holds up the colorful box. "It's called a Pop-Tart."

I glance at the toaster. "Because it pops up when it's ready."

"Right?" she says, picking hers apart with her fingers and eating it one small piece at a time. "I shouldn't like it but…"

"It's just so good."

Everything we ate at Serendee was grown there. Everything natural. We had all natural sweeteners, from fruits or honey, but nothing like the gritty substance in this tart. It feels luxuriously defiant, sitting in Camille's kitchen, eating foods that would make Anex's blood boil.

I take another bite.

"I think I should call Agent McNair," she says, resting her half-eaten tart on her plate. "Maybe if I talk to her directly again, I can get her to understand."

"Camille said we should let the lawyers handle it."

"I just think that maybe if I can explain everything, she'll let them go."

I shake my head. It may be my first time eating a Pop-tart, but I'm more familiar with the secular world than Imogene. "It's easy to say the wrong thing and make it worse."

Because of our positions in the community, we'd been instructed on how to talk to authorities outside of Serendee. Primarily—don't. And if you have to? Tell them nothing. Anex believes the government is filled with lying bureaucrats who will go to any length to keep ordinary citizens under their thumb. They want to control our lives, our health, and autonomy.

She runs her thumb over the edge of the table. "I don't want to make things worse."

I take her hand, linking our fingers together. "I know. It wouldn't be on purpose, but what we see as normal, they don't. Rex and Elon were involved in a lot of illegal activities. Especially the drugs—"

"They didn't have a choice," she argues. "No more than you had one to run the brothel, or I had in choosing my mate."

"You and I both know that, but to outsiders it's confusing. The police won't see it that way." I tug at her hand, and she stands, moving from her chair and into my lap. I circle my arms around her and hold her against my chest.

"Camille said she'd try to do something," she says.

It'd felt like a miracle when I'd woken up with Imogene that morning. Soft and warm. Just her scent was enough to evoke an emotion, something I'd been suppressing for weeks now—too afraid to hope we'd survive Anex's will.

Then she told me about what he'd done to her. The purification ritual. He's so full of shit. Always manipulating and trying to get the upper hand. There's nothing he loves more than demeaning women. Never again. Not with Imogene at least. Those days are over—she's free.

We changed into secular clothing. Soft yellow shorts for Imogene and an oversized T-shirt. She'd tossed me a shirt from the drawer. It had a worn lettering across the front, *Whittmore University 5k*. I tugged it on along with a pair of flannel pajamas and followed her to the kitchen.

Camille had been gone when we got down there. Leaving us a note and the box of Pop-Tarts to eat. There was an apology saying they were all she had and were normally for kids that came through the house. She didn't give a time for her return.

"Maybe if I go down there, it'll work. Barter with information. I worked in the Center. I know things—where he keeps his paperwork." Her finger traces the faded lettering on my shirt. "I could demand to see him."

"I want to bring them home as much as you do, but we have to be smart about this—safe." She frowns. "I don't think we should leave the house. He could be watching."

Imogene's eyes dart to the window. "Do you think?"

"I don't know, babe, but we have to be careful, and patient." I know for certain Anex isn't going to let us go this easily. Especially not her. He had plans for Imogene, dark and obsessive. There's no way he's going to give her up. She doesn't need to know that—not now. I just want her to feel safe. To feel loved and I'll do everything I can to make that happen.

"I'm pretty sure I'm not known for my patience," she says. "That's why my journal is filled with so many lapses."

Grabbing her thigh, I hitch her leg over my thigh until she's straddling me. Her hips rock into me and my cock responds immediately. I groan, and she laughs.

"Since you won't let me call Agent McNair, and we're trapped in the house, maybe you have some ideas about what we can do with our time?"

"Are you sure?" I ask. "I don't want to rush you after—"

After what he did to her. Us.

Her eyes meet mine, intense and determined. "He hurt both of us, Silas. Played games with our bodies and used us to advance himself." Her lips are a hair's breadth away. "I won't let him be part of this."

It's easier said than done. I know that. Anex has been in our brains for years. In the way we use our bodies, but he's gone and all I want is this woman. My heart nearly bursts when she adds, "I just want to feel something other than this aching fear."

I know it. I feel it. Our whole world has been turned upside down, it's scary as fuck. I want Elon here to protect us, and Rex to tell us what to do and Levi to make sure we're doing it right. They're not here, but we can comfort one another. Bending, I capture her mouth in mine, and glide my fingers between her legs until they brush against her clit.

She's sticky, ready, but I kiss her temple and ask, "How do you want it?"

Our eyes lock and I know she wants to tell me to decide for her—that she doesn't know—but my girl knows her body. What it can tolerate and what gives her the most pleasure.

"It doesn't matter. As long as you're with me."

I ruck up her shirt, lifting it over her head. I palm her tit with one hand, firm but not too much. I know they're tender. Then lick the nipple of the other, working it into a hard peek. When her back arches, I look up and ask, "That good?"

She nods, eyes closed and lifted to the ceiling. "So good."

I haven't fucked anyone since Imogene. That would've been too easy for me to lose myself into. Anex sent me there to pimp out the Fallen—force me to be the one that made the trades for their bodies. It would've hurt less to have done it myself.

But fuck, those weeks of celibacy have made my dick ridiculously hard and I lift her, setting her ass on the table. I drop my pants, kicking out of them and nudge her inner thigh. She spreads for me like the wings of a butterfly, and I hike one leg over my hip. A deep shudder rolls through me as her fingertips touch me for the first time in weeks, spreading precum over the head of my swollen cock. I don't wait for permission, I just kiss her, mouth crashing into hers as I push into her wet, tight, pussy. She gasps, followed by an exhale and she takes me in deeper.

"You okay?" I ask, searching her eyes. "You have to talk to me."

"I'm good," she says, fingers curling into the hair at the back of my neck. "You always make this good for me, Silas. Always."

I draw out, then punch back in again, wincing. "I hope you're ready, because I won't last long."

"You don't have to." Her jaw slacks and I ease my hand between us, reaching for the spot that makes her pant.

"Lean back," I tell her, reaching behind her to clear off the table. Plates and discarded Pop-Tarts push to the side. Leaning her back, it gives me space to trail my lips down her chest, to kiss those bruises, to suck her perfect nipples, to kiss my way down her flat, smooth, stomach.

"Silas," she hums. "Don't stop."

"I won't," I promise, flattening my tongue over her nipple. Her hips buck against me, fucking back in a frantic rhythm. I feel the sharp pain of her nails as they dig into my shoulders, legs spreading, allowing me in as deep as I can go. "I won't ever stop. I won't stop cherishing you. Protecting you." I lick her mouth. "Making love to you."

Because that's the difference. The depravity Anex encouraged wasn't about something good. It was about greed and lust. This—

what Imogene and I are doing is about love. That makes the pain worth bearing.

She pulls me close, until there's nothing between us, her body writhing against mine. I pound into her, wanting to feel every inch of her fall apart in my arms.

"Ah!" she cries, back arching, pussy clenching tight. Every muscle in her body tenses, rigid with release. I ride it out with her, thrusting everything I've been holding back for weeks, the fear, the rage, the disappointment, the loss. I pound into her body—into the woman that makes me feel real—the woman I am *never* letting go.

Hugging her to me, I come, the tight grip of her pussy milking my release. "Fuck," I grunt, her hair sticky on my face. I pull back and look at her red cheeks and shiny eyes. I close my fingers around her chin. "That was me and you," I tell her. "All of us. No one else. No one gets to claim that, especially not him. Do you understand?"

"I do." I don't know if she really does, but I plan to spend every day we have together proving it to her.

∼

After we redress, Imogene follows me to the toaster. I unwrap the pastries and she pops them in the slots. The door opens at the front of the house as I push down the lever. Turning, I see Camille. A tense line slashes across her forehead.

"Good, you're awake," she says, gripping the door jamb. "We need to go."

"Go?" Imogene asks. "What's wrong?"

She shifts her hips. "Agent McNair thinks it's best for you both to move somewhere more secure."

The hair on the back of my neck rises and I rest a hand on Imogene's hip. "Has he made a move?"

"She hasn't told me, but I'd assume something has changed." Her eyes dart to her daughter. "I don't want you to leave, but we know he's aware of this place. He sent the package."

"It's fine," Imogene says stiffly, then looks at me with soft eyes. "As long as we're together."

"Always." I grab her hand and kiss the back. "Go grab whatever we've got upstairs. I'll clean up."

She nods, and exits the room, leaving me and Camille alone.

"What aren't you telling her?" I ask.

Her eyes shift to where Imogene left, making sure she's out of earshot. "There was a threat. Down at the jail."

"What kind?"

"Explosives. Enough to level a city block."

"Shit."

"They discovered it in time," Camille adds, "which was probably intentional, but it's clear Timothy isn't going to give up easily. And even if he has left the country, he still has loyalists willing to do his dirty work."

I cross my arms over my chest. "He's not giving up." I nod at my girl. "Especially not when it comes to her."

"That's how I felt, too, and what I told the agents. The threat on the building that is holding his son… it's obvious that he's willing to go to any lengths to fight the government." She takes a step forward. "Silas, I'm trusting you to take care of her."

"That's not in question. Imogene is my priority."

"That's what I don't understand. Why are all of you so invested in my daughter?" She looks me in the eye. "The fact you don't think it's unusual for four men to be interested in one woman is a signal of how fucked up your understanding is of appropriate societal norms."

I lean against the counter, forcing myself not to be offended. "You're right. Societal norms are lost on us. We were raised differently. We didn't get to go to school or the university like you and Anex did. We weren't allowed to socialize with the opposite sex, past the age of twelve. We lived in the donums—raised by house monitors. We grew up under a rigid structure of documenting Lapses, receiving

Corrections, and forced to listen to hours and hours of Anex's lectures. We went through intensive training and ultimately were singularly focused on building the community Anex wanted. Then one day Anex decided we were different—we were brought into the inner circle and told the secrets of Serendee. The consequence of that is that we were removed even further from 'normal.'" I inhale deeply before immediately releasing it. "Imogene was given to us as a toy, another object for Anex to use to distract and control us. The difference is that over time, it became more than that. She became our reason to push back. We became her reason to challenge her beliefs."

"But don't you see that outside of Serendee, this type of relationship isn't sustainable?"

"That's not for you to decide."

We both look at the door leading from the dining room into the kitchen. Imogene stands there, a small travel bag clutched in her hand. Her words ring loud and clear.

"Honey, I—" Camille starts, but Imogene cuts her off.

"I've spent my entire life being controlled and manipulated." Imogene's voice is clear and convicted. "Everything from what I ate, to what I wore, to where I slept, and ultimately who I was mated with—and even that was taken from me." She moves to stand beside me, her small hand sliding against mine. "Silas is my choice. Rex and Elon and Levi are my choices. Just because you don't understand it, doesn't mean you're right. Not about this." She swallows. "I will not allow anyone to take this choice away from me."

She lifts her head to look at me, and I cup her behind the neck and say, "I love you," then brush my lips across hers.

"I love you, too," she says, pushing up on her toes to kiss me back. When we pull apart Camille's expression has softened, although the line of worry is still etched on her forehead.

"You're right. It's not my place to judge. And arguing about it isn't how I want to spend my last few minutes with my daughter."

"You're not coming?"

"They want me to stay here and pretend like everything is

normal." She jerks her hand toward the door. "There are two agents out there ready to take you to the safe house."

Imogene releases my hand and walks over to her mother. Next to one another it's striking how similar they look. There's no mistaking their connection. And when Imogene wraps her arms around her mother's shoulder and says, "Thank you for coming for us," something shifts between the two of them. Camille's arms cinch around her daughter and the two cling to one another like this may be their only chance.

If Anex has his way, it may be.

23

Imogene

Two agents were on the porch when we left and were ushered into a black SUV. My mother looked small and sad on the front porch, arms wrapped around her body, as we drove off.

"You'll see her again," Silas says, pulling me against his side.

I nod, but there's a knot of worry in the pit of my stomach. I don't know much about the police or federal agents, or the crimes Anex has committed, but I do know that none of these are things he likes—things he approves of—and every day that passes we've betrayed him more and more.

The bomb sets all of this in a new direction. It was a warning—a clear threat—that he's willing to take out his biggest assets. I lean forward between the seats.

"I need you to turn around."

The agent's eyes flick to mine in the rearview mirror. "Those aren't our orders."

"I don't give a fuck about your orders," I say, pulse quickening. With every word, I know this is the right move. "I need to talk to Agent McNair. Immediately."

He holds my gaze for a moment longer then jerks his chin at the man in the passenger seat. He pulls out a phone and presses a button. "Yeah." He says once she's picked up. "We're enroute. There's just a problem." He pauses, twisting to look at me. "I'm not sure. She can tell you herself."

He sticks his arm out between the seats and hands me the phone. I've never used a cell phone before and it feels strangely heavy. I hold it up to my ear like I've seen others do. "Hello."

"Imogene, Agent Kane tells me there's a problem?"

"I want to talk to you."

"We can arrange something when you get to the safe house."

I look at Silas. His expression is both concerned and curious. I take his hand in mine and link our fingers together. "We need to meet before the safehouse. I promise it'll be worth it."

She's quiet for a moment. "You're ready to talk?"

"I'm not only ready to talk, but I'm ready to give you everything you need to bring Anex down."

"I'm glad to hear that—"

"I'm not finished." I cut her off and draw a deep breath for courage. "I'll give you everything you need to bring down Anex but I want something in return."

"What are you requesting?"

"I want my men back."

∼

I TELL Agent McNair that I need two things. One, for her to meet me at the Center. Two, to bring Rex, Elon, and Levi with her.

Our driver, Agent Mallory, makes a pass on Main Street, three times before bringing the SUV to a stop outside the building. Leaving us with Agent Kane, he exits the building, hand on the butt of his weapon, and checks everything out.

"Is this really necessary?" I ask, eyeing the way the front door has been barred with police tape crisscrossing the glass. Seeing the

Center shut down like this brings home the reality of everything: Anex is out of business.

At least this business.

"After that bomb threat," he asks, eyebrows raising, "hell yeah, it's necessary."

A crackle comes across the walkie talkie along with Agent Mallory's voice, "All clear."

"Stick close," he says.

"What about—" I start, worried she's not holding up to her end of the deal.

"Agent McNair will be here. I promise." He opens the passenger door and then my back door. "We're too exposed on the street. It's safer to wait for them inside."

I exit the car and Silas follows. People on the street watch us as we enter the building and I'm grateful to be in secular clothing, although if I've learned anything, outsiders can sense our differentness just like we can tell theirs. Inside, I'm struck by a wave of surrealness. Everything is exactly the same, but not. The Center is eerily quiet but has the lingering evidence of the Fed's raid. I walk over to my desk and see that it's rummaged through, desk drawers open. Pencil cup tipped to the side. Calendar removed. Mindlessly, I start to put things back in place.

"Don't touch anything," Agent Kane says, passing me.

I step back, unsure of what to do with my hands.

The doors swing open, bringing in a bright ray of afternoon sunlight. Agent McNair walks in, but my eyes skirt past her to the men that follow: Rex, Levi, and Elon.

Agent Mallory shuts the door behind them and stays outside.

"Thank god," I say, noticing their wrists are bound as I run over. I throw my arms around Rex and he plants a kiss in the crook of my neck. Reaching out, I squeeze Levi's hand. "Are you okay?"

"We're fine." Rex answers for all of them. "What is this?"

"I had her bring you to me," I say, looking to Levi. "A trade. Information for you."

Elon shakes his head. "You don't need to do this, Imogene, we can handle it."

I step in front of him, reaching up to cradle his face in my hand. "I know you think that, but this is bigger than our pride. This will be over soon."

He blinks, his tired eyes creased with worry. "What did you do?"

"What I should have from the beginning." I turn to the agents. "Do they have to be handcuffed?"

"Yes," Agent McNair says, gaze holding mine. "At least for now."

For now.

That means there's a chance *if* I can give her what she wants.

"I brought them with me just like you asked. As you can tell, we've already done a clean sweep of these offices and removed anything incriminating."

I turn and make eye contact with Levi. He and I worked most closely with Anex in this office—he as a teacher, me as his administrative assistant. "We need to show them," I say. "*Everything.*"

Awareness flickers on his exhausted face, and I sense his hesitation. I get it. What I'm about to show them will prove the enormity of Anex's crimes, but in the process, it'll show how twisted and depraved he really is. He grimaces. "Are you sure?"

It'll also show all of us, all of our friends and community members, in a compromising light. Him. Me. All of us.

"I need to do it," I tell him. "Or we'll never be free."

Levi nods. "Then do it."

I cross the room and enter the hallway, Agent Kane pushes in front of me, insisting on leading the way. Fair. I could be leading him to a room of booby traps. Instead, I point to a small storage room door, one that holds all the records. The lock is busted, and a quick look inside of the open, empty cabinets, I can see that the files have been removed.

"I told you," Agent McNair says, "We got everything."

"I don't think so. Anex recorded everything," I tell the agents. "Every meeting, every educational session, every midnight lecture, basketball game, ceremony." I swallow. "Every Correction."

"Correction?" Agent McNair asks. "What's a Correction?"

I inhale deeply. "You're about to find out."

I nod at the bank of floor-to-ceiling cabinets attached to the wall and open one of the middle drawers. I press my fingers against the back wall, feeling for the right spot, but can't find it. Panicked, I look back at Levi.

"Let me do it," Levi says, stepping forward. He brushes past me, his arm warm against mine, sending shivers down my spine. He holds up his bound hands. "It'd be easier if my hands were free."

Kane and McNair share a look, but ultimately, she nods. A moment later the ties are cut, and Levi rubs at his wrists. "That's better."

"Don't do anything stupid," Kane says, hand on his gun.

"It's just a lever," Levi says, reaching into the drawer. "I'm going to press it and it'll release a latch." A loud click follows, and he slowly withdraws his hand at the same time the cabinet detaches from the wall.

"What the hell?" Rex asks as Kane assists Levi in moving the cabinet. Next to him Elon shakes his head. Rex looks at me. "You knew about this?"

"Your father trusted me," I reply. "And Levi. We were his most devoted followers."

Just saying it makes me feel a pang—guilt maybe. There's no time to dwell on it. With his gun drawn, Kane steps through the small doorway and into the hidden room. "Holy shit," he mutters, then calls out, "It's clear. You can come in."

A moment later we're inside—all six of us in the narrow space. The room is filled with a variety of electronics. Nothing I understand how to use, but I'm aware of their importance. Against the back wall are computers and monitors.

"He's got everything," Kane says, pulling on a pair of latex gloves. "VHS, CDs, tapes, flash drives."

"He's been documenting everything for the last thirty-five years," Agent McNair says. She looks at Rex. "You really didn't know about this room?"

He shakes his head. "I knew he kept recordings, but nothing this extensive." He looks at the sheer size of the collection. "Imogene is right. He didn't trust me, Elon, and Silas the way he did her and Levi. They were devoted to him—and Serendee. He knew I had my issues with how he ran the community."

Agent McNair turns to face the shelves, eyes landing on a section titled 'Corrections.' Each recording marked with a name and a date. I pull one out and hold it out to her.

Imogene Montgomery.

The date is from two months ago, before the banishment and Reeducation. I know that she'll find sessions between me and Levi. Possibly the aftermath with me and Elon. She hands it over to Kane who pops it into one of the electronic devices.

"Stop," Elon says, lunging for the screen. Levi and Silas block him, holding him back. He shoves against them. "Get the fuck out of my way. No one has the right to see what is on those tapes—"

"It's okay, Elon." This is what I need to do to get my men back. Honesty and transparency. I look at the agents. "Watch it. You need to know the truth."

Kane presses play and an image comes on the screen. It's me and Levi standing in the middle of the room—talking. The table is next to me, the leather strap on the flat surface. My cheeks burn and I look to the floor as the recording progresses. The whole room watches as I bend over that table and take Levi's punishment.

An arm comes around my shoulder and Levi pulls me against his chest. I look up at his handsome face. "I'm sorry," he says. I'm not sure if it's about the Correction, or the fact this video is being exposed, or about everything that's transpired in the last few weeks.

"Don't apologize," I whisper, under the sound of leather snapping against my skin and my following screams. My body lights on fire. Humiliation. Desperation. Confliction.

I turn, pushing past everyone and leave the room. I stop in the hallway and press my shaking body against the wall, trying to remain upright. A person emerges from the file room. The shoes stop in front of me. Black. Feminine.

"Imogene," she says, her voice quiet. "I had no idea."

I look up at her, past the blur of tears in my eyes and ask, "Is it enough?"

She nods. "It's enough."

I sink to the floor, relief rushing through me.

I have my men back.

24

Imogene

The ride to the safe house is long, and my stomach aches with panic. Agent McNair had to handle release paperwork for the guys before they could come. I didn't like the idea of being separated from them, but there wasn't any other choice. They'd meet us there.

Wherever "there" is. All I know is that it's dark, and we turned off the highway and onto a dirt road fifteen minutes ago. Nothing about being surrounded by the thick forest of trees, tall pines that shoot straight up into the night sky, quells my nerves.

"Hey," Silas says, nodding out the front window, "looks like we're almost there."

"There" turns out to be a small cabin tucked away in a forest. The car slows with the crunch of gravel under the tires, easing to a stop next to an identical SUV. The two agents get out, doors slamming behind them. "You really think he won't find us here?" I ask, peering out the window.

"I think only a fool would underestimate Anex, and you're the smartest person I know."

"Although I appreciate the compliment, that's not very comforting." I roll my eyes and check out the other vehicle. "I wonder who that is?"

Neither Mallory or Kane seem concerned, and they open the back of the vehicle, removing the small amount of belongings we brought with us.

I climb out of the car just as the screen door whines and closes with a snap. Agent McNair steps out on the porch. My heart drops. "Did something happen?"

"Everything's fine." She gives me an unexpected smile. "Actually, I was able to handle everything over the phone. We just took a different route in case anyone had tracked us from the Center."

"We?" I ask, rushing up the steps. She jerks her thumb over her shoulder, and I run past her, wrenching open the door and bursting inside.

They're there. Hands free. Skinny and tired.

Mine.

"Oh my god." I want to go to them, but I'm just struck by deep and sudden exhaustion. My arm presses into my stomach and I bend, a deep, unrecognizable, wail coming from inside.

I turn and a figure falls in front of me. Elon, down on his knees. I meet him on the floor. "Babe," he says. I feel the press of his lips against my forehead. "What is it? What's happening?"

"I thought I'd lost you forever."

To Anex. To prison. To all the terrible things he said would come if we betrayed him.

"Never," he says, looking back as the guys come to stand behind him. His hands cup my face, and he thumbs away my tears. "We will never stop fighting for each other."

Silas' arms wrap around me, his body heat warm and comforting, and a moment later Levi's there, rubbing my back and pressing a kiss to my temple. Over Elon's shoulder, I feel Rex's intense gaze, his blue eyes sweeping over me, looking for wounds or injuries. Both of us know they're there–he just can't see them. I lift myself off the ground and go to him, brushing aside the tears on my cheek. "I've been so worried about you." He was inside the longest, left with nothing but his worries.

"Don't be," his thumb wipes away a tear. "I was fine."

That's impossible, but it'll take time.

He lifts his chin, some kind of silent signal, and Elon's got me in his arms, lifting me. He carries me across the room and up a flight of stairs, stopping when we enter a bedroom. He eases me to the floor and steps into the bathroom, turning on the faucet.

"What are you doing?" I look toward the door, to the sound of masculine voices downstairs.

"The guys are going to make dinner." He comes back to me, kissing my nose, then the underside of my jaw, my collarbone. A shiver runs across my skin. "And I'm going to run you a bath."

"You just got out of prison, I'm the one that should be cooking," I tell him, those old routines and behaviors falling into place. "You know I like to."

"I know you do, but tonight, let us take care of you, babe."

The idea sounds nice, and completely foreign. I'm also too tired to do anything but watch him run the bath, filling it with soapy, clean smelling bubbles. I haven't moved and he returns to me, hands pushing under my shirt, lifting it over my head. Kissing the center of my chest, he reaches behind my back and unhooks my bra, gently pushing it down my shoulders. His eyes go to the fading bruises, and he rubs a thumb over the side of my breast.

"Rex told me what happened." He tilts his head back, closes his eyes and swallows thickly. "I should've been there to protect you."

"You had no choice," I tell him, running my hands under his shirt to feel the hard muscle underneath. "None of us did, but we do now."

He looks down at me, eyes filled with dark intensity. His hand cups around the column of my throat and he draws me to him, kissing me on the mouth. A surge of warmth runs through me—the strength of his tongue, the taste of his lips. I allow myself to relax, to sink into him, knowing we're all home—and for the moment—safe.

Kisses down my body, reverently, taking his time. When his mouth closes over a taut nipple, lathing against the peak, I cry out, desperate for more. His breath is hot, spreading over my skin, down my belly as he licks and tastes. He stops at my hip and my hand falls to cover the brand, but he lifts it gently, kissing my fingers and the skin around the mark.

"He'll pay for this one day, love."

As much as I hate the brand, I appreciate that they don't ignore it —that they accept that it's part of me—just another scar left from Anex's domination.

There is no man more domineering than the one before me. The sight of him down on his knees spreads warmth between my legs. He's controlled and diligent as he explores every inch of my body.

He eases off the cotton pants I'd found in a drawer that morning. The drawstring is untied in a sharp yank. Exposed, he sets me on the edge of the tub, pushing my legs apart with his palms. He bends, teeth nipping at the delicate flesh of my inner thigh. The tease of pain makes me hotter, wetter. He looks up at me and says, "I've been dreaming of this for weeks."

"Me too."

"Hang on, babe," His tongue glides over my slick folds, delving into them, teasing and tasting. My fingers grip the sides of the tub, the steamy water curling up my spine. My breath is short, coming in hot, needy bursts, but It's when his tongue finds the bundle of nerves, the ones wound tight and desperate, waiting for him to discover, as I unspool, spinning toward ecstasy.

I cry his name out, the sound echoing off the bathroom tiles and buck against him.

"Elon," I say, again. "That was…"

"Just the beginning." He stands, pressing his hand against my back and easing me into the warm, steamy, tub. My limbs are jelly, my heart pounding like I've just finished a race. I watch him strip, then climb into the tub behind me. Water sloshes over the sides as he fits his massive frame in with me, cradling my back against his chest.

"Is this for real?" I ask, threading my fingers through his. "Me, you, this tub, the guys downstairs?"

He pushes the hair off my neck with wet fingertips and plants a kiss on my neck. "It's for real."

There's two words he's left off, but I allow it, not wanting to mar this moment with the world outside.

It's real—*for now.*

After what we've been through, I'll take what I can get.

~

"Did we really eat all that?"

I stare at the empty dishes on the table, the plates that are scraped clean. Levi and I offered to clean up after dinner while the others took showers and unpacked.

No, *dinner* isn't the right word. We had a feast. Agent McNair had arranged for a grocery delivery, apparently thinking it would last a while. Unfortunately, she didn't anticipate the appetite of my four men after subsisting on prison food and Serendee rations.

They ate a lot. *I* ate a lot, more than I should. Lately, I've found it hard to stop, even when I know I'm full, because there's this gnawing hunger in my belly all the time. I know in my heart that this is because of the limitations and restrictions we had on food in Serendee, but my brain hasn't been able to separate that yet.

"We did," Levi says, taking a stack of plates back to the kitchen. "I think I may have witnessed the definition of the word gluttony."

I grab two platters and carry them over to the sink. "If I keep this up, I'm going to gain more weight." Pressing my hand to my stomach, I feel the way it pooches out a little. I can't decide if I like it or not.

"You look good like this," he tells me. "Rex was always right about girls being a little meatier. More to hold onto."

"I keep reaching for my journal—like I should be documenting every lapse."

"It's okay to write things down," he says, as if he's reminding himself as much as me. "Just don't let it rule you."

I nod and head back to the dining room, bringing back another pile of dirty dishes. More than once, I glance over my shoulder, looking out the dark windows, searching the room for anything I or the agents missed.

"What are you doing?" he asks.

"I keep looking for cameras. I know they aren't here, but it's hard to shake."

Paranoia.

It was bad before but seeing that stash of recordings made it worse. Levi turns on the faucet, letting the water run until it turns hot. I don't miss how he keeps his hands under the water until it turns hot, turning his skin pink. He takes the first dish and rinses it off. "You were brave to show them the videos."

"I did what I had to. She wasn't going to let you go if I didn't."

"You don't have to justify it, Imogene. You did the right thing."

"Maybe." It still feels wrong, exposing not only myself but my friends and neighbors. My *lovers*. I scrape a pile of chicken bones into the trash. "I can't imagine what else they'll reveal."

"More than I'm willing to think about," he says quietly.

"There are so many shameful moments—some you may not even know about, like the exams in Healer Blooms clinic or how awful the branding was. How we turned on one another or how we treated one another to gain his favor. The farther away from it I get, the harder it is for me to reconcile."

"I know," he agrees. "I can't help but think about the way we bowed and doted on Anex every time we were in his presence. How quickly I did everything he asked." He glances at me. "How willing I was to hurt you for his bullshit belief system, when all he really wanted me to do was break you down."

It's an apology, one I'm not willing to take. "You weren't the only one seeking Enlightenment, Levi." I'd asked for that as much as he gave it. I wanted the pain. I still do, and that's something we have to figure out. "Do you ever feel like…" I start, then shake my head back and forth looking for the words. "Like we've been underwater?"

"Underwater?" he asks, eyebrow raising.

"I just feel like I have these moments where I'm clearing out the cobwebs, or running my hand over a fogged-up mirror, trying to see everything clearly."

"Yes," he says. "Absolutely, especially when we first got out. I could barely function. Elon was supporting us, and I was just... trying to figure out how to get back in." He glances at me. "Back to you."

"But you feel better now?" I ask.

"Food, sleep, getting away from the lectures and non-stop input seems to help."

"Sleep is good." Full nights. No music blaring through the grounds. No late-night basketball games or random work assignments. That doesn't mean I'm able to get a full night's rest, but it's better. More consistent.

He turns off the faucet and grabs a towel, drying his hands. Then he rests a hand on my hip. "You know, when he banished us, it gave me weeks to get ahead of where you are right now, maybe even more than that when you consider the other things you went through." He keeps his eyes pinned to mine. "The conditioning and control—over your body as well as your mind... it was a lot, Imogene."

I think about Rex at the dinner table, hungry but quiet. Elon's need to just be with me, to take care of me, to touch me under the dinner table with every opportunity. Silas' sleep, deep and long. "We're all going to have to heal in different ways, aren't we?"

"I think so." His hand drops down and squeezes my hip. "I've been reading a lot of the books and information Camille had at her house. It's overwhelming, but helpful. It makes me feel less crazy."

"I just want to feel normal."

He laughs. "I wouldn't even know what that looks like, would you?"

I push up on my toes and kiss him.

"What was that for? *Not* that I'm complaining."

"I like seeing you smile."

He grins wider. "I like seeing you smile, too."

"Are we going to be okay?" I ask. It's a big question. But Levi is my Guide. He's always been there to answer my questions and keep me on the path. It's just now we're on a different one than before. Before he can respond, I blurt out another one. "How long do you think will we have to hide?" Then another, "And where will we live when it's over? Do you think we'll have to testify against Anex?" My heart pounds, thudding hard against my chest. "What happens if no one believes us?"

He takes my face in his hands. "I want to answer all of those things for you, Imogene, but I can't. And for the first time, I won't lie or pretend that I can. That's what I would have done before. Just made up something to convince you that I knew better than you did or spewed a bunch of Anex's rhetoric to keep you in line." His thumb strokes my cheek. "But I'm not that person anymore—or I'm trying not to be. I can't tell you the future. I can't promise that by doing the right thing Enlightenment will follow. I can't do anything but tell you that I love you, and I'll stay with you, and we'll get through this together."

Fresh tears build in my eyes and press my cheek against his chest. "That's all I need, you know that, right?"

He nods and I hug him tight, maybe tighter than ever before and even not knowing what comes next, I feel more secure than I have in years.

∾

I leave Levi and Silas downstairs reading and head to bed. I pause in the doorway of my darkened room, finding Rex under the covers, deep asleep. Even at rest, his face carries the weight of exhaustion.

"He's beat." I turn and see Elon coming down the hall. He's shirtless and in a pair of black sweatpants. "He barely slept at the jail."

An unease sits in my bones. Anex was relentless with him, mentally and physically. I want to go to him, make sure he's okay but I feel the barrier between us. "Are you sure he's okay?" *We're okay*, I want to add, but don't.

"All he wanted was to get back to you." His hand slides behind my neck, and he pulls me against his chest. His tongue licks at my lips, seeking entrance. It's easy to get lost in him, easy to want kisses and touches to last forever, but he pulls back and declares, "It's all any of us wanted."

"He made me a promise," I say, looking into the room. Rex's blond hair shines in the glow of the hallway light. "That he'd come home to me at night. No matter what." I step into the room. "Like it or not, I'm upholding it now." I reach out a hand. "Sleep with us?"

He looks between his best friend and me. "Are you sure? Because once you invite me in bed with the two of you, I'm not leaving."

My cheeks heat at the thought of Rex and Elon together. What that means for them and me. "Until I know for sure that Anex isn't going to come for me—for us—I want every minute I can get."

"I'll kill him first, Imogene." It's not a threat—it's a promise.

"Hopefully, it won't come to that," I say, leaving him in the doorway. "At least not until we're ready." I cross the room and stop at the edge of the bed, removing my clothes, before climbing into the bed and shifting to the middle, close to my Mate. I leave the covers down, an invitation. His hesitation slips away, and he follows, dropping his pants. His cock bobs between his legs and it takes everything in me not to reach out and stroke it.

Rex doesn't stir other than to wrap his arm around me, and I burrow against his warm skin, eyes pinned to Elon's.

"Thank you for saving us," he says quietly, hand gliding down my arm.

"Thank you for saving me," I reply. "You pulled the veil from my eyes, and as difficult as that has been, I owe you everything."

My own exhaustion supersedes the feel of want between my legs, and the way Elon struggles to keep his eyes open, I know he feels the same. I don't know if it's the sense of freedom, or the security of being between the two of them, but when sleep drags me under, I allow it to take me.

A tremor wakes me, running down my spine and between my legs. Hot breath at my neck, nipples pebbled and hard.

"Little Lamb, open up," I hear, before my legs are pulled apart, a hot tongue licking a hot path up my inner thigh.

I blink, seeing the shine of blond hair between my legs. I'm barely awake, but a jolt of energy rushes through me when Rex's warm tongue dives between my folds.

"God, you taste so good. Fuck I missed this." His words are quiet- a whisper. "I missed you."

My hips rise to meet him, a burst of desire shooting through me. My toes curl, fingers twisting into the bedsheets and a deep moan builds in my throat. With the gentlest of touches, he sucks at my clit and a cry rips from my throat.

"You like that?" he asks, lifting to his elbows. Rex's eyes meet mine, his blue eyes liquid heat. "I thought about you the whole time I was in that cell. How you taste, what you feel like." He palms my breast, lifting the nipple to his mouth. His tongue swirls around and around, building the heat between my legs, forcing my back to arch. "It's better than I remember. You're better." He shifts and looks over his shoulder. "Don't you think?"

It's then that I see Elon sprawled beside us, hand fisting his cock. He grunts his approval.

"Show him your pussy, Little Lamb. Elon wants to see." His hand grips my thigh, pushing my legs apart. The cool air meets the damp heat and Elon licks his bottom lip, focused between my legs. Rex rubs his fingers over my entrance, spreading me apart while his friend watches. My skin itches, like it's about to burst into flames, but I'd die first. All I want is for these men to make me come.

"One finger or two?" Rex asks, toying with my body, fingers dipping in and out.

"Two," I breathe.

"Three," Elon commands, chin lifting. "Take three, baby. Get ready for us."

A swirl of butterflies explodes in my belly, but I lean back on the pillow and let my thighs drop to the side. Rex's fingers, sticky from my excitement, push into me. One at first, gliding in and out. Then the second, adding more pressure. "That feel good?" he asks, brushing his thumb over my clit.

"Yes," I hiss, biting down on my bottom lip. "More."

He slides in the third finger, pumping in and out, the stretch feels good. He leans over and captures my mouth with his, kissing me hard. I want to curl into them, fuck them. I want them to claim me—make me their own. My whole body starts to shake, desperate for more.

He pulls back, eyebrows knitted together. "What's wrong?"

"Nothing," I say, although we both know it's a lie. "I want you in me."

Elon rises to his knees, cock thick and straining. "She needs us." A look transpires between them, and I know when understanding strikes Rex. He nods. Rex played games with my mind, not my body. He used me for his own whims, a battle with his father, but other than the strapping in Anex's room, he didn't take his emotions out on my body. Elon understands my desires better. He's helped me through the pain before. The unrelenting, *aching* need that can only be relieved by one thing.

"On your back," Elon tells Rex. He does as his friend demands, removing his fingers from inside me and stretching out on the bed, abs taut, erection hard and wet. I mourn the loss of him in me, but I lick my lips and bend to kiss him, licking the salty tip of his penis. He hisses and grabs for my breasts, tugging my nipples between his fingers. The sharp pain is exactly what I want, and I bob my head, taking his cock deep down my throat.

Elon moves behind me, grabbing my hips like I'm nothing but a rag doll. With his fingers digging into my flesh, his cock slides between my cheeks, rough and demanding, poking hard at my entrance. Rex's chest rises and falls as I suck him off, fingers twisting in my hair. He yanks at the scalp, and I cry out. His hips thrust up, his cock hitting the back of my throat.

God. *Yes.*

"Open for me, baby," Elon says from behind me, hips rearing back before he drives into me. He fills me, both deep and wide, pounding with deep slow strokes. The feel of him inside is better than anything in this world, that is until Rex removes his cock from my mouth, scooches down the bed and presses the tip against my already full entrance. "And now you're going to open for him, too."

I nod, my eyes meeting Rex's as he works his way slowly inside. This time the stretching hurts, God, it hurts, and I suck in a breath.

"Too much?" Rex, asks, hand cupping my cheek.

"No, just give me a second."

They do, Elon still behind me. Rex's jaw tenses. "Little Lamb, I gotta move."

The tendons in his neck strain, he's holding out for me. I nod, giving him the go ahead and he pushes in an inch more. This time the burn is better, slicker, and I breath deep and push down, taking him in the rest of the way.

I've never felt so full.

"Holy fuck," Elon mutters. "Christ. Do you know how good this feels?"

"So fucking good," Rex says, pulling my face down to his, our foreheads pressed together. "But if I don't move, I'm coming like this, just sitting inside of you."

I laugh, like that'd be the worst thing in the world, but I rock my hips, nudging them along. Both men groan, something deep and animalistic. After the first thrust, there's nothing gentle about it. The friction is too much—frantic and hungry—all I feel is them. It's all I *want* to feel—leaving the bad darkness of Serendee behind us. The manipulation and mind games. I just want my men, to feel them, to love them, to let them love me.

That hollow pit in my stomach, the one I can never seem to fill, vanishes.

Elon's thrusts send me into Rex, whose hands cup my breasts and squeeze them together. He mouths my nipples. My head falls back, resting on Elon's chest. His hand comes around my throat, and he twists my head, sweeping his tongue into my mouth.

"I'm gonna come," Elon says, teeth dragging down my jaw. He fucks into me, hard and furious, until he buries a strangled groan into my neck. His cock pulses into me and he drops his fingers, catching cum, and swiping the wet, slippery, fluid over my clit. I shudder, the start of my own orgasm rippling through me.

"Fuck. Fuck. Fuck," I chant, body going rigid.

Rex swears under his breath as my muscles clench around him. His cock slippery from Elon's slick cum. "Hold on, Little Lamb," he says, lurching to his knees. Both men lift me, fill me, holding me up as Rex drives into me with a final thrust.

"I love you," Rex says, breath heavy and hot on my ear. "I love you and you're mine, never forget that. You're Elon's and Silas' and Levi's. You belong to us, Imogene. Us and only us. And if we have to fuck you every goddamn day of your life to prove it to you, we will."

My body is numb, spine lax, as he whispers these things, and I barely feel it as they lower me back to the bed, body sticky and warm. And as we curl together, I'm struck by the awareness that even after they've pulled out, and are no longer in me, I still feel full.

25

Elon

Hack. Hack. Hack.

Chop.

Clunk.

I push aside the curtain and peer out the kitchen window at the continuous sound, day after day, since we got here. It's the sound of irritation. Restlessness. Distraction.

Hack. Hack. Hack.

Chop.

Clunk.

Rex heaves the axe over his head, biceps straining as he gains the momentum to chop the massive log. He'll split this it into smaller pieces before tossing it on the ever-growing pile. He's been out there since sunrise, his gray shirt two shades darker from sweat, showing no signs of slowing down anytime soon. Other than the night he and I shared with Imogene, he's been withdrawn. I know she's nervous about it. Insecure.

Hack. Hack. Hack.

Chop.

Clunk.

My eyes shift to the ridge behind him, scanning the narrow space between the trunks. Nothing but trees.

Nothing but the five of us settled into this close quartered, temporary situation—living, but not living—a different sort of life altogether.

It feels like we're still in exile.

It's not the life we expected and it's not easy. The cabin is small for a group of people that is used to living in an expansive, wide-spaced, nature-driven community. Our outdoor time is limited due to constant surveillance by the FBI, and as Levi continues to remind us, we're all struggling with our own trauma that we carried out of Serendee.

I'd argue with him, but I see it myself. How Imogene cooks, making elaborate, spice heavy, intricate meals, while barely taking a bite of it herself. She won't admit it, but I catch her counting calories, fingers twitching with the need to write each and every one down.

Levi's no better—having stationed himself at a desk that overlooks the yard with a wide window. He's surrounded by stacks of books that have spilled over to a pile on the floor. Each and every book is about a single topic: Cults. Surviving them, escaping them, defining them, rejecting them, recovering from them... His academic and intellectual drive has shifted from obsessing over Anex's doctrine, to analyzing cult behavior. I'm not sure the last time he slept, really ate a meal, or took a shower. I do know him well enough to understand that he won't stop until he considers himself an expert.

My eyes shift to the living room, where Silas has been sprawled on the large couch, eyes glued to the flat screen TV mounted to the wall for the last five days. The shows are mostly shiny things—plastic looking men and women parading around shirtless or in bikinis. They're called reality shows, but I don't get it. Everyone is playing a game. There's nothing realistic about it at all. I'm not sure what Silas is getting out of this, or if that's the point, it's nonsensical and mindless. Whatever it is, he's enraptured.

Me? Paranoia has settled in deep. I feel it in my bones, in every shadow and movement outside the window. I know in my soul Anex will never let us be free. We weren't just part of his inner circle—he believed he owned us—and that doesn't change just because he's on the run.

I keep track of the news. Looking for any information on Anex or his remaining circle that didn't get picked up during the raid. I find myself scrolling the tablet Agent Mallory gave us to use—one Anex's people shouldn't be able to track—searching to see if Margaret had the baby, or if any arrests have been made. I have alerts set up, dozens to chime if something comes up, but day after day it's nothing until...

I stare at the message that flits across the screen. "Silas, give me the remote."

"They're just about to decide who gets voted off the isla—"

I'm across the room in three strides. "Give me the fucking remote!" I snatch it out of his hands, the commotion bringing Imogene from the kitchen and forcing Levi to look up from his book.

"Can you keep it down?" he shouts from his corner.

"No," I reply, stabbing at the buttons. There are forty news channels, but I don't know how to get there. I throw it back at Silas, the plastic device hitting him in the chest. "Put it on the news. Now!"

He finds it quickly, and the press conference is already in progress. A tall black man stands behind a podium, a large set of columns behind him. At the bottom it says, "*State Attorney General, Michael Morris.*"

"Shut up," I tell everyone, although the room is quiet.

"Today, Timothy Andrew Wray and co-conspirators were indicted for the crimes of sex trafficking, false imprisonment, money laundering, racketeering, and tax evasion."

"Oh my God," Imogene whispers beside me. Her fingers brush against mine and I hold onto them tight. Silas sits up, possibly for the first time in a week.

"Prior to this, Timothy was wanted for tax evasion and questioning, but due to the discovery of an enormous amount of irrefutable evidence by the FBI," the camera widens, revealing Agent McNair standing just to the side, "the state had no choice but to expand the scope of our investigation and alter the charges."

"Holy shit," Levi says, closing the book in his hand.

"As of right now, all four of the people indicted are unaccounted for. We are asking the community to report any sightings or information you may have on the following people to the tip line below." Photos appear on the screen, "Timothy Wray, who goes by the name Anex, and his followers Margaret Ackerman, Erik Heisman, and Jasmine West, heir to the Cobra Tequila empire."

"Fuck," Silas says, running his hand through his hair. "Rex and I," he looks back at me. "We recruited her."

"I remember her," I say. From the frat parties. She'd been on the hook for a while. I guess Rex and Silas locked her down.

"We caution you not to approach any of these people on your own. They are dangerous, their compound had extensive explosives and weaponry. We must assume they are armed and should be approached with caution."

We watch the rest of the press conference, but the attorney general declines to answer questions from the press.

"What they're saying," Levi rubs his chin, "is that they have no fucking clue where he is."

"Maybe it's a trick," Imogene argues. "Like, they're trying to pretend they don't have anything on him, making him more overconfident."

"I need some air," I say once it's over. I walk to the door and open it. Mallory is on the deck, watching the press conference on his phone.

"Where are you going?"

"For a walk," I reply.

"Not sure that's a good idea, Elon."

"Fuck good ideas!" My patience is hanging by a thread. "No one has a fucking clue where Anex is. We've been cooped up for a week. I need some goddamn air before I lose my mind."

Imogene steps out of the house and shuts the door behind her. She looks at Mallory. "I'll go with him."

"That doesn't make me feel more secure, Ms. Montgomery."

"We'll stay close. I promise."

He frowns and shakes his head, but says, "Fine, but I want you in sight of the house at all times. I'll be watching."

"Don't worry," she says, grabbing my hand, "we're used to that."

Gravel crunches under foot, and I try to steady my breathing as we walk farther away from the house. My skin itches knowing the agents are nearby but I suspect it's less about them and more like what Imogene said, we're used to having a lack of privacy.

"Talk to me," she says, tightening her grip on my hand.

"I just needed some air, that's all." I glance over at her, at the boots and fitted jeans. At the button-down plaid shirt with the sleeves rolled up to her elbows. "That press conference… it just feels like more games, you know?"

"I believe in Agent McNair," she says, leading me to an outcropping of rocks. They're mossy on the sides, but smooth on the top. I grab her hips and lift her to sit on top. She lets me fit in between her legs, linking her arms around my neck. "I believe she'll catch him."

"How?" I ask with complete sincerity. "How do you still believe?"

She shrugs and plays with the hair at the back of my neck. It's grown out, longer than I wore it at Serendee. "I grew up thinking the outside world was scary and dark. That people were conniving and ruined by the Secular world. That all they wanted was money and to exploit our bodies."

"When really Anex was already doing it," I add. "I know, but that betrayal, it should make you more pessimistic. If he could convince an entire community, he'll be able to talk his way out of all of this with that attorney general, or a jury in a courthouse."

"He may," she admits, "but until then I just want to live my best life."

I look around the woods, taking in the quiet, the cold. There are no leaves on the trees other than the pines. This far away from the house, other than the occasional bird, or snap of a twig, it feels like we're the only ones alive.

It's peaceful. Better than fighting or running drugs or living under Anex's omnipresent rule.

"What's your best life look like, Elon?" she asks suddenly.

I think about it, but the answer is elusive. Finally, I say, "I thought I'd live forever in Serendee. Working for Anex and Rex. There was no mate in the picture, not for us. Not until you came along, and I didn't think that would last either. I thought my Enlightenment would come from doing everything Anex asked of me, including what he asked me to do to you. But now I understand how so much of what he expected of me was wrong." My eyes flick to hers. "How could that not include you?"

"Because in the end we chose each other."

I shake my head, blinking back the emotion I can't seem to hold back. "I just want to be a good man for you, Imogene, and I don't know if I know how to do that."

She pulls back, removing her arms and gives me a glare. "You're fucking with me, right?"

I laugh. I can't help it. Swear words sound so weird coming out of her pretty mouth. "No."

"Baby, you've always been good to me," she says. "Even back when we were kids, playing on that merry-go-round, being the big older kid that watched out for the rest of us." She presses her hands to my cheeks. "You saved me on the street the night of my Ordering. Those guys wouldn't have stopped."

"That wasn't just me—"

"No, you were the one that walked me home, made sure I was safe." Her hands lower to my chest. "You taught me how to be Rex's ideal mate and lover, and you saved me from that backwoods farmer at his vegetable stand."

She doesn't know what happened after that—when we went back for him.

"And you came back to Serendee for me after being Banished. Nothing has stopped you from being good to me, from taking care of me no matter what obstacle."

"None of this was supposed to happen, Imogene. I think that's why I'm struggling. And what if he comes back? What then?"

She sighs, exasperated with my questions, but it doesn't stop her from answering. "If we peel apart what Anex taught us, that there's only one path, a path he laid for us, then the possibilities are endless. There is no supposed to be, it just is what it is. And what this is... well, I love you. So much. And I'm just grateful I don't have to hide it."

My heart thuds, from how beautiful and smart she is. How did that happen? We were supposed to educate and train her, but this girl didn't need it. She's always been leaps ahead of us. I press a kiss to her neck and whisper in her ear, "I'd show you right now how good I can be to you, but Mallory is watching."

"Then take me back to the cabin and show me there?'

I kiss her, capturing her mouth in mine, making sure she knows how much I love her—want her—but she knows. It's in my bones, the way I look at her, the way I get hard every time I'm near her.

I help her off the rock, wrapping her legs around my waist and carry her in the direction of the cabin.

"Is this necessary?" she asks, grinding into my waist.

"Your legs are too short." I can't wait to get the clothes off my woman. "And it makes you walk too slow."

I press another kiss to her neck too distracted to process the branch snapping in the distance. I do look up at the crack that follows, a zing cutting through the air by my ear. I drop Imogene to the ground, covering her body with my own as another bullet flew past.

"Mallory!" I shout, but I hear his footsteps pounding off the porch. I look down at her, "Baby are you okay?"

"Y-yes," she nods. "What was that?"

Kane appears from the opposite direction and I push Imogene at him, snagging the gun off his belt in the process. "Get her back in the house."

"Elon—" he starts, realizing what I've done.

"Elon, no!" Imogene shouts.

Rex runs across the yard, shirtless, body worn from chopping wood. I pin my gaze to his. "Get her inside. I'm going to deal with this."

He nods, pulling her back to the cabin and knowing she's safe with him, I load the chamber. Making a mad dash into the woods, I press my back into the nearest tree. Bullets land, spraying shards of bark everywhere.

I knew Anex would come for us—for *her*.

And there's no fucking way in hell I'm going to let him have her.

26

Rex

"Stay here." I pull the shirt over my head and fling open the closet door, looking for a coat. "I'm going to help Elon."

"Please don't," she says from the corner of the living room. It's a blind spot in case anyone tries to shoot at the house. Silas has his arm wrapped around her. "It's bad enough that Elon's out there."

Raking my fingers through my hair, I spin and look at her. My girl. My Mate. "He tried to kill you. I can't let that go."

"You don't have to." She looks to Levi and Silas. "Tell him not to go out there."

Levi's pressed to the wall, peeking out the window. "Looks like you won't have to."

"What does that mean?" I head to the window, not giving a fuck if someone sees me. I'm exhausted and burned out—past the end of my rope. If today is the day this ends, then I'm ready for it. But before I reach Levi, the front door kicks open. Elon enters, a dirty, bloody mess. Behind him, Mallory and Kane drag in a man wearing head-to-toe camouflage, fighting against the restraints cinched around his wrists.

It takes me a full heartbeat to realize who they caught.

Erik.

"You're fucking with me." Rage pumps through my veins like lava, and I lunge at him, grabbing him by the collar. "You came here to kill my Mate? My best friend?"

The crack of my fist hitting his chin comes before Mallory jerks him aside. When the agent looks up at me, I see the agent's split lip. Erik put up a hell of a fight.

"That," I tell Erik, "was for all the shit you put me through the last few months."

"Fuck you," he says, spitting blood next to my shoe. "You fucking traitor."

I lunge for him again, but this time Kane jumps between me and Erik.

"Damn it, Rex," he shouts. "We've got him under arrest. A team is coming to pick him up and take him to interrogation."

"Is he the only one?" I ask, heart thudding. "Did he come alone?"

"We didn't find anyone else on our sweep," Kane says, but he shifts on his heels, knowing it's not enough.

"Leave him here," I say. "We'll watch him."

He laughs. "You'll kill him."

"He won't," Levi says, "because if we kill him, we won't be able to find Anex." He gives me a hard look. "And that's our priority, right?"

I push the image of wrapping my hands around Erik's throat and watching the life drain out of his eyes. Reluctantly, I agree. "Right."

Kane nods at Mallory. "We'll check the perimeter. You stay here, out of sight, away from the windows."

Weapon drawn, he eases out the front door, taking caution that no one is out there. Mallory removes his gun from the holster on his side.

"Hey," I call before he follows Kane. "Can I interrogate him?"

Mallory touches his puffy lip. I notice his knuckles are bleeding, too. "As long as he's alive when we get back."

The door slams and the room is quiet. Silas brings a dining room chair into the middle of the room, his eyes more focused than they've been in days. Good. He needs to get off his ass and get pissed. Elon hands me a weapon, one I'm assuming he took off of Erik. I tuck it behind my back and help him hoist our hostage off the ground, then toss him in the chair. Levi moves to retie his binds behind his back, securing him to the chair.

"They're bad enough," Erik says, eyes focused on Levi, "but you're the worst, you know that? He thought you were a real believer. A teacher. Enlightened."

Levi stills, his expression blank, but there's no doubt a million emotions are running through him. His fingers curl into tight balls at his sides and I look to Silas. "Get him out of here." I jerk my chin at Imogene. "Her too. Upstairs until I'm finished."

"What?" Imogene cries, voice panicked. "I want to hear what he has to say."

Silas nudges Levi up the stairs, and I move to her, taking her face in my hands. "What I'm about to do? I don't want that to be how you see me. Elon either. There are tactics Anex taught us that you don't know about and that's a good thing."

"I'm not afraid of you, Rex."

She should be. After all the things I did to her. The pain I allowed her to suffer at my hands and my father's. "Please go. Don't fight with me on this."

"You don't even have to do this—you can wait for the agents to get back. Let them do their job." She looks past me to Elon. "I don't want you to lose yourself in all of this again—either of you."

"We won't." I shake my head and rub my thumbs along her cheeks. "But you know we're the only ones that can stop him, Little Lamb. We can't trust the Feds to do what really needs to be done."

She nods and I press a kiss to her forehead. Her hands squeeze mine. "I love you."

"I love you, too."

She goes on her own, heading up the stairs. I wait until I hear the door snap close before I pull the gun from where I'd tucked it in the back of my pants and face Erik.

"I should put a bullet through your head for how you treated me back in Serendee."

"You were Fallen. The dregs of our community. You deserved worse." He scoffs. "I held back on your pathetic, traitorous, ass because your father held out hope that maybe you could be redeemed."

Crack!

Elon beats me to the punch, slamming his fist into Erik's jaw before I even have a chance to swing. He winces, shaking out his knuckles, but the smug grin on Elon's mouth tells me it was worth it. "Shut the fuck up, asshole. You only got to that position because we were Banished. You gained from the bullshit, trumped-up charges Anex threw at us. Otherwise, you would have been a low-level lacky for the rest of your pathetic life."

I step forward, towering over him. "You think he won't turn on you the way he turned on us? Because he will. He's loyal to no one."

"You fucked up," he says, eyes shifting to Elon, then back to me. "Putting your carnal needs above your duty to Serendee. You betrayed your father, Rex. You still are by hiding out with his woman and working with the government."

"She's mine!" I lean forward, grabbing him by the collar. "And who do you think ordered us to do everything? For Elon to sleep with Imogene? For Silas to train her to become a proficient lover? To escalate her Corrections? Who invited her to the women's group and required her to write down the collateral that exposed us? It was a fucking set up, Erik, from the very beginning. It was a way to remove obstacles. To get me to kneel. To force Elon and Levi out because of his insecurities. To control Silas in order to increase his wealth." I release him, thrusting him back so hard the chair skids. "You think he won't do the same to you? You're not even blood."

The smug intention in his eye wavers, flickering for a moment, but then snaps back in place. "You're the one that betrayed him with all your accusations and blasphemy. You started this, Rex."

There's only one accusation that means anything to me and I'm not afraid to say it out loud. "He killed my mother. I don't know how, but he did it, and one day I'll prove it."

He snorts, holding my gaze. "Even if you do, you'll never find him."

"Then I guess you'll have to be the one to tell me." I whip out the gun and press the nozzle to his head. "Where is he hiding? What are his plans?"

He lifts his chin defiantly, making the barrel dig deeper into his temple. "Do it. I don't give a fuck. But understand that this doesn't end with me. He'll send another. And another." He grins, teeth a pale pink from his bloody mouth. "His followers are wide and strong."

"His followers are in jail or scattered like the wind," Elon says, arms crossed over his chest. "You're delusional, Erik."

"You think so? Not everyone is a traitor like you." He looks around the cabin. "This is your life now. Running until he catches you and gets her back."

I let his words sink in. "You weren't shooting at her."

"Fuck no. I was shooting at him," looks at Elon. If it hurts my friend's feelings that my father wanted him killed, he doesn't let on. "Your father wants his property back. The smartest thing for you to do is to give her to me and let me go before anyone else gets hurt."

There's not a chance in the world Anex lets us go even if he has her.

"She'll never be his Mate," Elon says.

"Oh, he knows that, and he no longer wants her for a spiritual wife. He wants her to pay. To punish her. To make her beg and scream for mercy." He laughs, enjoying this. "He has plans for your Little lamb. Dirty and depraved things that'll make her wish I'd put a bullet in her head."

"Shut up," Elon roars, foot kicking out and flipping over an end table.

Erik doesn't heed, continuing, "He's already got it lined up. The house. The dungeon. The cameras." He smirks, although it's mangled from his puffy lip. "And if you're lucky you'll survive long enough to wat—"

He doesn't get the last word out before I shove the gun in my pants to free up my hands, wrapping them around his throat. My fingers squeeze tight enough to make his eyes flutter shut, his body jerking from the lack of air.

"Rex," Elon calls, but his voice is faint, a distraction lost in the years of pent-up anger. The grief over my mother. The rage at my father. "Anex set you on a fool's errand. If he wants to keep sending people after us, then go for it. We'll take you out one by one."

"*Rex!*"

A voice cuts through the fog.

Her voice.

"Rex, please."

I release him, and he makes a loud, choking, gasp for air. My hands shake and it takes everything in me not to finish him off. I want to. More than almost anything else in my life. Anything but her.

I turn and see her standing at the bottom of the stairs, expression worried. Silas and Levi stand behind her, watching me closely.

"She did this," I tell Erik. "She saved your ass. Remember that."

I storm off, pretending I don't hear Erik gasping for his life. Or feel the eyes of my friends as they witnessed me turn into a monster. I find myself in the hallway off the kitchen and open the only door—the room the agents are using, and slam the door behind me.

"Fuck," I mutter, running my hands through my hair.

The door opens behind me and then shuts. I don't have to look to know it's her. And as much as I want to push her away when she wraps her arms around my waist, for her own good, I don't.

"Hey," she says, "what happened?"

"I wanted to kill him," I reply simply, sinking to sit on the edge of the bed. "He threatened you and I just... snapped."

"It's understandable. He attacked us."

"It's not understandable." My skin feels hot and my stomach churns. "It's not okay to strangle the life out of another person. If I'd killed Erik, how would I be different from him? Or my father?"

She sighs and pushes her way closer, nudging my legs apart to stand between my thighs. "It's understandable that you reacted this way. You've been pushed to the edge, Rex. Tortured. Forced to torture others. Watching your friends get sent away. Watching me get carried off with the explicit intention of becoming your father's wife. You've sold yourself as much as Silas has. Demeaned yourself to keep others safe. Fought as much as Elon. All under the pressure of being your father's heir."

"I tried so hard not to turn into him. Everything I did was the opposite." I rub my eyes with the heel of my palm. "I pushed to live outside Serendee. I partied and drank and smoked. I fucked around, and lived hard, Imogene. All I wanted was to get away from the son of a bitch."

"But you stayed for me." She reaches for my fingers, linking them with her own.

I snort. "It wasn't a selfless act, little lamb."

"I begged you to stay. I'm the one that foolishly thought there was good in Serendee. That I could reach Enlightenment."

Her tone is filled with disappointment. In herself or in Serendee, I don't know. What I do know is none of this is her fault.

"I hurt you, Imogene. Not just that day in my father's chamber." I wince at the memory of beating her with that paddle, how I bruised and battered her tender flesh. "I hurt you the day of the Ordering. I hurt you when I forced you to your knees, humiliating and exploiting your innocence and naivety. I was cold and callused when I forced myself on you and took your virginity." I feel sick thinking about it but I can't stop. Not now. "So many times, I had the chance to treat you better and I didn't." I look down at where our fingers curve together like links on a chain. "I don't deserve you. Especially not out here in a world where women get to choose their fates."

"I don't blame you for those things."

"You should. You should never want to be around someone like me again. You have the opportunity to start new. Go live your life with someone that isn't a monster who is still fighting the urge to go back in that room and end that man's life."

"You know what I think?" she asks. When I don't look at her or answer, she continues. "I think that's why Anex sent him here. He wanted you to lose control and question everything. He does know us. He knows you, he programmed us to fall into line. He knew exactly how to get you to react and behave like he would." I swallow and look into her blue eyes. "Like a ruthless leader who will do anything to get what you want."

I let her word sink in, a bit of the fog and anger clearing. "You mean like how he killed my mother to ascend to the position of power that he couldn't while she was alive or while Camille lived in Serendee."

"Exactly."

I pull her hand to my mouth, kissing her knuckles. The adrenaline slowly starts to wane. "I don't deserve you."

"That's not for you to decide."

God, this woman. "He won't give up until he destroys us all, you know that right?"

"Then we find a way to stop him."

I shake my head. "How?"

"By giving him what he wants."

"He wants you, Lamb, and that's not going to fucking happen." She's quiet—staring at me—an intent in her silence. What she wants dawns on me. "No."

"Why not? My mom did it to get into Serendee, and that's how they got me out. Why can't we do it again."

"Because Anex isn't dumb enough to fall for that twice, and I'm not stupid enough to risk you." She gives me a look, determined yet pleading. "No, Imogene. It's not going to happen."

"It's the only way to end this."

I struggle to get air to my lungs. The thought of putting her in harm's way is too much to bear. "I won't risk losing you again."

"It's not about losing anything. It's about ending this for good."

Hopping up, I pace the floor. "No, you don't! This is the kind of crazy move he wants us to make! Something impulsive and dangerous." I eye her. "But that's what you want isn't it? The danger. The risk. The feel of adrenaline when you're doing something wrong."

"What?" The hurt is clear on her face. "Why would you say that?"

"Because we're fucked up and broken, Imogene. All of us, and we fall right into old patterns. Yours is to see how much pain you can handle." I stride to the door. "Mine is to be an entitled prick, but for once," I open the door and step into the hall, "I'm not going to let it happen to me or to you either."

27

I mogene

The house feels different that night, like we're in limbo, waiting for the next attack. Erik, neck ringed with red bruises, is taken away in a van with blacked out windows, still refusing to speak. Additional agents arrive, assigned to help Mallory and Kane until the FBI moves us to a new safe house.

The events of the day are enough to make me wired, but that's not why I can't sleep. It's memory of Rex's anger and accusation. In the past I would have deferred to him, pushed aside my nagging impulse to fix this once and for all. He's my Mate and I was raised to let him make the decisions. And what if he's right? What if I just want to feel that rush of danger? The temptation of being bad?

That tell-tale twist of defiance churns in my stomach and it's not long before I finally give up and get out of bed, already knowing where I'm going—who I'm looking for.

I pass Silas sleeping on the couch, the TV down low, light flickering in the dark room. At the desk, Levi sits in the leather chair, absorbed in a book. The title is visible, *Healing the Mind: The Psychology of High Control*.

He looks up when he notices me and swivels the chair to face me. "You're up late," he says, closing the book, but keeping his thumb in it to mark his place. "Everything okay?"

My heart rattles in my chest and my skin feels hot, prickly. Shifting on my feet I finally say, "I need you."

Levi's back straightens, his thumb slides out of the book, and it falls to his side. "What's wrong?"

My hands twist in front of me, twisting at the long T-shirt I'm wearing as a nightgown. Agent McNair left me soft shorts and pants, I can't wear them, not after so many years of wearing dresses. "I need you to Correct me."

"Why?"

"Because I'm having Regressive thoughts." I swallow. "I want to disobey my Mate."

He takes a deep breath. "First, you shouldn't use the words, Regressive and Corrections. They aren't real and are only give Anex power he doesn't deserve." He rises, standing tall in front of me. "Second, I'm not going to punish you for having free will, Imogene. You don't have to do everything Rex tells you to do. He doesn't control you out here."

"Do you really believe that?"

"I'm trying to." He takes my hand and tugs me toward him. "Why don't you tell me what's going on and we can try to work through this?"

He sits and I go with him, perching on his lap. It feels good to be close to him, but that desire to pay for my Lapse is still strong. A war of conflict wages inside of me.

"Talk to me. What's made you come to me like this?"

"Instinct," I blurt. "When I do something wrong. When I have a Laps—" He frowns, and I swallow the word. "When I feel like I've been *bad*, my instinct is to come to you and you Cor—*punish* me."

"What did you do that made you feel like you're bad? How are you disobeying Rex?"

"I want to go after Anex—to let Agent McNair use me as bait to draw him out."

He weighs this, ultimately admitting, "It's not a bad idea."

"Thank you."

A smile flickers on his lips and then vanishes. "But I understand his hesitation. We just got you back. The idea of putting you at any risk is terrifying."

"It wouldn't be dangerous. I'd talk to Agent McNair. Do it the right way."

"Honey, there is no right way when it comes to dangling you in front of Anex like a piece of meat. He's unpredictable—probably more now than ever before."

The rejection of my idea stings—more than it should. It's irrational, a deep-seated need that I can't shake. Maybe Rex was right. I want to feel pain and putting myself in harm's way is one way to get it.

"You just said I have free will—then you'd be okay with me going against your wishes too?"

"I'd want us to keep talking about it and come up with a solution we all can agree on."

Well, now his reasonableness is just pissing me off.

"What if I ran out that door right now and snuck past the agents? What if he has one of his men out there and they catch me? What if I finally lured him out—getting him to expose himself?"

His forehead creases. "You're trying to get a rise out of me."

Grinding down on him, I say, "I'm trying to get *something* on you to rise." He holds my hips, forcing me still. A dark laugh bubbles in my chest. "So this is how it is."

"How what is?"

He's going to make me say it. Fine. "Without the Corrections you don't want me."

"What are you talking about?" His eyebrows knit together. "I don't understand what you're saying."

It's a lie. He knows exactly what I'm saying, but if he wants me to, I'll spell it out. "I know what we did together was messed up. I know it was Anex manipulating and controlling us—forcing us to break down our boundaries so that he could exploit them later, but…"

"There's no but, Imogene, it was wrong," he swallows thickly. "Treating you like that wasn't right."

My heart sinks. I thought if anyone would understand it would be Levi. That what we did together in the dark of his room, or down in the basement of the Center, was more than just punishment. Humiliation rises to my cheeks. "I'm sorry," I say, scrambling to get off his lap. "This was stupid—I should go."

I turn to rush out of the room, to anywhere but here, but a figure steps in front of me and grabs onto my upper arms.

"Silas. You're awake," I breathe. "I was just going to bed."

"You were running away." He releases me and runs his hand through his hair and glances over at Levi, who is frozen in his chair. "So yeah, I heard all of that."

My cheeks burn even hotter. "Well, forget it. I made a fool out of myself."

"Babe, you didn't. Look, all this stuff is fucking confusing. I get it. I'm confused. Just so fucking confused. There's real and not real. Our desires mingled up with manipulation. Where our wants end and Anex's conniving begins." He scrubs his face. "Trust me, I know."

Silas' body has been used for Anex's whims and greed for years. It's fair for him to be conflicted. Me? I'm not so sure.

"Then what do we do?"

"We don't let him continue to control us."

I look to Levi and after days of reading and focusing on moving ahead with his life, it's clear he's struggling. With clenched hands, he admits, "I don't know if I can give Imogene what she wants without losing myself." His voice drops. "And I don't know if I can give her what I want without her losing herself."

"Go on," Silas says, crossing his arms over his chest.

"Every escalation of our Cor—" he fights the word—"*sessions* was at Anex's hand. He encouraged me, he gave me the strap, he pushed you to the brink so you'd come to me begging for absolution."

"Did you give her absolution?" Silas asks.

"There *is* no absolution," Levi says. "Not in Anex's world. It's all a façade."

Silas turns to me. "If he didn't give you absolution, what *did* he give you?"

I think about those sessions. The welts he left on my back side that left me dripping with want so intense that Elon had to fuck it out of me. The night Levi cut me with the knife and then fucked me with the handle, bringing me to one of my most intimate and intense orgasms. I didn't just take the Corrections because I deserved it. I took them because I craved it.

"Relief," I say. "Because I have this emptiness in the pit of my stomach all the time. A hollowness that is only filled by my love for all of you. Every time I'm with one of you I feel more complete. Steadier." I look at Levi. "And when you bring me to the edge like that, I feel like I can fly."

"Are you sure that's not just old habits making you say that?" Levi asks.

I shake my head. "Are *you* sure that by asking me all of these questions you aren't just falling into *your* old habits?" The question seems to stun him. Shock him on an innate level. "I think you're doing all of this because you don't want to accept how much you liked our sessions. You liked them, not because Anex told you to do it, but because you got off on it."

He rushes me, slamming me into the wall. The impact hurts, but it's the good kind of hurt. The only sound is my heaving breath when he says, "Why are you doing this to me? My brain is finally clearing, and you're trying to drag me back in!"

"I don't want to drag you anywhere, Levi." His hands have my wrists pinned and the look in his eye is dark and feral. "I just want to be us. The real us."

"I'm afraid of what I'll do to you if I'm allowed to go untethered."

"I trust you. Unequivocally, but Silas will keep you from going too far, won't you?" I look over at him and he looks more awake than he has been in days. Helping makes Silas feel good, like he has a purpose, and if anyone can get us through this, it's him.

"I will," he agrees. "If this is what you both want."

His promise makes the tension in Levi's shoulders unwind, but he doesn't release me.

"I don't want to punish you because you're a bad girl," Levi says, his green eyes darkening a shade, "I want to tease and taunt you because you're sexy as hell." His hand runs up my shirt, fingers splayed over my stomach. "I want to bring you to the edge, make you cry out in pain and desire because it makes me so fucking hard I can barely see."

My belly drops and warmth spreads between my legs. "Yes, please."

His mouth hovers barely an inch from mine. I can feel his breath and I'm dying to kiss him, to feel his tongue in my mouth, but he steps back, removing his hand, his warmth. Crushed, I think maybe he's not into this after all.

Then I look down and see the hard line of his erection pressing against the front of his pants.

"Strip," he says, matter of fact. I glance at Silas who does nothing but watch quietly. Dropping my hands to the hem of my shirt, I pull it over my head and stand before them in nothing, but my panties. The room is chilly. Exposed. My nipples tighten from both the air and anticipation. We're playing a dangerous game, one where an agent could walk out at any moment. The idea shoots adrenaline down my spine.

He sits back in his chair, hand shifting his erection. "Are you wet?"

"Yes."

He leans back. "Show me."

Hooking my fingers in the sides of my panties, I pull them down. The crotch is damp. He holds out his hand and I give him the panties. He runs his fingers over the wet spot and presses it to his nose.

"Fuck," Silas mutters, shifting next to me. Levi's eyes flick to his friend, a coy smirk toying at his lips.

"Touch her."

Silas follows his friend's direction, his hand gliding down my hip, fanning over my pussy, and dipping between my legs. He feels around and my hand grabs his shoulder, bracing myself. He holds up his fingers. "Soaked."

Levi nods. "Spread her legs. I want to see her scars."

Silas drops to his knees, grazing his knuckle against my clit as he parts my thighs. I suck in air and my knees instinctively try to slam together, but he keeps them apart. His thumb brushes gently over the pale scars on my inner thighs.

"How did it feel when I gave you those?" Levi asks.

"Good." My belly flutters at both the memory and Silas' face being so close to the hot pulsing nerves between my legs. "A rush. A release."

"Do you need a release now?"

I nod, hopeful. "It's been so long."

"Is that why you're being defiant?"

"Maybe," I say, willing to agree to almost anything if one of these men will touch me the way I need them to.

He reaches into his pocket and pulls a long object. A pocketknife. A tremor works its way from my belly to between my legs. Fear. Panic. Need. He flips it open, exposing the blade. It's long. The handle thick.

"You can choose, Imogene. Do you want me to cut you, or to fuck you?"

"What if I want both?"

"Greedy." There's an old glint in his eye, like he's calculating the Lapse.

"You make me that way." I tell him, without the least bit of shame. "I want the rush. The feel of you." I look down at Silas, run my fingers along his cheek. "Of him."

"I can give you what you want." Levi stands, unzipping his pants, pulling his erect cock out of the flap. "So can he."

Silas, who has been holding on far longer than he'd like, plants a single, hot kiss on my pussy. He then works his way up my body, stopping for a sharp tug on my nipple. I hiss, "Oh, God," wanting him to do it again, but he steps aside. Levi stands before me, knife in hand.

"Is this where I ask either of you if this is going too far?" Silas asks, rubbing his palm down the front of his pants.

"We're good," Levi says, licking his bottom lip. "But you may want to brace her for this."

I don't mind the feel of Silas behind me, his hard erection pressing into my backside. But I don't know what Silas means until he gently presses the tip of the knife under my ear.

"You'd look lovely painted in red," he says, voice a whisper. Silas' hands clench on my hips, this scene unfamiliar, but in my bones it feels right. I know Levi won't hurt me—no more than I want it.

No more than I crave it.

He trails the blade down my body, circling my breasts, and slashing my abdomen with phantom cuts. The touch feels like a flutter, a whisper against my skin, toying and teasing, making goosebumps rise and my nipples tighten into hard peaks.

He settles the tip on my hip, just below Silas' fingers, above the brand.

"He doesn't deserve to be marked on your body," he says. "You don't belong to him."

I feel what he is saying, deep down, like a siren calling my soul. I grab the handle and his hand. Applying pressure, I force the blade into my flesh. Levi's eyes widen. "Imogene, no—"

At first, it's a prick, just a slice, but I press harder, slashing through the mangled flesh, pushing over the fresh, still healing scars. I hurts and I bite down on my bottom lip, keeping the scream inside. Silas must sense it, the way I'm about to unleash, and turns my head, kissing me, swallowing the scream into his mouth.

Blood coats my hands and the knife falls to the floor with a clatter.

"Shit," Levi's mutters, pulling off his shirt to cover the wound. But I lick Silas' tongue and face my redheaded partner.

"Let it bleed," I tell him, catching the slippery warmth in my fingertips. I laugh, feeling a rush—*the rush*—freedom.

I grab his length, fingers slick and greasy with blood. He pulls back, as if he wants to recoil, but his cock pulses thick in my hand.

"Fuck," he mutters, liking it. I stroke him, gliding the blood up and down.

"You're right," I say, pressing my ass into Silas' crotch, "he doesn't own me. You do. Claim me. Make me yours."

Silas' hand wraps around my body, palm bloodied and flat on my stomach. Behind me there's the rustle of fabric and the hard poke of his cock as it's freed from his pants. He drops into the chair and drags me with him, bringing me down.

"You ready for me?" he asks, rubbing my clit. I buck and the tip of his cock slots against my entrance, pressing into me until his hands steady my hips and he punches inside. He fills me, his cock deep inside and I exhale at the feel of him, stretching me wide.

Levi closes the gap, taunting me with his cock in my face. I grab it, pulling the tip to my mouth, licking the salty, warm blood off the head. His legs tense, and he groans, thrusting deep to the back of my throat.

"I take it back," Levi says, fingers tugging at my hair. "You are a bad girl. So fucking bad."

This. This is when I feel right. When my body is in motion, filled and stretched. I love the taste of Levi in my mouth and the feel of Silas deep in my core. Silas' teeth bare down on my shoulder, and he palms my tits. They're everywhere. Slippery and hot.

Mine.

The urge for more consumes me and I ease back from Levi's cock, sucking at the tip. I look up at him, skin pink, a swipe of blood across his hip. His fingers brush hair off my cheek and I say, "I want you in me when you come."

Silas kisses my neck and starts to lift me up, but I press back down. "No. Both of you." I know from Rex and Elon I can take both of them, and that need to feel full is overwhelming. My legs spread and Levi lowers himself. It's awkward, with limbs and dicks and fluid everywhere, but when he straddles the two of us and slides his cock next to Silas' my eyesight grows fuzzy, black spots clouding the edges. It feels so good. The stretch so intense—so right, that my orgasm rips through me on the first thrust.

"Oh!" I cry, struggling to stay coherent.

"That's it, baby," Silas says, grunting in my ear. His arm wraps around my waist and he holds me to him. I fall into the sound of his breathing, the little words whispered in my ear, the final hiss as he comes, spilling his hot seed inside.

The two of us are lax, slumped in the chair while Levi continues to pound into me with absolute abandon. This man. My partner. *My guide.* He led me here, to this moment, to this depravity of blood and sweat and semen. His hair flops over his forehead, the long line of his jaw clenched tight. He's an angel—fallen like the rest of us. A long groan building in his chest and he grips the base of his cock and I close my eyes as he makes his final thrust.

Then it's just the three of us, a pile of heavy breath, sticky skin, fused bodies.

"Jesus Christ," Silas says, shifting beneath me. "I knew you two had your thing, but fuck, it looks like a goddam massacre in here."

I open my eyes and all I see is blood, smeared across the three of us. Levi bends over and kisses me gently. "Are we okay?"

"We're perfect."

"You two are monsters," Silas says, easing me off him and stretching his legs. "I'm not sure if I'll ever be able to walk again."

Levi rolls his eyes, but helps me stand. He wraps his arms around me. "What are you going to do about Anex? Still determined to play bait?"

"I still want to do something. I mean, I plan on it, but you're right. It should be something we all agree on."

"Any ideas?" Silas asks, cleaning up with his T-shirt.

"Yeah," I say. "But to make it work, I think I'm going to need some help."

28

Silas

"Do you think we should go up there?" Rex asks, glancing at the staircase.

"No," Levi says, continuing to read and flipping the page of his book.

"I'm just not sure they should be alone."

"Rex," I say, "she's talking to her mother. I think she can handle it."

He runs his hands through his hair, a clear sign of agitation. It's not a surprise Rex is possessive of Imogene, he chose her after all, but this isn't jealousy that he's feeling. It's insecurity. For all their time estranged, Camille is still her mother. And mother's carry weight.

"She just may want some support—a little back up as she presents her idea," Rex continues, pacing in front of the fireplace. "What if Camille tells her it's shit? Or encourages her to do something different? Her idea is good, but Camille can be a little...."

"Controlling?" Elon says. He's holding a stick in one hand and a knife in the other. Somewhere along the way he decided to take up whittling. I suppose it's better than fighting for money.

"Bossy?" Levi tosses out.

I roll my eyes at both of them. "I'd say protective."

After talking it over as a group, Imogene had the idea to talk to her mother about ways to lure Anex out without putting herself at too much risk. At first, Camille didn't want to discuss it—any level of danger was too much. But after Imogene pled her case, they came up with a plan. They're in an upstairs bedroom on a call right now.

A call we weren't invited to participate in—hence Rex pulling his hair out.

"So what's this really about?" I ask. I've worked with enough anxious people to know we're talking about a bigger problem. "Why are you so stressed about her being alone with her mom?"

"I'm not—"

"Son of a—!" Elon curses, staring down at his thumb where the knife slipped. "Fuck."

I hop off the couch and rush over. "Are you okay?"

"It's fine," he glares down at the spot. "It's just a graze."

Looking him over, I agree. Not too deep, but still bleeding. I walk into the kitchen and grab a clean cloth, running it under the faucet. Back in the room, I hand it to him and glance up at Rex. "You were saying...?"

He sighs. "What if Imogene does this interview and like they said, the whole world learns about us—about Imogene. Once it's out, she may want more."

"You mean she may want normal," Levi says, finally looking up with his book.

"Fuck normal," Elon growls, applying pressure to his thumb. "None of us are ever going to be normal."

"We played in the Secular world a lot," I remind him, "or have you forgotten the frat parties?"

"Yeah, that's the thing," Rex says, dropping into an armchair. "We did frat parties. And clubs. We drove cars and got our licenses. We had money. All kinds of shit. Imogene, she didn't get to do any of that, and once this is over, once we leave this house, the whole world is going to open up for her."

And that's it. Rex is scared. Maybe for the first time in his life, he's scared.

Levi frowns. "You don't think she'll want us anymore?"

"Or," Elon points out, "maybe she'll only want one of us."

My stomach clenches. We haven't talked about this. About how we want to handle the future. I know she loves us and I'm pretty sure she wants to be with us—all of us—but Rex is right, there are a lot of unknowns.

"Living here made the transition seem possible," Elon says, toying with the cloth, "but we've been pretty isolated. No one knows we're here. We've been able to pick up where we left off."

"Rex may be right," Levi says, "From my reading, as her mind clears, and the further we get away from Anex's control, she's going to want to live a normal life."

"Fuck." Rex deflates in his chair, as if Levi's statement confirms all his fears. He thrusts his fingers into his hair and tugs at the root. "I don't know if I can live without her. I love her."

"She loves you too." My heart thuds anxiously at the thought of letting her go, but he's right. They may not be Ordered anymore, but Imogene is loyal and she clearly loves Rex. If she's choosing anyone, it's him.

"She may, but that's not the same as wanting to be with us," Rex says, then adds, "*all* of us."

"Wait," Elon straightens, "you'd want that? To let us be part of this?"

"Why not? I love you too. You're my family, the only one I've got left." He frowns. "You know, if that's what she wants too."

Hearing Rex put someone's desires above his own, especially a female's, is big enough. Big enough to make me wonder if maybe we can make this work.

Elon stands, blood seeping through the cloth wrapped around his finger. Rex rises to meet him, but before he catches his balance, Elon throws his massive arms around his best friend and gives him a tight hug.

Rex looks at me over his shoulder, eyebrows raised. I clear my throat and say, "What Elon is expressing is a thank you. For being our best friend, our brother, and allowing us the chance to be with the woman we love. You don't have to, even outside of Serendee, you could have coveted her and kept her for yourself."

"He's right," Levi says. "Anex was never going to let us have a mate, but you did, and that bonds us together."

Elon steps back, clapping Rex on the shoulder. "And if she doesn't want all of us?" he asks, wiping at his eyes.

"Then we fight for her," Rex says, looking calmer than he did moments before. "She could maybe say no to me, but all of us?" A grin tugs at his mouth. "She doesn't stand a chance."

29

Imogene

The lights are glaringly hot, and my armpits feel like the inside of a damp swamp, but I've just survived the first segment of my interview with Jane Morgan. Across the room, behind a crew managing cameras and microphones and the swamp lighting, my mother gives me a smile of encouragement.

This interview, it's the compromise to me playing bait. Turns out my mother had been fielding interview requests for weeks, buffering me from the hordes of journalists that had been vying for an exclusive.

Apparently, everyone was curious about the Sex Slaves of Serendee and due to statements I'd made to the police about my time in captivity, the branding, the secret women's club, and Timothy Wray's plan to make me his mate, my name was at the top of the list.

"Are you ready?" Jane asks. Her hair is perfect, a thick helmet framing her symmetrical face. Her eye makeup is thick, making her seem a little unreal. Can someone's eyes really be that color blue?

I think of Rex. Yes.

The weird thing is she's exactly how Anex would have described a member of the media: a superficial puppet whose only goal is to exploit the Enlightened out of jealousy.

Which is not how *I* view her. It's not, but those mental assumptions are hard to shake.

"You've already told us a little about your childhood and what it was like growing up in Serendee. We'll start with a few more easy questions before we build up to the heavy stuff, then we'll bring in your mother."

"Sounds good." I smooth out my black skirt and shift on the couch cushion, a lame attempt to hide my nerves. I don't think it works. "I'm ready when you are."

The camera man gives his cue, and around us the lights dim, other than the bright ones directed at us. My mother gives me a tight smile, and I'm reminded why I'm here.

Timothy Wray can hide, but we're going to expose him for his crimes. We're going to reveal the world to who he really is even if it means having to expose myself to do it. Camille and I were intentional when picking out which show to give an exclusive interview. Popular, with a big audience, and a reporter that would make me look strong but sympathetic.

Jane Morgan was the winner.

"Imogene," she starts, "for the majority of our audience... well, they're going to have a hard time believing you and the other residents didn't know about Timothy Wray's illegal activities." She looks down at a sheath of papers. "Tax evasion, money laundering, distribution of illegal substances and of course, the horrifying charges of sex trafficking and imprisonment. Is it possible for all of that to be going on and no one being aware of it?"

Way to start with an easy one, Jane.

"I won't justify our ignorance. And that is what we were, ignorant and naive about the truths of our home—in Serendee. We were very isolated from what we called the "secular world" and Anex controlled the access we had to information coming in and out of our community."

"Including media, right?"

"Correct. We had no televisions or radios. We relied on Anex to let us know what was important and to make the standards for how we lived and worked. He gave us skewed views of government and laws." I swallow, feeling the heat prick the back of my neck. "It feels foolish to say we just didn't know, but we didn't, and even if we did, what would we do about it?"

"You were afraid of him."

It's not a question but I answer it anyway. "Yes, very much so and the more I learned, the more I understood how much danger we were in."

She leans forward. "In what way?"

I take a deep breath and try to formulate my words. Camille, Levi, and I spent hours going over possible questions, but now that I'm here it's a struggle to articulate it accurately. "Timothy Wray controlled our minds and bodies. He managed what we ate, what we wore and when we slept. We spent hours listening to his lectures and absorbing his propaganda." I give her a small smile. "That's a word I just learned. It wasn't part of our vocabulary."

"Did he punish people?"

I'm not going to talk about the corrections. I'd already made that decision. I'm also not speaking about my relationship with my men. Anex already used that against me once, I won't allow it to happen again.

"In his own way. The biggest reward you could get from Anex was his attention. It was the most coveted thing in Serendee. He knew it, and he doled it out carefully and strategically. He didn't have to punish people often because all anyone wanted was his approval."

"Is it true you were arranged to marry his son?"

"Yes." *Mate.*

"And that allowed you to become part of what people refer to as his 'inner circle.'"

"It did."

"And being part of that inner circle allowed you more access to Timothy Wray and his activities?" she asks.

"I don't think it allowed me more access to him," I struggle to breathe just admitting it. "I think it allowed him more access to me."

Jane leans forward, hand covering mine. "What did Wray want from you, Imogene?"

I look to my mother, and she nods. We knew I'd have to tell the truth. Reveal to the world what kind of person he really is.

"I was flattered by his attention," I admit. "And I was asked to join a special group of women. To join we had to tell our deepest secrets." Collateral. "And we were marked—branded—with a symbol. One we thought represented Serendee."

"But it didn't represent Serendee, correct?"

"No. We were branded with Anex's initals." Tears burn in my eyes at the memory. The pain and humiliation. The utter mind control he had over me. "Anex wanted me to be one of his wives and the months leading up to my escape were spent either in isolation, being groomed, or being manipulated by him."

"Did you say wives? Plural?"

I nod.

She lets that sink in, then adds, "You understand that people will say that you could've left at any moment. You're eighteen. Your mother had left the group years before. But you stayed and willingly participated in these activities. People will say this isn't a cult, that he's just a con man who convinced the weak people in the community to believe in what he's selling."

"I would tell those people that I was born and raised in Serendee and that I was taught that even though there are times the community hurts, we believed it was less than the world outside. That our family and friends, that our rules and our leader, would keep us safe on our path to Enlightenment."

"Why are you here, Imogene? Why tell a story so many will find hard to believe?"

"Because it's time for Anex to practice what he preaches. He's always telling us obstacles are just another test we have to endure. That only the weak and fallen fall victim to outside interference." I straighten my spine. "I believe *this* is his test. One he needs to be present for. He taught us to believe in our convictions, in the truth of our community. If he has nothing to hide, and he did nothing wrong, then why is he on the run?"

Jane nods, her expression pleased with my response. She waves Camille to come over and my mom crosses the small space and sits on the couch next to me.

"Is it true you two have been estranged from one another for years?"

"Yes, since she was twelve," Camille says. "Leaving her was the hardest thing I ever had to do."

"Then why did you? Most parents wouldn't leave their children in that situation."

"I refused to go," I tell Jane. "She tried to get me and I refused. Serendee was my home."

Jane looks back at Camille. "Do you regret it?"

A tremor runs through my mother, and I reach for her hand. "Every day, but I also know how scared I was at the time and I did what I thought I had to. That I don't regret."

"Scared of Timothy Wray? You thought he was going to hurt you?"

"His first wife was my best friend. We all started Serendee together. Timothy changed over time, he started gaining power and control over the residents. He wanted an open marriage and his wife, my best friend, Beatrice, refused." She looks at me. "She was dead two months later and he wanted me to take her place. There was no way that was happening, but it became clear; fall in line, become his wife, let him continue his tyranny or my fate would be the same as Beatrice's."

My stomach rolls with queasiness. Back then I never would have believed Anex was capable of such things. Even a few months ago when Rex told me his suspicions, but now I know better.

"You think he hurt his wife?" Jane leans in slightly, eager for an answer.

My mother doesn't let her down. "I know he did. He took away my best friend, he stole my daughter's innocence, and he's ruined hundreds of lives."

"Wow, that's quite an accusation." Jane's expression softens and she looks between us. "What's it like having your daughter back?"

"I never gave up hope that one day we'd be reunited, but I also wasn't sure if it would happen." Mom looks at me and smiles. "It feels like a miracle."

"And now?" Jane asks, looking at me.

"Now it feels like we have a second chance," I say, holding back tears. Camille and I have a long way to go, but the fact that she's here, doing this my way, is a huge step. "One of the tactics Anex uses to control people is to separate families. He managed to get my mom away from me, but that's another one of his cycles of abuse we're ending."

I say this more to the camera than to Jane. I'm talking to him.

"Everyone in Serendee now has the opportunity for a second chance, but we won't experience true freedom until Timothy Wray and his associates are brought to justice. He needs to understand what it's like to feel the walls closing in, to have your choices taken away from you, to become isolated and removed from your loved ones." I squeeze my mother's hand. "But until then we will keep living —surviving—because that's who we are. Ironically, he's the one that taught us to be that way and ultimately, we will be his downfall."

30

Imogene

In the end Timothy Wray isn't found on the beach of some tropical island, or deep in a forest rebuilding his community. Because of the popularity of my interview with Jane Morgan the whole world started looking for Timothy Wray.

Ultimately, four days after the broadcast, they find him in Las Vegas. Photos are plastered all over the news—images of Anex sitting at a table in the middle of a smoke-filled casino. He's got a cigarette between his fingers, a drink at his fingertips and he's wearing a baseball cap and jeans. Two women sit on either side of him, watching him gamble.

Jane Morgan announces from the TV that these are sex workers. Not his sex workers, but ones he hired in Vegas to be his companions.

"I mean…" Rex says from next to me. His arm is around my shoulder, and the five of us have been glued to the TV since the reports started rolling in.

"Right?" Elon adds, not able to formulate a full sentence.

"It's just so—"

"Anticlimactic?" Levi offers.

"Yes," Silas nods. "Exactly. It's anticlimactic. Not to mention fucking hypocritical."

The entire scene is surreal. Our leader, the champion for health and clean living, is caught in a smoky bar wearing polyester clothing surrounded by bright lights and gluttony.

"You know what?" I say, dragging my eyes from the screen. "I fucking hate that guy."

Rex laughs, pulling me into his side and kissing my temple. "Me too, Little Lamb."

"Can we skip to the best part?" I ask.

"I've got it," Silas says, fast forwarding a little until he gets to the next part of the report. I snuggle into Rex's side as the images on the screen flip, shifting to the scenes of the police surrounding Anex in the parking lot. He's shoved to the ground, arms behind his back.

"After Timothy Wray was taken into custody his partner, Margaret Robinson, who is eight months pregnant, was found in their lavish penthouse suite at the Royale Casino," Jane says, voice short and clipped. She's not doing a person-to-person interview here. She's reporting the news and her persona changes like a chameleon. "She was found with Jasmine West, heir of the Cobra Tequila empire, and another one of Wray's followers, Robert Carrington. Carrington is reportedly a self-made millionaire from the tech industry who hasn't been seen by family or friends in months."

The three of them are escorted out of the hotel by police, the bright lights of photographers' cameras flashing in their faces. Margaret looks huge, like she could give birth at any moment. The screen shifts again, this time to a press conference with Attorney General Michael Morris.

"We're thrilled to learn of the capture of Timothy Wray, Margaret Robinson, Jasmine West and Robert Carrington. We look forward to extraditing them from Nevada and bringing them home where they will face the charges brought by the state." He looks directly at the camera. "Many people have asked about the remaining members of the Serendee community. We continue the process of determining the roles residents played in Wray's schemes. Many, including dozens of children, are victims. It will take time to figure this out. We ask for your patience and consideration." He rests his hands on the podium. "And last, due to new evidence, I'd like to announce that investigators are looking into the allegations of foul play in the suspicious death of Beatrice Wray, Timothy's wife. Thank you. That's all for today."

Shouts come from the media, their voices drowning one another out. Morris walks off the stage, clearly not planning on answering any questions. Next to me, Rex disentangles himself from me and stands. "I think I need some air."

He walks to the door, closing it with a sharp snap. I look at the guys. "Go," Silas says. Elon nods.

He's out on the porch, leaning against the railing. I wrap my arms around him. "I doubt anything will come from it, but it's nice to hear they're looking into it. Thank you for getting this started."

"Me? I didn't do this, Rex. You did."

He turns, facing me. "What are you talking about?"

"The day you picked me for the Ordering, that's the day all of this fell into line."

"Careful, you sound like my father." he snorts and gestures to the house. "Or like Levi."

"Anex's talk about The Way and Enlightenment may have been self-serving, but there's a reason people wanted to be part of his world. This connection between us—this need for something bigger than us." I place a hand on his chest. "We found that. Me, you, Elon, Silas, Levi—we're bigger than Anex."

"I worry about everyone left behind."

"Me too."

"I wonder if there's anything we can do for them."

"I know who we can ask." I smile. "I have you to thank for her, too. You opened that door for me."

"One of us should have a mother in their lives, don't you think?"

Sitting here like this reminds me of the day up on the cliff, the day we first spoke, when we'd both just lost everything. The difference now is that we're no longer divided by power. By Anex's rules, or the lure of The Way.

We've found one another. We're true.

We're mates.

I feel it in my chest, when he looks at me with those brilliant blue eyes or touches me with his strong, steady hands.

The veil that kept us separated has been torn down. We've learned the truth and have survived. We escaped and will flourish. We went against all our beliefs but for the first time in my life, I feel it.

Enlightened.

EPILOGUE

I mogene
Three Weeks Later

Music fills the darkened room and I lurch up, body moving like I'm pulled by strings. Anex. He's calling us for a lecture.

"Hello?" A low voice says. A light flashes, glaring in the dark and the weight of a hand on my hip draws me back to the present. We're not in Serendee. We're at Camille's house. Anex is in jail.

"You're safe," Silas says, drawing me to him. "That's just Rex's cell phone."

I exhale slowly as Rex speaks low into the phone. "Now? Okay. We'll be there."

Silas and I both sit up and Rex comes back to the bed, sitting on the edge. He's wearing nothing but a pair of shorts, his body filled out after months of starvation and abuse.

"Who was that?" Silas asks, stretching his arms over his head.

"The jail."

Panic grips me. "Is something wrong? Did Anex—"

"The *women's* jail. Margaret's in labor." He looks at me. "She asked for us—me and you—to come to the hospital."

"Oh." My heart still pounds. Two scares too close together. I push back the cover and swing my legs over the side of the bed. "Do you know what she wants?"

"Nope," he shakes his head and offers me a hand, "but I guess we'll find out."

∼

The car is quiet as Rex drives us to the hospital in my mother's car. The streets are empty in a way I'm unfamiliar with. I'm still not used to being in this world, the freedom of picking up at 2 AM and getting in a car, wearing jeans and an oversized sweatshirt, hair still messy from sleep.

"They didn't say anything else?" I ask. "Just that she wants us at the hospital?"

"That's all," he says, hands tight on the steering wheel.

"Then I'm sure everything's okay." I settle back in the seat, willing that to be true. I have no fondness for Margaret, she's responsible for much of my hurt as Anex, but that baby is an innocent. I just want it to arrive in this world safe.

Rex grunts and it's like every muscle in his body is tense. I rest my hand on his thigh and squeeze. "Are you worried?"

A car's lights flash as it drives past, highlighting the tick in his jaw. "No."

He's been a little distant, but it seemed normal to me. He watched his father get arrested, our whole life crumble, we've had to move from the cabin back to my mother's house. There are hearings and trials coming up. Testimonies and depositions. It's been scary and unknown.

He pulls into the hospital driveway, easing the car into an empty spot in the visitor lot. Turning off the car he clutches the keys, unmoving. "Rex, what's going on?"

"We need to talk," he looks out the window, up at the bright hospital sign. "But I don't think now is the right time."

"Why not?" I ask. "We have no obligation to go in there just because Margaret wants us to. She can wait."

A smile tugs at the corner of his mouth. "So independent."

"I'm just making you a priority." I take his hand. "Tell me."

"The guys and I," he starts, and I feel the tremor in his hand, "we've been trying to give you space—room to make decisions about the future."

"The future? What does that mean?"

He inhales sharply. "We've never really talked about it since leaving. Back there everything was set in stone. You belonged to me. It was determined. But out here, those rules don't apply."

"That's what you're worried about?" I move my hand to his chest where his heart pounds erratically. "I'll always belong to you. I love you."

He exhales, a little of the tension easing. "Is that all you want? Just me or…" he swallows, "because I know it's not traditional and the guys are prepared. We're all prepared to do what you want. And everyone has just been following your lead."

At night we sleep together, taking turns in the king-sized bed. Tonight, it had been Silas and Rex. Before that, Elon and Levi. Night after night I get to spend it with the men I love. We cook together, watch stupid television shows, shop and explore the city with new eyes. They explain this world to me, help me understand it. They're healing me, one moment at a time.

"We're hanging by a thread here, Little Lamb," he says, breaking into my thoughts. "I need to hear you say it."

"I couldn't give any of you up for the world," I say, tears pricking at my eyes. "The four of you are the only good things I brought out of Serendee. I want you. All of you."

He moves suddenly, eyes lit with emotion. His hand traces my jaw, and he whispers, "I love you," against my lips, before his mouth claims mine. A slow burn spreads through me, like the glow of daylight, despite the dark surrounding us. Rex is my sun. Elon, Levi and Silas are the rays that keep me alive. "I'll tell them when we get home. I should have been clearer. I took you for granted."

"Never," he says, hand clasping my face and kissing me one last time. His forehead presses against mine. "I guess we should go inside."

He exits the car and walks around to open it for me, hand clasping mine. One thing is for certain; whatever is waiting for us inside, it seems easier knowing that we'll handle it together.

∽

On a wing filled with soft mauve décor and teddy bears on the wall, a guard waits outside the hospital room door, a stark reminder of who we're here to visit. There hasn't been a trial yet—Anex, Margaret, and Erik are all in jail awaiting hearings. Jasmine and Robert, with the strength of their family connections, personal finances, and denials of involvement of the more serious charges, were able to get bail.

"Spread your legs," the guard says, insisting on patting us down. I went first, but her hands seem to linger on Rex's large frame. "She's still on security measures," the square shaped woman with blunt bangs says. "You're to keep your distance at all times. Do not offer or accept anything. There are cameras." Her hands pat Rex's butt and he frowns, eyes narrowed. "Understand?"

"Has she already had the baby?" I ask.

The guard nods, actually giving me a glimmer of a smile, and opens the door. The room is small, but Margaret looks tiny in the oversized hospital bed. Her left wrist is attached to the rail by a chain and handcuff. Her right arm holds a bundle—a blanket rolled up so tight that all I can see is a little, squished, pink face in the crook of her arm.

A flood of emotion rushes through me. I'd always assumed I'd be there for the birth of Margaret's baby—assist actually. I feel a strange sense of loss at not being here, but also understand that I have no right. Margret looks tired. Deep purple shadows hang under her eyes. Her cheeks are gaunt and her hair stringy. I'm not sure if it's from the delivery or from life in detention. Could be both.

"Are you okay?" I ask, eyes shifting to the bundle. "Is the baby okay?"

"As good as a woman can be after pushing a nine pounder out of my vagina." Margaret works to sit up a little, wincing from what I assume is pain. "But the birth was beautiful. Not what I wanted, obviously, but still."

"It's a..." Rex starts, peering at the baby and taking in the pink hat, "a girl?"

"Meet your baby sister." She lifts her arm, offering the baby to Rex. "Go on, take her."

Rex shakes his head, eyes glazing over. Shock? I step in, bend, taking the tiny newborn from Margaret. She's so lightweight and fragile, yet firm and compact. Her mother watches me closely as I settle her into my elbow. "She's beautiful." I peer at her face at those blue eyes. I look at Rex. "She has your eyes."

"What do you want, Margaret?" He asks, visibly distressed. "Why have us come down here because if you think that you can—"

"Do you remember the story I told you about meeting your father?" she asks, cutting him off.

"Yes. At a café in town. You were a student, and he wooed you with his intelligence to come down to the Center for classes."

Her lips quirk. "Well, that was a lie."

Rex stiffens next to me, snapping out of his fog. "Then what's the truth?"

"I met your father when I was fourteen. I was working at my father's restaurant and Serendee was one of his suppliers. Back then Anex used to make the deliveries himself. He'd show up in that old red truck, the back filled with crates of organic vegetables. He was handsome as sin. All blue eyes and a smile that made you feel like you were the only person in the world." Rex shifts next to me, and I reach out, taking his hand. "He'd drop off the food, come in for a meal. I'd serve him and we'd talk." She laughs. "Well, *he'd* talk."

"Ow." She hisses, and the movement from laughing makes her wrap her free arm over her belly, wincing. "Sorry. They said to be careful about that." She takes a slow, settling, breath. "Anyway, his visits lasted for years. Sometimes he'd take me around in his truck, making deliveries to all the other markets and restaurants on his route. He told me all about you—" she looks at Rex, "and your mother who had died. He said he liked having the company of someone who didn't know his trauma or past."

An uneasy feeling tickles my spine. I've learned over the last year that everything about Anex is a well well-designed façade. But Margaret... even in her darker moments she always seemed so true.

"When I was sixteen, I started running wild. Staying out all night. Going to parties. Drinking, smoking, nothing big, you know," she winks at Rex knowingly, "but my father was at his wits end. He was a single father—my mother had been gone for years—and he just had no idea what to do with me. Then Anex came by the restaurant one day with a delivery, and my father told him all about it. I guess Anex suggested that I could come live at Serendee, that he'd straighten me out with fresh air and a wholesome environment. When I was better, he'd send me back."

"Were you angry?" I ask, rocking my hip a little when the baby lets out a yawn.

"God, yes. Furious. I felt betrayed that my father would just send me away and to some stupid, boring commune. I wanted my internet and TV. My cell phone, weed and my boyfriend who was a drummer in a band. Twice I tried to jump out of the car. Once, I succeeded, but he chased me down and dragged me back. By the time we got to Serendee we were both dirty and worn out. He'd also convinced me to give it a shot. He's amazing at that, you know, convincing people into things they're skeptical about. It didn't hurt that he was so good looking. Charming and charismatic. I was half in love with him the first day we met. By the time we got to Serendee I was head-over-heels. The all-consuming kind that threatens to swallow you whole."

She tells this story in a faraway voice, like she's a million years away from being that girl. In truth, that's exactly what she is. The woman in front of me is the aftermath of a man like Timothy Wray.

"I don't remember you being in Serendee when you were sixteen." Rex regards her with suspicion—like this is just another game.

"That's because your father didn't allow me to join the regular population," she says. "Not at first. He put me in an empty house on the edge of town, this was before the Main House was finished, and kept me there."

"How long?" he asks.

"A few years."

My throat threatens to close off, but I manage to ask, "He locked you in a house for years? Alone?"

"He *educated* me in that house. I didn't have the privilege of growing up in Serendee, like you two did. There were a lot of things I needed to learn before I would be worthy of living among the other residents. Of being worthy of him."

My fingers tighten around Rex's, a chill settling in my spine. "You were one of the Fallen."

"I was the *first*." She says this with pride. "A success too. It took a lot of work. A lot of Corrections. One step forward and one back, all of that. He trained me, just like you. I was broken down and built back up. It was my own journey. My path to understanding The Way." She smiles warmly at me. "It's why I had such an affinity for you, Imogene. I understood your spirit, and he felt the same connection to you that he had to me all those years ago."

Bile rises in my throat, bitter and overwhelming. Panicked, I hand the baby to Rex, pushing her into his chest, before bending over, fighting off a gag.

"I'm sorry my father did that to you," Rex says, a tremor in his voice. I take a deep breath, willing my stomach to settle. Looking up, I see that the bundle is so small against his broad chest. "You were a child and deserved better. I'm sure if you tell the DA your story, they'll reconsider, and possibly allow you to testify for the prosecution."

"You misunderstand." Her eyes widen. "Your father saved my life. He introduced me to the philosophies of The Way. He chose me and I will eternally choose him. I will never speak out against him. *Ever*."

Rex and I look at one another, neither sure of what to say. "Then why did you call us here? Just to see the baby?"

"I want you to take her."

I blink. "Excuse me?"

"I can't raise a child in jail, Imogene. And the judge isn't giving me bail. I believe Anex and I will ultimately be proven innocent, but someone needs to care for her while we're fighting for our freedom."

"You can't be serious," he says.

"Dead." She levels an intense look at Rex. "You're her family. She needs to be with you. Her big brother. Not tied up in some foster system with strangers."

The nausea of finding out the truth of Margaret's past is overwhelmed by the request she's making. I'm finding it hard to breathe. To think. "Please. Just consider it."

Before there's a chance to reply, the guard opens the door, allowing a nurse inside. "I need a few minutes with the new mommy." She takes the bundle from Rex and says, "How about you push this sweet angel down to the nursery?"

We step outside, the square bed on wheels in front of us. The guard points down a hall to the nursery.

"That..." Rex says, voice so low I almost can't hear him, "that was fucked up. Every day I think my father can't be worse than I already think he is and sure enough, I'm proven wrong."

"I know."

"And a baby? We can barely function ourselves much less take care of an infant."

"Life is chaotic," I agree. "We've just gotten on our feet."

Rex stops, pressing his back to the wall and dropping his head to his hands. "Why is this so fucking hard, Imogene? When does it stop being hard?"

I know what he's asking. As terrible as those last few months in Serendee were, the majority of our lives there seemed stable. Familiar. It would be easier to go back to what we knew than living this life of unknowns.

"We can't take her…" his forehead is creased, and he gazes at me and then back down to the little girl, "can we?"

I look down at her, at those same blue eyes that Rex has, and I want to say no. That we're moving forward and leaving all of this behind, but Margaret is right. She's family. She's Rex's only blood relative that he has left. We can't allow Anex to destroy this little one's life too.

"We can," I say, feeling it in my chest. "But we should talk it over with the guys first—"

"They'll say yes," he says with zero hesitation.

"And probably my mom," I add.

He reaches into the crib, running his finger down her pink cheek. "We'll need her help."

"But we can do this."

He smiles at me, handsome and strong. "We can definitely do this."

18 Months Later

A lot can happen in a year and a half.

A community, a family, can be torn apart.

A leader can be held accountable for the terrible things he's done.

A new, different kind of family can emerge from the ruin.

And something so precious can be born, a reminder of the true meaning of life.

"Mom," I say, trying to formulate a response. "This is isn't necessary."

"Honey, I don't need it anymore. I spend all of my time over at Beatrice House and there's plenty of room for me to stay there."

I stare at the key she's holding out. "But it's your house, and you know I can afford something on my own."

When the evidence of the Fallen was revealed in court; the imprisonment, sexual abuse and trafficking, the jury delivered a swift and decisive judgment. It only took them two hours to convict Timothy Wray on all charges. The following day the sentencing was issued, and the judge gave him a hundred-and-sixty-seven years in prison along with the ruling that he pay restitution to his victims. *Millions.*

Anex claimed to be broke, that he'd gambled away his stolen fortune, but the government seized the Serendee property. An arrangement was made for Anex's victims to have the option of receiving land as part of their restitution, which allowed families to be reunited in a safe space. The community center was transformed into a resource center with social workers and job counselors. They also gave Rex his family home, since the title was in his mother's name. He, in turn, donated it to Camille to use as a new center for cult survivors and their families.

During this transition, we'd been staying at my mothers' house and while we figured out what to do next. The idea of moving back to Serendee doesn't appeal to any of us, but we also don't know where to go. The world is big and intimidating.

Mom leans against the porch railing, arms crossed over her chest. "Have I told you about buying this house?"

The porch swing creaks when I sit down. "No."

"When I left Serendee, I had no credit to my name. No bank account or savings. Everything had been tied up in the community." She runs her hand over the painted wood rail. "I didn't have any family to come back to. No siblings. My father died when I was in college."

"What about your mother?"

She laughs. "Things were already tense when I dropped out of grad school and moved to the property. She called it then—outright —she said I was joining a cult and to snap out of it. I told her she was closed minded and didn't understand how we were going to change the world." She laughs, but it's lacking humor, just filled with a tinge of sadness. "It didn't help that I borrowed money for school and invested it in the vision of Serendee. And later, the fact that I left you behind… well, she never forgave me." She looks down at her feet, the only sound is the whine of the swing chains. "I came out of Serendee alone, scared, broke, but eventually I got a job, saved every dime I could, and had enough for the down payment on this place."

In a matter of minutes my mother had filled in the gaps about much of my family history that I never knew about.

"The lack of support is why I started this program in the first place. I wanted to make a place for people to go to that needed help. And for people like my mother who needed support when she lost her child into something like this." She smiles at me. "I knew I needed to make up for what I helped start—for leaving you."

"Thank you for telling me all of that, but you don't need to give me your house, it's too much."

"I should have given you everything, Imogene. I should have been there for your first dance, your first date, to help you apply for college, to get you ready for life. I failed at all of that, but this is something I can do for you." She stands upright. "I can give you a home. One to make your own."

"You know I'll be living here with all of them, right?"

"And Bea. Yes, they're your family, I understand that." She's fought me on this. Encouraged me into therapy, worried I'm stuck in old habits. But I'm not. And my therapist agrees. This is just who I am, and they are who I love. How we came together may be unconventional, but nothing is going to change how we feel about one another. "I was thinking you could use some of your money to tear down a few walls and make a big bedroom and a room for Bea next door." She grins. "Maybe add a family room to the back?"

As she talks, I can envision it. The six of us in the kitchen where Silas and I ate our first Pop Tarts. A freshly painted living room with a sectional and big TV. A room decorated just for Bea—the sunshine in our life.

A place for us to continue to heal, to grow, and figure out what to do with our lives.

Together.

"Please." Mom holds out the key. "Take it."

I hold out my hand and she drops the key into my palm. I rush over, engulfing her in a hug. This is what Anex took from me. My mom. My history. My truth. But in this house, I'll rebuild it, we'll rebuild it, one indulgence at a time.

.

.

AFTERWORD

First, don't forget to join Monarch's on Facebook for all the good stuff! All of my books can be found on Amazon.

Readers,

Writing this series has been interesting. I started to develop the idea for Serendee during the early days of the pandemic when I was walking a lot. There is a "cult-ish" community in my neighborhood and it got me thinking deeper about the topic. Not that cults aren't something I'm curious about anyway. I first read Helter Skelter in high school and Jim Jones and the People's Temple sucked me in during college. I won't deny there are elements of many different cults in this series. Heaven's Gate, NXVIM, Scientology, The Children of God and various other extremist religious groups, and a few off-the-wall cults that no one has ever heard of.

The interesting thing I noticed during my research is that all of these high control groups behave the same way. They build, they flourish, and ultimately their downfall follows predictable patterns.

Anyway, I appreciate you all "indulging" me in this possibly made up trope, cult romance, that allowed me to deep dive into my personal obsession + my love for reverse harem + giving all the characters I traumatize a happy ending.

The time period of writing this series was tough. I wrote the first draft of The Order before Lords of Pain was released. Obviously, once that book was out there, Sam and I were focused on the Royals. I also had no idea how to market/cover/or categorize a "cult romance" because seriously, this is not a thing. It took me a year to come up with a cover design (this was right before discrete covers became popular. I should have waited another 6 months!) and I rewrote the first draft to be a little darker, something I was more comfortable with after working on Lords.

By the time I released The Order my husband had been diagnosed with cancer. During the last 18 months he's had chemo, surgery, radiation, another surgery, and is coming up on his final *fingers crossed* surgery next week—typically, the day before this releases. Sam and I have written 6 Royals Books, are midway through Princes, launched a kickstarter campaign and I had covid!

Y'all it's been a LONG two years. Thank you for sticking around during all of this and allowing me to play in this side sandbox of delicious, deranged darkness.

Angel

Printed in Great Britain
by Amazon